A BETTER CLASS OF PERSON

A BETTER CLASS OF PERSON

Tessa Barclay

severn
House

This first world edition published in Great Britain 2002 by
SEVERN HOUSE PUBLISHERS LTD of
9–15 High Street, Sutton, Surrey SM1 1DF.
This first world edition published in the USA 2003 by
SEVERN HOUSE PUBLISHERS INC of
595 Madison Avenue, New York, N.Y. 10022.

British Library Cataloguing in Publication Data

Barclay, Tessa
    A better class of person
    1.   Millionaires Greece - Fiction
    2.   Detective and mystery stories
    I.   Title
    823.9'14 [F]

    ISBN 0-7278-5902-1

Typeset by Palimpsest Book Production Ltd.,
Polmont, Stirlingshire, Scotland.
Printed and bound in Great Britain by
MPG Books Ltd., Bodmin, Cornwall.

One

M r Crowne was in Greece, which was good. It was April,
which was also good. He was on a small island with
only about a hundred other people, which was even better.

But sad to say, the island was owned by an heiress whom
he had known when they were both children and whom he'd
never liked, which was bad. He was at a social event to which
the hundred other people had been invited, which was worse –
Gregory Crowne didn't care much for social gatherings unless
music was involved. He was here on the orders of his family,
which was worst of all, because there had been long, loud
arguments about who should attend.

'I went to her father's funeral,' his father had contended.
'Elissa made a big fuss about the way the floral tributes were
displayed and I found her very displeasing. I shouldn't have
to go to this birthday affair.'

'I went to her wedding, which was vulgarly ostentatious,'
said Grandmama Nicoletta. 'And anyway, I'm too old for all
that air travel and hopping into ferry boats.'

She was in her seventies, which these days wasn't old, and
moreover, in the course of her interior-decorating business she
ran up and down ladders with assurance and lots of energy.
Yet they were all three aware that if she went as a guest to
Elissa Paroskolos's party, she'd be so icily polite that it would
freeze anyone within twenty yards.

'They only want a Hirtenstein there so they can say they've
got royalty,' Gregory had protested. 'Or at least ex-royalty.
You can bet they've canvassed the Windsors and the Rainiers
and got a polite brush-off.'

The Windsors and the Rainiers, however, were in the happy
position of not owing gratitude to Elissa Paroskolos. The

1

Hirtensteins were indebted to her – well, not exactly to Elissa, but to the memory of her dead father, Yanni Dimitriouso.

A long time ago, when the Hirtensteins had been chased out of their homeland without a pfennig, their kind-hearted friend Yanni had come up with a substantial loan. Such good deeds can never be forgotten by the blue-blooded, so by a majority of two to one, ex-Crown Prince Gregorius von Hirtenstein, known outside his family circle as Gregory Crowne, had been elected, despite his protests, to attend Elissa's celebrations.

This was only one more negative entry in the mental balance sheet. He'd been outvoted, and if he'd been strong-willed he'd just have said, 'I won't go.' But his sense of duty, confound it, had made him agree. For not only had dear old Yanni made a substantial loan to the Hirtensteins, he'd quietly cancelled the debt when they'd paid off about a quarter of it.

So here was Gregory Crowne, sitting on the edge of a swimming pool on the island of Kerouli, trying to get the better of his feelings of vexation and hostility – and succeeding rather well, because sitting beside him in a steamer chair was the lady of his heart, Liz Blair.

The invitation to the party had been worded 'and companion'. Mr Crowne had insisted that 'and companion' should mean Liz Blair. Grandmama Nicoletta had been indignant. 'That girl!' she'd complained. 'She's so *unsuitable*!'

Very true, from Grandmama's point of view. Liz hadn't a drop of royal blood in her veins, from any side of any blanket. She wasn't distantly related even to the aristocracy. She was a commoner through and through.

Grandmama Nicoletta might have forgiven that, had she been a star of some minor firmament – a great artist, an opera diva, a writer of distinction, even a well-known couturière. Alas, no. Though Liz was in the dress trade, she was a buyer – a nobody who went to fashion shows and then either bought saleable designs for a wholesale dress chain or prepared designs of her own that were more or less copies. Not a lofty profession.

Liz had been thrilled when Gregory had asked her to accompany him to Kerouli. A lot of the Beautiful People would be there, and they would, of course, be wearing beautiful clothes. Although not exactly planning to raid their wardrobes, Liz intended to take lots of notes and lots of photographs, to help her in choosing next year's resort clothes for the stores. So here she sat, wrapped against a rather chill sea breeze in a cerise cotton sweater and with her wet toffee-coloured hair wrapped in a towel. Grandmama Nicoletta would have disapproved of her entirely. Yet by her very presence, she cancelled out all the debits in the mental ledger and made this jaunt bearable for the ex-crown prince of Hirtenstein.

'So is she really horrible?' she now asked. 'In the pictures you see in the society mags she looks rather angelic.'

'Who says the camera can't lie?' the prince enquired. 'From what Papa and Grossmutti say, she's still the same objectionable girl who learned one-upmanship in the cradle. I suffered from it myself, years ago.'

'What, you mean she was one of your lady-loves and gave you the air?'

He grinned. 'Hardly. I was fifteen and she was nine. She came to stay with us at Bredoux for the mountain air – she'd had some chest infection or something and it was thought it would do her good. But she didn't like the house, which of course wasn't up to the standard she was used to, and she was scared of the horses – Papa didn't believe it, he thought she was just being difficult—'

'But by what you tell me, your papa thinks the world is divided into two kinds of people: human beings and horses,' she laughed.

'That's true.' Greg's father taught equestrianism in a little hamlet outside Geneva where the family had settled after leaving Hirtenstein rather hurriedly. It sometimes seemed, even to his loving son, that ex-King Anton was descended from centaurs. 'Anyhow, she was very rude – said we smelt all horsey – and spent a lot of time in her room watching TV and stuffing herself with chocolates. I remember she mixed up the pages of my music manuscript just before I was going for a piano exam . . .'

'On purpose?'

'Well, what was she doing ferreting around in my music case? She couldn't read music – didn't know Bach from

3

Bernstein. What's more, she squashed a chocolate in the middle of page four. She'd heard me say page four was difficult.'

'What a philistine!' laughed Liz. 'Did you play through the chocolate? How did it sound?'

'Sweet, of course, which was quite inappropriate because the piece was by Sibelius.'

'Oh, him,' said Liz. She had actually heard of Sibelius, which was more than could be said of some of the composers her beloved talked about.

Gregory Crowne made his living as a concert arranger on a small scale. He had adopted this career on realizing that he would never be a good enough pianist to make it in the competitive world of classical performance. It earned him an adequate income, giving him pleasure and satisfaction; he was happy in his work, although he might have made more by allowing his name to be added to various boards of directors.

Liz, by contrast, knew almost nothing about classical music. To tell the truth, she had something of a grudge against it, because it meant that Greg was always flying off to New York or Vienna or somewhere to play nursemaid to some neurotic performer. The idea of spending almost a whole week with him on some idyllic island had sent her into an emotional spin; and the island really was idyllic. The main house, which she'd seen as the motor boat drew in to the jetty, was on the highest point, a lovely white building embowered in olive trees and with a wrought-iron balcony round the upper floor.

She and Greg had been taken by a tiny little electric vehicle, something like a golf buggy, up a steep path to a cabana on a platform cut into the rock, with glorious views out to sea. A short walk from their cabana there was another, and then the swimming pool, sheltered by a wrought-iron grille interwoven with the evergreen leaves of passion flowers still in bud.

It had seemed absolutely imperative to go for a swim, because almost no one Liz knew had a pool, let alone a whole island; but despite the shelter of the trellis, the sea breeze had been a little too keen. They'd scrambled out and

4

dried off, to be offered hot coffee almost at once by one of the attentive waiters.

So here they sat, filling in the lazy hour before it was time to dress and meet the other guests at a cocktail party in the big house. Greg was lying back in his steamer chair, long legs extended, feet crossed, hair plastered to his skull, and his nose rather pink from the cold water. Liz looked at him with fondness. Blue-blooded people went pink with cold like everyone else, it seemed.

'So she was sneaky and ill-natured. But pretty, of course.'

'Was she? I thought of her as podgy, completely spoiled by her doting father and given to tantrums. She turned herself into a good-looking girl by the exercise of her iron will, I think.'

She chuckled. 'You really disapprove of her, don't you?'

'Well, she made me fail my music exam! I had to take it again three months later. As to having anything wrong with her chest, I never believed it, because she had enough breath to scream like a banshee when she couldn't have her own way.' He sighed. 'Looking back, I don't think there was anything wrong with her. Her mama just wanted to get rid of her for a couple of months.'

'Her mama. Is she here for the birthday?'

'Not she. She took off with some real-estate salesman just after Elissa's mountain visit and negotiated a huge divorce settlement. From all I hear, Elissa hates her.'

'I'm glad I asked. I might have put my foot in it.'

'Well, it's a pretty foot.' He reached out a bony hand to pat it.

She swung the pretty foot about at the ankle. 'But though you thought there was nothing wrong with her *then*, this time it's been really serious.'

'Yes.' Gregory was silent a moment. 'I shouldn't be unkind about her. She's been through a dreadful time. The word is, she's had a serious form of meningitis – lucky to recover, by all accounts, and it's taken months.'

She could see he was feeling guilty. She stretched and got to her feet. 'Come on, it's getting a bit chilly. I need to dry my hair and get ready for the cocktail thing.'

A few other guests had been sitting about on the perimeter

but now they too were heading towards their rooms to get dressed for the evening. The ex-crown prince and his lady-love fell in with them, exchanging friendly nods and seeing some of them peel off along other paths, presumably to other cabanas.

'This place must be quite big?' Liz ventured.

'No, I think it's just been very well planned. Yanni Dimitriouso hired one of the great architects to do the job – I think it was Telbeger or somebody. Cost millions, even then. But he felt he needed a retreat from the pressures of piling up the dollars. I've never been here before, but I think I heard there were cottages and cabins enough for about a hundred and fifty.'

'And the posh guests get to stay in the main house up on the hill?'

'No, I think the house was designed just for family living. We'll see when we get there.'

The cocktail party was to be held in the house. It proved to have an open-plan ground floor, the entry merging into the drawing room and then into the dining room and into the games room and the garden room. The only places with doors were the kitchen and what might be the master's study.

The master – that was Niki Paroskolos, whose name figured in the list of the world's hundred richest, and whose photograph figured almost as often as his wife's in the society magazines. He was a handsome man, without a hint of grey in his thick black hair despite the anxieties of high finance. He moved about among his guests, stopping for a hand-clasp here, a hearty embrace there.

'Where's Elissa?' Liz whispered to Greg.

'I don't see her. Perhaps she's not going to be here for the entire evening.' He glanced about, able to see over the heads of most of the guests. 'I don't see many of her relations.'

'Maybe she's quarrelled with them?'

'Wouldn't surprise me. I overheard the boatman saying it would be a comparatively small affair.'

She smiled at him in admiration. He could speak Greek, and also French, German, Italian and almost every language that his international clientele called for. Then she remarked,

6

'A small affair? There must be about a hundred people here!'

'Well, that's small by the standards of the Paroskolos family, or the Dimitriousos. Grossmutti said there were about four hundred people at Elissa's wedding.'

'What, on this little island?'

'Darling, don't be silly. They'd have fallen off into the water. No, Elissa and Niki were married in Paris, which in my opinion is the only reason Grossmutti agreed to go.'

'I saw a picture of her wedding dress,' she sighed. 'A long slinky satin gown with a train . . . Gorgeous. But I don't even remember the bridegroom.'

The said bridegroom now approached, hand outstretched. 'Your Highness,' he said in a cordial tone. 'We haven't met, but I know you from reading about your musical projects in the newspapers.'

'How do you do,' muttered Gregory. He hated to be addressed as a Highness. 'Miss Blair, let me introduce our host, Niki Paroskolos.'

'Welcome, welcome to Kerouli,' cried Niki, taking Liz's hand in both of his. 'I hope you're comfortable, have everything you need?'

'Oh, more than I need,' Liz said. 'It's all absolutely delightful.'

'How is Elissa?' Greg enquired. 'Haven't seen her so far.'

'No, she'll be down a little later. She's very nervous, you understand, so Dr Donati is giving her a little something to shore up her confidence.'

'Elissa is nervous?' Greg echoed, with some surprise.

'Oh yes. I'm afraid you'll find her very changed, Gregory. Pyogenic meningitis, you know – it takes a heavy toll. We were lucky to have it recognized early enough to get proper treatment, but even so . . .' His voice died away. The dark eyes seemed to fill with sorrow, but he rallied. 'Well, you'll see. She's doing very well, and Dr Donati thought this would be a good opportunity to launch her back into the social round.'

'I look forward to wishing her well,' Greg said.

Niki thanked him, then, with a polite inclination of the head, moved on to speak to other guests.

'She's nervous, and this is a "good opportunity" for a relaunch?' murmured Liz, 'in front of a hundred people?'

Greg shrugged. 'I said it already – this is a relatively small gathering.'

'But surely a little family party would have been better.'

'She's probably done that already, wouldn't you think? Not that a little family party would be much fun for her, because she's on bad terms with almost all her folk.'

'She sounds awful,' sighed Liz, who had parents and a brother whom she loved.

She was glancing about, estimating whether she'd made the right choice in clothes. Some of the other women had the glint of diamonds about them but, on the other hand, some of the men were in dark business suits. Gregory was looking handsome in an evening jacket. Liz had curled her shoulder-length hair on top with a diamante comb, and was wearing a black silk skirt and black taffeta top that left one shoulder bare. Her escort had told her she looked delicious; but, of course, he was biased.

They drifted about the big room, which seemed only a little crowded by the guests. They stopped to chat and introduce themselves now and again. Gregory Crowne observed that most of those they met were friends of Niki Paroskolos, either personal or business. The few who seemed to be from Elissa's side of the marriage were elderly cousins, the kind obliged to turn up and look happy because they were on some kind of family pension.

There was a stir among those in the big entry area. They turned to look. Coming down the wide staircase from the bedroom floor was a dark girl on the arm of a middle-aged, paunchy man.

The guests murmured in greeting. The pair reached the foot of the stairs. The man made an encouraging movement with the arm on which her hand rested. She stepped forward, then paused.

She hesitated, her eyes searching the gathering. Niki moved towards her through the guests. She put out a hand, palm upwards, inviting him to take hers. He obeyed, clasping it gently, then taking it to his lips.

8

The guests offered a little spattering of applause. The couple stood for a moment, acknowledging the greeting. Niki made a motion as if to take his wife forward. She drew back, shy, almost frightened. He said something in her ear, so that she took a step or two into the party area.

She was beautiful – a cloud of dark hair in buoyant waves, fine dark brows over wide brown eyes, a mouth that trembled between smiles and sorrow. She was wearing a short evening dress of creamy voile scattered with dreamlike coppery flowers. Thin straps held it against her slender body.

'Oh wow,' Liz breathed.

'What, "oh wow"?' Greg asked.

'She's changed her dressmaker.'

'How do you know?'

She cast him a glance that said, 'You're a very clever man but you're an idiot.'

He acknowledged this complicated message with a slight shrug. 'But really, how do you know?'

'Well, of course, I only understand her wardrobe by what I've read in magazines; but for evenings she wore Versace and Matthew Williamson mostly – glittery things. That dress is from Gucci. And heels – she's always worn stilettos.'

'Stilettos?' he said in alarm.

'High thin heels. But of course, if she's weak on her pins from the illness, Cubans are safer.'

'Are you speaking English?'

'Catwalk English.' She took pity on his bafflement. 'All I mean is that her clothes always seemed to have a touch of aggression about them. But not tonight.'

'And that's so wonderful it deserves "Oh wow"?'

'It's weird – a really big change. And it's clearly important because this is a big occasion, right?'

'I suppose so.' He'd lost interest, but Liz was ferreting in her tiny evening bag for a pencil. She tugged at his sleeve, and he said, 'What?'

'I need a piece of paper – something to sketch on.'

'You're going to sketch her dress?' He was feeling in the breast pocket of his evening jacket but had nothing to offer.

'Oh well,' she said, philosophical, 'I'll jot it down when

9

we get back to the cabin.' She watched Elissa's slow progress through the gathering, taking in the rather shy look with which she accepted good wishes. 'You're sure she's a monster?' she asked.

'Always has been so far.'

'She looks rather sweet to me.'

He nodded a puzzled agreement. 'As you just said, it's weird. This is quite unlike her.'

'Well, she's been ill a long time, Greg. And meningitis – isn't that something to do with the brain? Maybe her outlook's been affected.'

'Um,' said the prince. 'That could be interesting.'

'Well, of course, you'd have to stop thinking of her as a horror.'

'There's more to it than that. Here we have a young woman who was her father's daughter where business was concerned, and who used her money as a weapon. Now she seems different, uncertain . . .'

'So?'

'Weakness in the world of high finance could be a danger for her.'

'Nah,' Liz contradicted. 'She's got that gorgeous husband to protect her.'

Further consideration of the matter was postponed as the trio approached them – Elissa Paroskolos and her husband with her doctor in attendance. Elissa's expression was faintly apprehensive, something like a girl on her first date – afraid of saying the wrong thing, of making herself look gauche.

'Darling, you remember Prince Gregory, of course,' said Niki.

His wife's face brightened; she put out a hand. 'Of course – Greg – how are you?'

'Well, thank you. And you too, I hear – you're well.' Her hand in his was thinner than he'd expected. Niki had said the illness had taken a heavy toll, and he was right.

'Yes, I'm a lot better. Still some way to go, perhaps.' Even her voice was different: lower, more husky.

Because he made his living by music, Gregory Crowne had a very keen ear. One of the reasons he'd disliked Elissa

10

Dimitriouso as a child was that she'd had a tendency to shriek. He couldn't imagine this young woman shrieking. There was, in fact, very little force behind the production of the voice.

She'd learned her English during a long education at the best American colleges and was justifiably proud of it. She spoke it tonight with hesitation and with a slightly different cadence, as if her breathing had altered or – more likely – she'd spent her convalescence catching the tone of too much American TV.

He introduced Liz, who said how pleased she was to be here on this wonderful little island.

'Yes, my father created it as a place to escape to,' Elissa said. 'It's been wonderful for me this past year, you know. Absolute peace and quiet . . .'

'Yes, but not so peaceful this evening, sweetheart,' Niki put in, smiling.

She turned to the man just behind her elbow. 'Just a few friends,' she said, as if repeating words of encouragement.

'That's it – just a few friends.' He had a jovial voice that went with his rather chubby, reassuring frame.

'This is my guardian angel,' Elissa said, 'Dr Donati – I owe him everything.'

He gave a little bow as salute. 'A wonderful occasion,' he said, glancing about at the well-dressed company, the spacious rooms glowing with lamplight and flowers. 'And, you know, you organized most of it yourself.'

'Oh no – really, it was Niki . . .'

'Well, well, the pair of you together.' He patted her arm. 'And that's how it should be, my dear.'

'Yes, that's how it should be.' She smiled for the first time – a real smile, not a little hostess simper.

'My word,' thought Liz, 'she's a real beauty.'

Her husband moved towards the next group. Obediently she moved with him. The doctor lingered a moment to say, 'Gregory – I may call you Gregory? – you know her well; how does she seem to you?'

'Oh, I can't say I know her well,' said Gregory with some embarrassment. 'Last time I saw her she was nine years old!'

'Really?' The doctor was thoughtful, running a hand through his thinning hair. 'Ah. Childhood friends, eh?'

'Oh yes.' Childhood enemies, thought the prince.

'So do you think she's doing well?'

'Certainly. I gather it's mostly due to your care.'

'Oh . . . I suppose I can claim some of the credit . . . So you approve of my work, eh?' He gave a proud smile, waited for Greg to nod in approval, and followed his patient among the guests.

Soon afterwards, the buffet was in service. Liz bagged a little table near French windows open to the freshness of the night while Greg went to fetch some food. He found himself caught up for some minutes alongside a young man having a foolish argument in Greek over which wine to take.

'Keirios Paroskolos, both are excellent . . .'

'But should I have white? It's from Chile, I never drink white wine except French.'

'Shall I order a bottle of French to be brought . . . ?'

'Chablis? Is there Chablis?'

'Oh, certainly, sir. If you'll just wait a moment I'll—'

'But Niki told me to behave myself. I'd better not be a nuisance. The red isn't Spanish, is it?'

'No, sir, it's Bordeaux . . .'

'I'll have the red.'

He accepted his drink and wandered off. The waiter turned an expressionless gaze on the prince.

'Who was that?' asked Gregory. 'You called him Keirios Paroskolos?'

'The young brother of Keirios Niki.' The waiter clearly didn't want to discuss him. 'What can I offer you, sir?'

Greg accepted a plate of seafood and one of smoked pheasant for himself and Liz to share. They already had drinks. When he sat down beside her he said, 'You read the society magazines. Isn't Niki's younger brother supposed to be a bit of a . . . now what's the word? . . . a bit of a tearaway?'

'Oh yes.' She picked a piece of salmon from the plate with her fingers. 'Rather a bad lot, but he reformed not long ago. Got himself dried out at one of those posh clinics in Switzerland. Why, is he here?'

'Yes, dithering about at the buffet like a lost puppy. How's the salmon?'

12

'Gorgeous. Let's eat a lot and go back to the cabin, Greg. I feel I've done my social duty for one day.'

This was a fine plan. They slipped away unnoticed by and by. Liz quite forgot to sketch Elissa's gown because she had better things to think about. Happy in the luck that had brought them to this little haven, they made love. Outside, the sky was softened to a pearly blue by a quarter-moon, and beneath it the sea of Greece lapped against the cliffs.

Despite the happy circumstances, Gregory Crowne found himself lying awake. A foolish and no doubt idiotic thought had returned to his mind: Elissa Paroskolos had been ill. She was alone in the world now, because her powerful father had died about eighteen months ago. She was very rich, and vulnerable. If anyone wanted to manipulate her, to gain control of her fortune, it would be easy.

But no. As Liz had said, she had her gorgeous husband to protect her.

Two

G regory awoke to find that Liz had left the cabana – gone out to run, no doubt. He squinted at the bedside clock: ten minutes past nine. Sad to say, it was time to get up. He hated getting up, yet he did it every day.

He was shaving when Liz returned, sweat-drenched in denim shorts and a T-shirt. She planted a kiss on his chin, receiving in exchange a shaving-foam moustache.

'Ten minutes to breakfast,' she said, shedding clothes and heading for the shower. 'I promised Elissa and Trudi we'd meet them at the pool.'

'Who's Trudi?' he called as the water started running.

'Sort of nurse-companion, I think. Nice type – seems very devoted.'

Breakfast came in three versions on the island: you could whip it up for yourself from the contents of the fridge in the tiny kitchenette, you could pick up the phone and order it delivered by electric runabout, or you could go to the pavilion along the north side of the swimming pool.

It was there that they found Elissa and Trudi. Trudi was crocheting something large, using very fine yarn. Seeing Liz eyeing it with interest, she said, 'A lace bedspread, for my niece.'

There was a trace of Austria in her speech. She wasn't old, but there was something motherly in her appearance: sturdy body, round face, baby-soft straight hair cut in a slanting fringe across her calm brow. She was wearing a very ordinary cotton dress, nothing at all like a uniform, yet you could tell she was a nurse of some kind.

Her charge sat across the table from her, with a cup of coffee and a copy of yesterday's *New York Times*. She put it aside as

14

they took their places. To Gregory she looked as if she'd slept badly. There were shadows under the dark eyes, fatigue in the droop of her eyelids.

A waiter appeared at once with menus. At other tables guests were eating: croissants and French jam, cheese and crispbread, smoked fish, or simply tea and toast. Liz decided in favour of some fruit from the self-service table; Gregory asked for scrambled eggs.

Elissa seemed to rouse herself to be a hostess. 'I already asked Liz; she said you had everything you needed at the cottage?'

'Yes, thank you, it's excellent.'

'And you slept well?' She looked from Liz to Gregory, blushed a little, and sought for a way to rephrase it.

'Very well, thank you – and you?'

'Oh, me . . . I sometimes don't . . . I sometimes get these bad dreams . . .'

'It was just reaction to the excitement of last night, madame,' Trudi suggested. 'You got overtired.'

'I suppose it was that. But snakes . . . why should I dream of snakes?' She shuddered.

'Oh, that's horrid,' Liz agreed through a mouthful of fresh papaya. 'Sometimes I get dreams like that, but it's always big insects – you know, the kind they show you in close-up on television.'

'But this was so real,' objected Elissa. 'Not just snakes, but you know – people were handling them, picking them up . . .'

'Like those evangelical types in the American South, you mean – in a revivalist tent?' Gregory asked.

'No, not that . . .' She was silent a moment. 'It was all white and bright, like a laboratory or something.'

Trudi put out a hand to pat her arm. 'You should just forget it,' she said in gentle admonition.

Gregory was inclined to agree. He preferred not to think about snakes first thing in the morning while eating scrambled eggs. He was searching for a way to turn the conversation, when Niki strolled up.

He dropped a kiss on his wife's head. 'Had a good walk, my love?'

'We did the all-around trail, twice,' Trudi supplied, 'and Madame enjoyed it.'

'Yes,' Elissa said, 'I enjoyed it.'

It was almost like a schoolgirl repeating a lesson. Liz and Gregory took care not to meet each other's eye – there was something embarrassing in it. For something to say, Liz announced that she'd run round the trail and found it quite hard work: 'A lot of ups and downs,' she explained.

'Oh yes, Papa had the paths quarried out of the solid rock,' Elissa said. 'There was nothing here when he bought it, it was just a big old rock sticking up out of the water with some tufts of seagrass and a few wild flowers that had survived the goats.'

'Goats?'

'Oh, my dear Miss Blair, the curse of Mediterranean gardeners,' cried Niki. 'Leave them for a couple of months on any stretch of land and they'll eat it bare. But Yanni banished them all, of course and, as I understand it, employed experts of every kind to make the island a little paradise.'

'It certainly is that,' Liz said, glancing about the pavilion. It was a beautiful building: long and low, open on one side this morning to the risen sun, its furnishings were chosen to give a feeling of lightness and space. The tables were of thick glass resting on aluminium legs, the chairs had white canvas seats and backs, and the guests in their bright casual clothes were the only colour.

'I remember some of the construction work,' Elissa announced after a pause. 'When I was small . . . Cranes were shipped over from Piraeus on barges . . . Yes . . . little yellow cranes moving about like big caterpillars . . . We made home movies of it.' Her eyes had a faraway look. Was she seeing that childhood show, so outlandish in its technical strength? – an illustration of her father's power?

Niki smiled and nodded. 'You wrote about it too,' he reminded her. 'You did an essay at school.'

'Yes. At school.' She paused. 'Niki, is there a place where people do things with snakes, pick them up and hold them, put something – pieces of glass – against their mouths . . . ?'

He stared at her but quickly masked his surprise. 'I don't think so, dearest.'

16

'It was just a dream, madame,' said Trudi soothingly.

'No, they do that; it's for a reason . . .'

'It doesn't sound likely, my love.'

'It makes you feel uneasy. The snakes struggle to get away . . .'

'Forget about it, madame,' Trudi urged. 'You'll give yourself another nightmare.'

'The Butanta Institute,' she said, as if plucking the name out of the air.

'What?'

'I think . . . that's the name of the place . . .'

There was an awkward silence. Gregory and Liz looked at their plates; Niki put a comforting arm around his wife. 'Let's go back to the house, Elissa,' he suggested. 'The latest boat brought back some letters.' He flashed an apologetic glance at his two guests, who smiled tactfully.

She rose. 'Is that the name of the place?' she asked in a puzzled tone. She looked at Gregory. 'Have you heard of it?'

'I'm afraid not,' he said and then, trying for lightness, 'but then I'm not a fan of snakes.'

'Neither am I.' She shuddered. 'So why did I dream about them?'

'Perhaps yesterday evening was a little too much for you, my dear,' said her husband, shepherding her away. He gave a little look over his shoulder as they went as if to say, 'It's nothing, please forgive it.'

Trudi folded up her crochet, put it in a beach bag, and rose to follow her patient. 'Perhaps she had some wine,' she mused. 'There was so much pressure upon her, she might have picked up a glass by mistake.'

'And she shouldn't have wine?'

'Oh no, sir; it's contra-indicated with her medication.' She sighed. 'But it's not so big a thing; she'll be all right by this afternoon. I blame myself, though. I should have been there last night but you know . . . it might not have looked so good: a nurse at her elbow.'

'But Dr Donati was standing in for you,' Gregory suggested.

'Just so, and he's so careful – like a father to her, you know,

Mr Crowne. Ah well, it is a long road still ahead of her. *"Nun weiter denn, nur weiter, Mein treuer Wanderstab!"'*

'You like Schubert?' the prince asked, pleased.

'*Bitte?*'

'That's from a Schubert song.'

'It's from a poem by Wilhelm Muller,' she said firmly, and strode away.

'What was that she said?' Liz enquired, rather taken aback at the brisk disappearance of the others.

'It's from one of Schubert's songs. It means, "Now onwards, only onwards, my trusty staff" – staff meaning a support while you walk, you understand.' He pondered. 'I suppose that's how she sees herself: as Elissa's trusty staff.'

'And cross because she wasn't allowed to be with her last night.'

'Perhaps.'

They finished their food. Their coffee cups were refilled at once. While they drank, Gregory looked up the music crits in the *New York Times* while Liz sketched what she could recall of Elissa's dress.

'What would you like to do today?' he enquired.

'Well . . . What is there to do, actually? We could walk around the island, but I've just done that on the trot and, though it's quite interesting, it'd only take about half an hour. Besides, aren't we supposed to turn up for this lunch thing?'

He was shaking his head. 'No, I checked with the major-domo—'

'Major-domo!'

'Well, what's the word in English? Butler? Male house-keeper? In French we'd call him *directeur*.'

'Okay then, major-domo,' she said, amused.

'He said Keirios Paroskolos wanted everyone to feel free to enjoy themselves. I gather food will be available here around midday, but we don't have to show up if we don't want to. There's a tennis court, and of course there's a billiard room and so forth round the back of this building.'

'Tennis?' she mused. She was quite an energetic person but felt she'd done her stint towards physical fitness with her morning run.

18

For his part he was glad to see her shaking her head. He wasn't very keen on competitive sports. He rode well, which was only to be expected since his father taught horsemanship; he could handle sail, he swam and liked angling, and in winter he made good time at cross-country skiing. These were all things he could do on his own. He'd only learned to play tennis as part of his social training.

'We could go to Hydra, if you like. It would make a nice boat ride, and Miltos said we were welcome to make use of the boats.'

'What's at Hydra?'

'Well now . . . You could say it's the Juan les Pins of the islands . . .'

'Ooh – trendy?'

'I believe so, but I really only know Athens. And by the way, this reminds me: I must get to Athens at some time. I've got to see a man about a *hydraulis*, as it happens.'

'A what? Spell it.' He obliged. 'If it's from Hydra, why can't you see it there?'

'It's nothing to do with Hydra – that's a coincidence.'

'"Hydra" – that means water. What is it – a washing machine?'

'No, it's a musical instrument'

'With "hydra" in it – are you telling me there's a musical instrument based on water?'

'Yes, there is.'

'What does it play – the theme music from *Jaws*?'

'I don't know what it plays. That's why I want to see it. It's been reconstructed,' he said with total earnestness, 'from designs drawn up by somebody called Ctesibius . . .'

'Oh, with a catchy name like that he can't fail!'

'Well, I think it's Ctesibius . . . in 300 BC or thereabouts.' He became aware that she was grinning. 'Oh, very well then: you can go shopping in the Plaka while I look at the *hydraulis* – but I think it would make a good evening's entertainment. There's a lot of interest these days in early music.'

'Can't get earlier than 300 BC,' she agreed. 'Let's go to Hydra, even if it hasn't got a *hydraulis* – I feel the urge to watch the fashionable world wind-surfing and water-skiing.'

'I can't guarantee that, sweetheart. From what I've heard, it's more – what word would you use? – arty.'

They found on enquiry that one of the little fleet of motor boats was of course available to take them to Hydra and that one or two other guests had already decided to go. Among these, Gregory espied Niki Paroskolos's brother. While Liz busied herself with a pencil sketch of Kerouli seen from the sea, he got into conversation with Costa Paroskolos.

'Miss Blair and I don't know Hydra,' he began. 'Perhaps you could give us a few tips?'

Paroskolos shrugged. 'Full of painters and sculptors these days,' he said. 'I don't go there a lot.'

'But you're going today?'

'Only en route to the mainland. I've done my duty, if you know what I mean. Last night was a bore.' He broke off – looked rather guiltily at Mr Crowne. 'Shouldn't say that, should I? But I've never really had anything in common with Lissa. She never approved of me in the old days, so I've always steered clear.'

'She seems to have recovered very well . . .'

'Glad she's better, of course – that goes without saying. A lot less domineering, seems to me.'

'Yes, perhaps she's rather nervy. She has Dr Donati at hand, of course.'

'Oh, Dr Donati, he's a miracle worker! I can't tell you what a difference he's made to my life! I owe him everything.'

'He's your doctor too?' Gregory said, rather surprised.

'Not now. I'm "stable" now, you know. But of course when Lissa was in such terrible trouble, Niki knew just who to turn to.'

'Donati is a specialist, then?'

'You don't know him?'

'Not at all – but then I'm not well up in medical things.'

'You're from Switzerland, aren't you? I thought you might have heard of him. He runs a clinic in Switzerland, not far from Mürren.'

'Oh, in the Bernese Oberland. That's a bit far from my part of the world; I'm from Geneva.'

'Geneva . . . I meant to drop in on Geneva when I left the

clinic, but somehow I never got round to it. To tell the truth, I wanted to get home, where it's less . . . well, I don't know . . . where you can relax a bit more.'

Mr Crowne took this reflection on his adopted homeland in good part, and they went on to chat about life in Athens. 'They're putting on a *rembetika* group from Athens for you on the island tonight. If you're ever in Piraeus, drop in on some of the clubs; that's where it's at its best.'

Without having any intention of following up on the suggestion – for *rembetika*, he recalled, was a sort of Greek mongrel born of the blues and *bouzouki* music – Gregory nodded approval.

At Hydra most of the passengers disembarked. The Paroskolos' boatman said he'd collect them at four o'clock. Costa waved them goodbye as he was carried on towards the pleasures of Athens. Liz, who'd spent most of the voyage trying to photograph a quartet of dolphins, asked, 'Was that the brother?'

'Yes, he's making his escape.'

'I thought I recognized him from the magazines. Escape from what?'

'The boredom of Kerouli. He was saying something rather interesting, you know.'

'What was that?'

'He says Dr Donati treated him at his clinic in Switzerland.'

'Oh, when he went into seclusion to get over his bad habits?' She thought a moment, then frowned. 'Is that what's wrong with Elissa? She's got the shakes from getting over a drug problem?'

He considered that. 'I can't believe it. Elissa was never the kind to get caught up in drugs or drink.'

'No, but if she was getting over the after-effects of meningitis, and inadvertently got hooked on something?'

'Do *you* think that's why she's so shaky?'

'No . . . well . . . I'm no expert . . . Of course I do see people in the rag trade who feel they need a little top-up of something. It always seems to make them rather bright and merry, whereas Elissa . . .' She was looking back over her short acquaintance with her. 'That dream thing this morning – about the snakes?'

21

'Yes, snakes. I suppose that's the kind of thing that people hallucinate about.'

'But, Greg, I don't think she'd had a hallucination. I mean I may be wrong, but I genuinely think she had a dream that scared her.'

'*C'est ça*,' said Mr Crowne and, taking her arm, led her in among the narrow streets of Hydra.

Since most of them led steeply upwards, they needed all their breath, so conversation languished. Then, in the pleasure of patronizing the little studios, fingering hammered-silver picture frames and escaping the purchase of post-post-modern sculpture, they forgot about Elissa.

Lunch was eaten rather late in a taverna that served delicious fried *barbounia*, which Liz found on enquiry was red mullet. As promised, the vaporetto called to take them back to Kerouli with the rest of the guests. Once back at the their cabin, Greg said he'd take the opportunity to make some phone calls, so Liz elected to go out with her camera to use up the film.

At the highest point of the island she came across their hostess sitting in the shade of a pepper tree, staring out at the waters gleaming molten gold in the westering sun. She turned at the sound of Liz's footfall on the path of crushed rock. There was something almost scared in her expression, as if she were playing truant and thought someone had come in search of her.

'Hello, admiring the view?'

Elissa nodded. She pulled off her straw hat, offering her hair and face to the breeze. 'It's nice sometimes, you know . . . just to be on your own.'

'I know what you mean.'

Elissa said nothing for a moment, then: 'I suppose you thought I was a bit weird this morning, going on about that nightmare.'

'Not at all.'

'People who tell you their dreams are the pits, aren't they!'

'Well, it was a dream worth talking about . . .'

'But the thing is, it wasn't just one of those wild roller-coaster rides where horrible ideas pop out of your subconscious. I felt as if I'd really seen it. I was *remembering* it in my dream, and how I'd felt when I was there.'

22

'It seemed as if you knew a lot about it. What was that name you came up with?'

'The Butanta Institute.'

'Perhaps you've been there.'

'But Niki said it doesn't exist.'

Liz wanted to say, 'Perhaps Niki doesn't know absolutely everything,' but instead enquired, 'Have you looked it up?'

'Looked it up?

'In an encyclopaedia.'

'I don't think there is one on the island.'

'Well, the Internet, then. You've got a computer?' She asked this in full confidence that the answer must be yes, because the running of the island's various establishments and systems practically demanded at least one.

'Of course. But it's in Niki's study.'

'But it's available to you?'

'We-ell . . .' Clearly this was something that the invalid had never thought of. 'I suppose so.'

'Then let's go and ask him to look it up.'

'But he's busy at the pavilion, setting things up for the *rembetika* group.'

'All the better. We don't need to bother him with it. Come on, let's go and see whether the place really exists or if you just imagined it.'

Elissa rose slowly, but fell into step with Liz's brisk pace. They reached the house within ten minutes. In the early-evening calm, its white stone facade seemed to offer peace and perhaps wisdom.

They went in. Liz glanced at Elissa for directions. Elissa led the way through the open-plan area to one of the doors at the back of the house. Here she hesitated. She seemed to be asking herself whether or not she should enter.

Liz solved it for her. She boldly turned the handle and in they went.

'It was really strange,' she told Gregory when she got back to the cabin about half an hour later. 'She seemed scared to touch the computer. Almost as if she were doing something wrong.'

'So what happened?'

'Oh, I just sat down and got a search engine going, and in next to no time, there it was: Butanta Institute, Sao Paulo, Brazil. Renowned centre for the provision of snake antivenom.'

'Snake antivenom!'

'With pictures. People milking venom from the snakes' mouths, on to glass slides. In a laboratory with white walls.'

'And that's what she described!'

'It knocked her for six, Greg. I had to help her up to her room and get her to lie down. Luckily the nurse type arrived just about then and took over.'

'This is very strange.'

'You can say that again.'

'But I just said it once . . .'

'Now you know very well that's just a phrase or saying – oh, it was a joke. I see.' She gave him a lightweight punch on the arm. 'Be serious. What do you think? Seems she's not having hallucinations after all.'

'Well, there must be some explanation. She knew the basic facts about this place. But why does it upset her so?'

'It's scary, Greg. You know what you said yesterday? – about her having control of all that money? You should have seen her just now: she was like a child, clinging on to me, shivering, practically in a state of collapse.'

He deliberated. 'What did the nurse say?'

'Not much. She shooed me out of the room, murmuring that Madame had these attacks sometimes.'

'Umm.' But if it meant anything – and he wasn't by any means sure of that – why should it concern them? Mr Crowne had little interest in the world of finance. Liz Blair had more, perhaps, because fashion these days was being taken over by big business; yet in her corner of the industry big deals on stock exchanges had little meaning.

'Did you make all your phone calls? Everything going well?'

'Mostly. Miriamne Voss has withdrawn from the programme I was putting on in Lisbon, so I got Zefera to stand in—' He cut himself off. 'You're not interested in any of that,' he said without rancour. 'Anyhow, I've just got to ring home now. I promised I'd let them know what I thought of the celebrations.'

She knew he meant he was going to ring his grandmother: ex-Queen Mother Nicoletta had a healthy interest in social affairs because it was among the jet set that she found clients for her talents as an interior decorator. Liz waggled fingers in farewell and went to the kitchenette for a cold drink. After the little drama in the study, she felt in need of something.

Gregory rang Bredoux. When Nicoletta picked up, he pictured her at this hour with a glass of dry sherry in her hand.

'Well?' she demanded. 'Did she appear in a dress falling off her plump bosoms?'

'Not at all, Grossmutti. Liz says it was a Gucci. Very pretty and virtuous. And her bosoms are a lot less plump these days.'

'Ha!' This expression of irritation was for both his opinion of Elissa's clothes and his mention of Liz; but she listened comfortably to his description of other guests, making mental notes of women who might be clients.

The prince was about to say au revoir when a thought occurred. 'Grossmutti, you know everybody: have you ever heard of a doctor called Donati?'

'No, doctors I don't concern myself with.' Diplomats, envoys and ex-prime ministers were more her type.

'He has an exclusive sort of clinic near Mürren.'

'Mürren?' she echoed, as if it were in Outer Mongolia. Nicoletta liked to stay near the warm shores of Lake Geneva.

'Could you find out about him for me?'

'Why are you interested in him?'

'Oh, it's just that he's here, looking after Elissa. And I was just thinking: if he has a lucrative practice to run in Mürren, he's making a big sacrifice in devoting himself to one patient on a tiny Saronic island.'

'Ah. Devoting himself? You mean exclusively?'

'It seems so. Moreover, I gather he's been here about a year.'

'*Himmel*, that is a wonderment. Either he's an idealist or they're paying him a fortune.'

'Yes.'

'So the girl has really been very sick?'

'I think so. And still is.'

'What? But this event was to celebrate her return to normality – if she ever has been normal.'

'Come come, Grossmutti; don't be catty. She was as normal as a spoilt very rich little girl is likely to be.'

'But, Gregory, my cattiness apart – this is a big risk for them, no? If she is not well, they shouldn't be putting her under the strain of holding this party.'

'I was wondering if it had something to do with financial affairs? Presumably her board of directors has been running her companies during the last year. Perhaps that's been causing them problems.'

'Or perhaps the handsome husband has power of attorney, and other financiers don't wish to deal with him.'

'Why should they not?' the prince asked in alarm.

'Who knows? He has his own great business to run, after all – it's transport, *n'est-ce pas*? Whereas dear Yanni's fortune was made in the world of money, of high finance. Perhaps the two concerns don't call for the same talents and they – I mean the business associates – don't have confidence in Niki.'

'That could be. Speaking of confidence, didn't I once hear that dear Yanni didn't have total confidence in Elissa's business ability in the first place?'

'Oh, that was just because she's a woman. Yanni was one of the old school, my child. He thought women should stay at home having babies. I think it was the greatest misfortune of his life that he didn't have a son.' She sighed fondly. She'd always had a soft spot for dear Yanni, although his only child had turned out such a vixen.

'Well, goodbye, my treasure,' she said, having enjoyed her little gossip. 'Ring me again to let me know how things—'

'No, wait, Grossmutti. About Dr Donati?'

'What about him? I told you, I don't know him.'

'Could you find out about him?'

'Well, of course. But why?'

'I don't know, really. He's *here* – that's what intrigues me.'

'You are an idle child with nothing better to do than see

problems where none exist. Nevertheless, I'll inquire about this idealistic Dr Donati of Mürren and let you know.'

Gregory reported this promise to Liz, who was taking clothes out of the wardrobe with a critical air.

'What d'you think?' she asked. 'This thing tonight sounds as if it's pretty casual. Not my glitzy see-through blouse, then, and not my Valentino . . .'

'Valentino? The old film star?'

'Darling, what you don't know about fashion would fill the Oxford Dictionary. I don't know why I asked your opinion in the first place.'

'Well, I can tell you this: from previous experience, *rembetika* is a boring sort of music mostly with a simple two-four beat, and people often dance to it.'

'They do?' Her eyes lit up. 'In that case – casual and danceable, eh?' She plucked a sort of camisole from the hangers. 'How about this? With my black skirt?'

'Is that by this dead film star?'

She tossed the camisole down, threw her arms around him, and kissed him with ardour. This led on to a very entertaining interlude that had nothing to do with clothes. When they eventually made their way to the pavilion for the evening's activity, they were clad in resort gear – Liz in her camisole top and a linen skirt, Gregory in Ralph Lauren.

Everybody else had taken the same line. People were sitting about in a relaxed mood with drinks, enjoying the evening air. Darkness had fallen, but the area around the pool was well lit with great standard lamps that sent their beams up towards the dark-blue sky. Further out, fairy lights had been strung up from palm-tree trunks.

The pool itself was covered with tailored wooden decking on which chairs were set out for the musicians. So far they hadn't appeared. Gregory explained that these were late-night birds.

'So what do we do meanwhile?'

He sniffed the air. 'I think we find the barbecue and have some food.'

This proved to be available behind the pavilion on a paved area with plenty of seats and little tables. Music, of the kind termed 'easy listening', was playing from an invisible sound system. They chose from among the kebabs on offer, decided what they wanted to drink and, within five minutes, the food was brought to the table where they were sitting. As they unskewered their chunks of lamb and courgette, they saw Niki in a white linen suit moving among his guests.

He came to them when they had had a few mouthfuls. 'Have you found something you like?' he asked. 'Please mention anything you'd prefer . . .'

'No, this is fine,' Liz said.

'Some people find barbecue food too simple—'

'No, no, this is lovely.'

Instead of moving on, as he'd done elsewhere, he lingered. 'I believe I have to thank you for being a great help to my wife this afternoon, Miss Blair.'

'Oh yes – glad to do what I could. How is she?'

'Very distressed. She feels she made a fool of herself. I hope you didn't think . . .'

'I just thought she was a bit overwrought – snakes seem to be her pet hate.'

'Yes, I suppose so. This was new to me. I don't know how it can have arisen.'

'Perhaps on her travels somewhere?'

He shook his head. 'In the United States? At Smith College or Harvard Business School?'

'Perhaps not.'

'I believe you called up something on computer?'

'Yes, technicians handling snakes at a place called the Butanta Institute. High-quality pics, very realistic.'

He sighed. 'What a pity she saw that.'

Liz was remorseful. 'That was my idea, I'm afraid. She seemed so perplexed about it I thought it would help to find out if the place really existed.'

A hard glint came into his eyes. 'How did you think that would help, exactly?'

The prince, instantly protective, thought it was time to play some part in the conversation. 'The point is, Elissa seems somewhat under the weather. Are you sure she's up to this ordeal of playing hostess over a week to a hundred guests?'

Niki seemed to sense that he'd stepped on an ex-royal toe.

28

His manner returned to its former mode. 'She's fine, really, quite fine. Dr Donati always said we must expect these little setbacks. Only' – with a little laugh – 'this one came out of left field. Snakes! Who could have expected that?'

They exchanged a few more remarks of regret. Liz sent a message of good wishes to Elissa. Niki resumed his progress among his guests.

'It's all very well,' said Gregory, spearing pieces of grilled pepper on his fork, 'but you can't just shrug it off so easily. That poor girl isn't up to all this *spectacle*.'

'You're saying she's round the bend.'

'Round what bend, exactly? Is she suffering from some form of mental instability? Is she having hallucinations? Delusions?'

Liz shook her head. 'I had a perfectly normal conversation with her this afternoon. I thought she was puzzled, bored, perhaps even a little scared. But she wasn't nuts.'

'Scared?' he repeated.

'Yes. When we were going into Niki's study. She seemed . . . I dunno . . . on tenterhooks, as if she was doing something wrong.'

'She didn't want to go?'

'Yes, in a way she did. She wanted to find out if she'd imagined this snake thing or not. But . . . let me try to explain . . . I think she felt Niki would disapprove.'

'And that set her on tenterhooks?'

'Well . . . I think it did.'

He gazed at her in wonder. 'Elissa Paroskolos was afraid she might meet disapproval from her husband?'

'Yes. Yes, I think that was it.'

'My dear darling Liz, Elissa Paroskolos is famous for not being afraid of disapproval – from man, woman or aliens from space. She and her husband have had public rows. She threw a tantrum at her father's funeral because Niki made a mess of having the floral tributes displayed.'

'Well, there you are. She's been ill; it's had an effect on her.'

'And that brings us back to what we were saying last night: she's a very very rich woman. Is she capable these days of handling it?'

They were joined then by a little group of other guests, who drew up chairs and tables with the intention of putting some warmth into the party. By and by the *rembetika* players turned up, to be listened to respectfully for a time until bold spirits decided to dance. Liz was one of those, dragging Gregory up. He obliged her by copying a few of her twirls and shrugs, only not so gracefully. They went back to their cabana about two in the morning, having had rather a good time.

Everyone was late to breakfast. The decking had been removed from the swimming pool and all trace of last night's barbecue had vanished. The newspapers were as usual set out on a table close to the door of the pavilion, so Liz picked up one of the English-language sheets, leaving Gregory to poke about between *Das Neue Blatt* and *Il Giornale d'Italia.*

He joined her at the table with a magazine in his hand and a frown on his brow. 'Look at this,' he said. 'I found it just like this.'

The magazine was opened and folded back at a page showing text and pictures. The heading, in bold type, was 'POISONOUS PETS!' Below that the strapline read: 'Workers at the Butanta Institute in Sao Paulo grow fond of rattlesnakes!'

Liz Blair felt a little frisson of shock. 'Good God!'

Gregory sat down slowly, drawing the magazine towards him to read. 'This is what you call a mega-coincidence . . .' he muttered.

Three

The coincidence wasn't so mega, after all. Gregory had taken a glance at the magazine cover and was reading the article when Dr Donati came bustling up.

'Good morning, good morning,' he called cheerily as he reached them. 'Ah, you saw it! I brought it to breakfast earlier, but of course people were sleeping late so I left it for you to find. Michael – that's the pavilion manager – rang to say you'd come in.' He took hold of a chair back. 'May I?'

'By all means.'

He sat down, looking with some eagerness at the others. 'So that explains it all, doesn't it?'

'In what way?' Gregory replied with an innocent air.

'Well, the snakes – the nightmare – this is the basis, you see.'

'But did Elissa tell you she'd read this?'

'My dear sir, I wouldn't dream of asking her the direct question. It might have a very adverse effect.'

'Then how do you know she's ever seen it?'

'Trudi told me.'

'Told you she'd read it?'

'No, no, she said she'd seen one of the servants reading it, about a week or ten days ago. That was Christos. He must have left it lying around somewhere and Elissa unfortunately saw it, picked it up and read it.'

'That would explain it,' the prince agreed. He ignored the fact that Liz Blair was frowning at him in ferocious disagreement. 'But why should it give her bad dreams?'

'Oh, my friend, snakes! They are so heavily symbolic in Freudian terms.'

'Symbolic of what?' asked Gregory, still innocent.

31

'Of . . . sex, you know, in the male sense.'

'So Elissa is having scary dreams about sex?'

'It's very possible, even probable.'

'But . . . forgive the question . . . Elissa seems so lovingly bonded with Niki, one wonders why she should have such dreams?'

'Ah, in the earlier years . . . children . . . they don't understand what they see, and you know if Mama and Papa were . . .'

'Making love,' supplied Liz, eager to help in whatever Gregory was up to.

'Yes, quite so, and you know, the mother . . . she deserted the child . . . there could be quite a complex, with its beginnings in that.'

'Dear me. Poor Elissa.'

'I unearthed the magazine last night. I meant to drop in at your cabana and show it to you, but of course you were listening to the *rembetika* and probably wanted to sleep late. So I left it for you to find and just wanted to have a word with you, to point out that here is one little mystery solved, no?'

'Yes. Very satisfactory. Elissa is relieved, no doubt.'

'Well, to be truthful, I haven't shown her the magazine. She already agreed that it was just something she must have seen on TV – one of those nature programmes, you know. So I've left it at that. Those pictures – rather too graphic.' This was true, for the largest of them featured a viper with its jaws forced open and its fangs showing in a most unpleasing grin.

Dr Donati got up, pulling his cotton windbreaker down over his slight paunch. His rosy cheeks creased in a smile as he picked up the magazine and rolled it to tuck under his arm. 'I leave you two lovely people to enjoy your day,' he said. 'Shall I see you this evening? There is a display of Greek dancing, if I remember correctly.'

'Wouldn't miss it,' said Mr Crowne.

They watched him go.

'Twit,' said Liz.

'Do you mean that in the male sense?' he asked.

'I mean that in the total sense. Elissa never read that in any magazine. She told me she was *there*!'

32

'But since her travels never seem to have taken her to South America, how can that be so?'

'Well, *I* don't know!' she said crossly, and turned her attention to her breakfast of fruit and rolls.

After they'd finished they went for a walk. There was a carefully tended path leading all round the island, passing now cabanas and now little cleared spaces where plants or trees in great earthenware pots brought colour and greenery to the barren rock. Often there were benches at these points. At one of them, shaded by a slender mimosa, Gregory sat down. Liz sat beside him.

For a time they gazed out to sea, where shipping could be seen through a faint haze moving out towards open waters. They breathed in the scent of mimosa and salt air.

'We're being manipulated,' Gregory said.

'Oh, is that what made me feel so cross with the dear doctor?'

'Very likely.'

'In what way are we being manipulated?'

'We're being asked to believe a pack of improbabilities. That magazine is supposed to have been left lying about by some servant. Oh really? Where is a servant going to leave a magazine lying about so that the mistress of the house is likely to find it?'

'Well . . . yes, that is rather odd.'

'You've been in that house. It's a model of perfection. You've seen how beautifully the pavilion is kept. Can you really imagine a servant sauntering about reading a magazine and then just dropping it somewhere?'

'Not without someone swooping down on it ten minutes later and putting it in the waste disposal.'

'Moreover, even if she saw it, why should Elissa pick it up and read it?'

'Well, on the other hand, sweetie, why not?' she countered.

'Because it's a backpacker's magazine for men. I took a look at the cover before I started to read. Lying closed, it shows a sweaty young man clambering up a jungly path. The magazine is called *Gung Ho*, and the advertising line was something like: "Offbeat thrills for trekkers".'

33

'Ah.'

'Does that seem like a must-read for a cosseted heiress?'

'I don't know. Perhaps if she was bored – and she seemed bored and restless yesterday—'

'Moreover, *mein Liebchen*,' he added, ignoring that, 'the magazine is three years old.'

'Three years old?' She studied him, perplexed. She'd no idea what the fact meant.

Another silence.

'I suppose if there *is* a servant here who's mad keen on backpacking, he might either save a magazine or buy it second hand somewhere.'

'Possible,' he agreed.

'Could you chat with the servant – what was his name?'

'Christos.'

'With Christos, and find out?'

'I could. But the point is, Liz, *should* we?'

'Shouldn't we? What's against it?'

'This is Elissa's home. We're her guests. She's clearly been very ill, and seems to be in a very edgy state. By meddling, we might make things worse. After all, she has a doctor and a nurse attending her. That means she's in good hands. Why should we bother about some dream about snakes?'

'Ye-es.'

'You don't agree?'

'Oh, all that you've said is true, darling. But then you see . . .'

'Yes?'

'Her doctor seems terribly anxious to explain away all that stuff about snakes.'

'So much so,' he rejoined, 'that he planted that magazine for us to find.'

'Planted? It was there, of course, but he came to us to explain why it had been left . . .'

'Were you convinced?'

'Oh, I'm sure he wanted us to see it so that he could link it up with Elissa's dream.'

'But were you convinced it solved things?'

'No. No, I wasn't. Greg, if you'd seen her when those

34

pictures came up on the computer . . . she was on the point of breakdown.'

'Did she say anything?'

'She gave a sort of half-scream and threw her hands over her face,' Liz said, trying to recall this moment of crisis. 'Then she moaned something about standing firm – I think it was "I must stand firm" or "I *will* stand firm". Then she began to shudder and moan sort of questions, like "Why? Why?" and – wait a minute – she said, "Am I going mad?" And then I saw she'd gone chalk-white and I thought she was going to faint, so I got her upstairs.'

'Leaving the computer on?'

She stared at him. 'Of course leaving the computer on. I never gave that another thought.'

'So then you explained to Trudi what had brought on this turmoil, and presumably she or someone else went to the computer and saw the pictures from the Butanta Institute.'

'Well, yes.'

'So because she's never been to the Butanta Institute a reason had to be exhibited why she got in such a state, and the reason is that she previously saw the same pictures or something like them in that magazine.'

'Well, it *is* possible that's where she saw them, Greg.'

'But then we come to the other question: why is it so important to show us an explanation and convince us by it?'

'Because . . . because . . . I don't know.'

'I think it's because it's important we don't think Elissa is crazy.'

'Oh.' She stopped to think about that. 'They want us to be convinced so we won't meddle. By meddling we might make things worse.'

'True.'

'Well, there you are.'

'Yes, here we are. We were specifically told not to talk to Elissa about it.'

'Were we?'

'Dr Donati said he himself hadn't asked her if she'd seen the magazine because it might have an adverse effect.'

'So he did.'

'It was a polite way of saying, "I'm her doctor and I don't want you upsetting her."'

'So it was.'

He got up and paced about, long legs taking up the tiny space between the bench and the great terracotta container. He glanced up through the mimosa blossom as if asking for help from on high.

'Have you got your cellphone with you?' he enquired.

'No, of course not. I don't carry it unless I have my handbag.'

'Then let's go back to the cabin and use the fixed phone to ring my grandmother.'

'The servants will be there cleaning the rooms.'

'Damn, so they will. Never mind, we'll get your cellphone and ring from some other spot.'

Liz looked doubtful. She'd arranged for roamer facilities but whether her phone would work from this nowhere sort of place, she couldn't tell.

To her relief, the little instrument behaved beautifully. Since it was now nearly noon in Bredoux, Grossmutti was preparing lunch for herself and Greg's father. 'I was going to ring you about sixish, dear. Just a minute while I wipe my hands; otherwise you'll smell the garlic.'

He grinned. When she picked up again he asked, 'Did you get any information about the doctor?'

'Certainly. It took me almost all evening, but just a minute . . . I've got it written down . . . here we are. Dr Donati runs a very élite sort of clinic near Mürren—'

'We know that, Grossmutti—'

'*Silence, mauvais enfant!* He specializes in patients who have mental health problems, mostly brought on by addiction of some kind. Some quite famous people have benefited from his treatment. I noted some of them down – do you want the list?'

'Was Elissa Paroskolos among them?'

'No, certainly not in that sense; but it seems he was called in after she fell ill during a skiing holiday at Mürren. When I say that, I mean, of course, that Niki skied and Elissa went shopping.'

36

'Grossmutti,' said her grandson in reproach, 'I think she really has been very ill.'

'But is now much better because Dr Donati came to her rescue. He plucked her away to his clinic, and after about three weeks – ' she paused and mumbled to herself as she checked – 'yes, three weeks, she was flown to Athens in a private jet. From there she went to Kerouli for what was expected to be a long convalescence. This is from about four different people who thought I was asking whether I should put *you* in Donati's clinic to have your brains tested.'

'Thank you very much, *chère madame.*'

'What is this about, Gregory?'

'I wish I knew.' He sighed. 'It would be nice to chat with Donati about Elissa, but I think this morning he warned me off.'

'Well, why don't you ask the family doctor?'

'Donati is the family doctor.'

'Is he? Well, it used to be . . . let me see . . . when dear Yanni had bronchitis . . .' A pause while she retrieved the information from her capacious memory. 'Ah, I remember! Dragorasie – that was it. He sent me a Christmas card the year before last. Basil Dragorasie – a very nice man.'

'Do you have an address for this very nice man?'

'Ridiculous! You can't really imagine I keep old Christmas cards? Look him up in the phone book.'

He did better than that. He took Liz down the winding path to the jetty, where two of the little private fleet of boats were tied up. He stepped aboard one and began a long and lively conversation with the boatman. Liz could make nothing of it except for occasional mentions of family names.

After about ten minutes Gregory stepped back on to the jetty.

'He's been in service here since Yanni Dimitriouso was alive. He says Dr Dragorasie lives on Spetses.'

'Spetses. That's another island,' said Liz, who'd looked in an atlas before leaving London.

'Yes. I think of going there now, to see if I can speak to Dr Dragorasie. Would you like to come, or would you rather stay here?'

'How long would you be gone?'

'Oh, about four or five hours in all, I suppose.'

'What's Spetses like?'

'Nice, I think. That author – they made films of his books – Fowles?'

'He lives there?'

'He used to. We could go and look at his house.'

'What a thrill. Well, I'll come, but not for John Fowles. I'd get lonely without you.'

He grinned and relayed her decision to the boatman, who swept off a battered panama to welcome her aboard.

Spetses was bigger than Hydra, and greener. There were a few cars but not enough to spoil the ambience. After the two-hour boat ride they needed a cup of coffee, which they found in a dockside taverna, together with a phone. Gregory found the doctor's number in the local phone book. A woman servant answered after some delay, to inform the caller that the doctor was having his afternoon nap.

'Oh, I'm sorry; I didn't think of that . . .'

'Who is it, Aspasia? Stop scolding and ask who it is.'

Aspasia said with less coldness, 'Who is calling, please?'

'Please tell Dr Dragorasie that my grandmother, Nicoletta von Hirtenstein, advised me to call.'

He heard this relayed to the doctor, who apparently snatched the receiver. 'You know Nicoletta von Hirtenstein?'

'I'm her grandson, *keirie*—'

'Her grandson? Gregory? Where are you speaking from?'

'The dockside in Spetses. I was wondering if I could see you for a few minutes . . .'

'Please, come – come at once. It's the pale-green house a few doors down from the monastery and with a Persian lilac tree at the gate.'

'Thank you, sir. We'll be there in about twenty minutes.'

Liz was looking sadly into the bottom of her tiny coffee cup. 'Hardly enough to be worth a swallow,' she said.

The café owner, having of course listened to Gregory's end of the conversation, refused payment from a friend of Dr Dragorasie. He gave them compass bearings for the house, standing in the doorway to make sure they started out in the right direction. After a stiffish climb, they arrived alongside the Persian lilac. The house door was open by the time they reached it, with an elderly maidservant curtseying a welcome.

Dr Basil Dragorasie turned out to have an impressive silvery moustache to match his silvery, well-barbered hair. He smelt of some expensive cologne. When Gregory presented Liz, he took her hand to bow over it in courtly fashion – a real old charmer.

'My dear boy, how is your beautiful grandmother? It's so long since I've seen her.'

'She's well, sir. May I ask, do you speak English, Dr Dragorasie? Miss Blair can't speak Greek and she has something to contribute to our conversation.'

'Of course. How thoughtless of me. My dear, you must think me an old barbarian. Now come, sit down, I have had the English tea prepared, for I know you must long for it after your boat trip. You came from Kerouli?'

'Yes, we're there for the birthday.'

'Ah yes. There has been quite a lot about it in the newspapers, but since I wasn't invited I took a spite against it, you know, and wouldn't read the guest list. Otherwise I would have known you were there, my boy.'

He spoke fluent English but with a stronger accent than, for instance, Niki or Elissa. He was clearly delighted to have been sought out by Nicoletta's grandson. Liz suspected some former flirtation there.

Tea was brought in by the maid: a beautiful porcelain teapot, cups painted with roses, and a plate of little cakes running with rose-water syrup and coated with almonds. Liz, who would normally have run from the sight, accepted first one and then another with eagerness. After all, it was a long time since breakfast.

After some polite conversation about the well-being of the Hirtensteins and their host, Gregory thought it time to broach the reason for his visit. 'You say you weren't invited to the birthday celebrations, doctor?'

'No, I am forgotten, I think.'

'Have you seen Elissa recently?'

'Not at all – not since she came back from Switzerland. Of course I offered my services when I heard she was back. After all, I brought her into the world, I have all her medical records. Her father – after the mother abandoned the poor child, he was so determined she should have every care, every attention. Even when she went abroad to school, he asked me to supervise, to ensure that she lacked nothing. Poor little thing: alone among strangers . . . She decided to diet. As a child, you know, she was very fond of sweets and so, of course . . . Well, her classmates made her unhappy about her weight – such a personal problem, but even in that I found a dietician for her by contacting friends in Boston; they thought I was crazy, but Yanni insisted . . . And her teeth – damaged by too much sugar; I saw to it that she went to one fo the finest men in the city so that now, when the paparazzi besiege her, she has the most beautiful smile. Don't you agree?'

'Indeed,' Greg said kindly. 'You must feel almost like a second father to her.'

'You put it exactly! So of course I was eager to see her, but Dr Donati said at first that she was still in an uncertain state of health. Later, when I telephoned again, he said he was in the course of restoring her memory, and was concentrating on her life at college and university.' He paused, almost out of breath in his indignation. 'My appearance, he said, would be a distraction.' He accompanied this account with a despondent shake of the head, as if asking for their view.

'I'd have thought having a visit from someone she's known all her life would be a help.' Liz remarked.

'That was my thought, Miss Blair. But then my subject has always been general medicine, I know little about neurology or psychology.'

'You didn't try a third time?' asked Mr Crowne.

'Well, I did . . . and was put through to Elissa herself.'

'And?'

'I don't think she remembered me. So you see, Dr Donati was right: I would only have been a complication if I had insisted on visiting. And since I am, as you see, getting old and suffering for my youthful indulgence in tobacco and brandy, I withdrew.'

There was a break in the conversation while they sipped tea, and Liz ate yet another almond cake.

The doctor gave a little shake of his silver head. 'You made a long boat trip just to exchange little nothings. Is there something you wish to learn from me?'

'Well . . .'

'Please, if I can be of help, I am all attention.'

'Do you know Dr Donati?'

'Only through two conversations on the telephone. Prior to Elissa's illness, not even by reputation. But since then I've been told by the gossips that the younger brother of Niki . . .' He hesitated.

'Costa?' Liz suggested.

'Ah, you know of that? Gossip among old Greek ladies reaches to England?' he countered with an arch smile.

'It was in the magazines and the gossip columns. He was rather famous for his good looks and his lifestyle.'

'So you knew that Costa Paroskolos had been in Dr Donati's clinic, Miss Blair?'

'I couldn't have told you which clinic. What was said ran something along the lines of: "I hear young Costa Paroskolos is leaving the party scene for the good of his health, on the sincere advice of his family. They've sent him off to one of those restful clinics in Switzerland".'

Basil Dragorasie shook his head in sorrow. 'That, of course, explained how it came about that Niki called in Dr Donati – he already knew of him – knew he had successfully treated his brother. In a way I was glad to have an explanation, because I confess I was very hurt at not being consulted. It became clear that the man is an expert on mental conditions, although I had never heard of him until he brought Elissa home to Kerouli.'

'But then? I'm just guessing, but you made enquiries?'

Dr Dragorasie smiled. 'You are as quick to catch a tone of voice as your dear grandmother. Yes, I looked him up and, as I deserved, I received what amounted to a professional rebuff. He is well established. He has published.'

'Published? Books?'

'One book – quite a list of research papers in respectable journals. I could find nothing to justify my ill will, and so I left the field.' He smiled at this good English metaphor.

'You learned that he runs a clinic in Switzerland.'

'Quite so.'

'Have you any views on the fact that he's devoted himself exclusively to Elissa for almost a year?'

The other man hesitated. Then with a shrug he said, 'The Paroskolos family can afford to hire even a highly prized expert on diseases of the nerves.'

Gregory made a little nod of acceptance. 'So what follows from that?'

'Follows? Why should anything follow?'

'Dr Dragorasie, you must have given this a lot of thought. Doesn't it worry you that Elissa Paroskolos needs the exclusive attention of a man like that, after nearly a year has gone by?'

'Yes, it worries me,' the old man burst out. 'Of course it worries me. And her memory is so poor that she didn't even remember me! But what is there to do? Niki is apparently satisfied with the treatment. He is rich; Elissa is rich. One does not approach beings like that with criticisms, with any questioning of their judgement.'

'Miss Blair was present when Elissa had a sort of hysterical attack.' He looked at her, and she took up the tale. She told it briefly, then they both waited for the doctor's response.

He sighed. 'That sounds bad. Understand, I am no expert in the treatment of meningitis. I looked it up, of course. The journals do say that there can be long-lasting effects, that sometimes the patient is handicapped in some areas afterwards. Modern drugs have made a wonderful difference to the recovery rate, of course. After my reading I came to the conclusion she was perhaps lucky to be alive.'

He tugged at his moustache, considering. 'And yet . . . what you tell me is very disquieting. You too have thought of it, I am sure. She is the owner of a very large fortune and will have even more in the future. She seems hardly fit to control all that. One wonders if there is not some court that could take her into its care.'

This weighty suggestion caused them all to sit in silence for some moments.

'In your medical career,' Gregory said, 'you've had patients to whom that has happened?'

'Yes.' The assent was weighted with reluctance. 'It's not an easy matter. Generally it is the family that asks for such a course. But you see in this case the family – her husband – is perfectly satisfied that she's in good hands.'

'The mother?' Gregory offered.

'They have not seen each other for, oh, seventeen or eighteen years. No court would accept a sudden intervention from her. Besides, Elissa has always hated her. It would not be a good thing to bring her in, even if she were willing.'

Very gingerly Gregory said, 'You yourself?'

'In what capacity? I am not her doctor now. I have no rights in the matter.' He was frowning and pulling at his moustache quite cruelly. 'There are members of the family at the festivity?'

'Yes, but they're what in English they call "poor relations" – the kind who are so delighted to be included that they wouldn't dare to do anything that might spoil things.'

'Ah yes.' He looked from one to the other of his guests, then said, almost with a groan, 'If only Yanni were alive . . .'

Gregory shook his head in regret. 'He died about two years ago, I recall. My father was at the funeral.'

'Yes, I had a word with him there.' The old man's eyes filled with tears. 'Ah, he admired Yanni as I did. He and I drank a toast to him. Anton kept saying, "It doesn't seem possible; it doesn't seem possible," but alas it was so: Yanni was gone.'

'I understand his feelings. Our family always hoped to repay Yanni's kindness in some way, but at his death all chance of doing that was gone.'

'You mean you think your father was regretting that? No, no, he was expressing wonder! That Yanni Dimitriouso should die in a boating accident! Yet, of course, old seadogs often die at sea, and an unexpected squall can defeat even the best.'

Aspasia, the maid, came in with an air of purpose. The visitors realized she was signalling the fact that they were tiring the old doctor – that it was time to go. They rose and began their farewells. Dr Dragorasie himself showed them to the door.

'You came here today because you were concerned,' he said to them. 'I thank you for that. For all her faults, Elissa was dear to me in the past and I earnestly wish her a complete recovery. Please tell her so, if you think she would like to hear it.'

There was no opportunity to discuss their visit on the way back, because Spiro the boatman felt conversational. To have had a long conversation between themselves would have seemed impolite.

At the jetty, who should be waiting but Niki Paroskolos. 'Hello there,' he greeted them. 'Had a nice trip? I'm just here to collect the boat logs.'

This was clearly unusual, because on seeing him Gregory had heard Spiro mutter, 'But there's Keirios Niki! What's he doing here?'

'Very nice, thank you,' Liz said as Niki helped her step ashore. 'We went to Spetses.'

'Yes, so I was told. A refreshing place, don't you think? Did you visit the sites they used for the film?'

'No,' Gregory said, to see what the reaction would be. 'We were paying a visit on an old acquaintance of my family: Dr Dragorasie.'

'Yes, one of the other boatmen told me you'd been enquiring after him. How is the poor old soul?'

'He seemed quite well. I'll be telephoning my grandmother to let her know. She met him at your wedding, I believe.'

'Oh yes,' Niki said, preceding them up the path. Over his shoulder he added, 'He wanted to take part in Elissa's treatment, you know, but Tonio wouldn't hear of it.'

'Tonio – that's Dr Donati, I take it.'

'He said the poor man was totally out of date even where general practice is concerned, but as to neurology – no, no, we couldn't have that. I'm afraid poor Drago took offence.'

'Mm,' said the prince. After a moment he said, 'I think he'd like to be invited to the birthday celebrations.'

'He would? I heard he was getting too frail for travelling about.'

The steepness of the path was now having its effect on

conversation. There was quite a gap before they reached a few yards of level walkway in which to regain their breath. As they moved on, Niki said, 'I really don't think I should invite him. Elissa's memory is so poor that she doesn't really remember him. That would only distress him, don't you think?'

They made the rest of the ascent in silence. At the top Niki gave them a smile. 'See you later.' They nodded, then went their separate ways.

'He doesn't like Dr Dragorasie,' Liz commented.

'Well, that's understandable, I suppose – an interfering old man . . .'

'He's not an interfering old man, Greg! He's an old family friend. I think it's rather callous to prevent him from even seeing Elissa.'

'What I think even more surprising is Niki's presence on the jetty when we got back.'

'Say what?'

'Our boatman was astonished to see him. So it seems he made an unusual trip down to the quay, and I ask myself why.'

'And what do you reply to yourself?' she asked in amusement.

'I think they're keeping an eye on us.'

Her amusement vanished. 'Greg! You're not serious?'

'I'm . . . half-serious. He'd been asking the boatmen where we'd gone, and he wanted us to tell him what Dr Drago, as he calls him, had been saying to us.'

'But why should they be keeping an eye on us?'

'That's the question. Why?' He walked on a few steps then said, 'I'll tell you another thing: I mentioned the magazine-reading servant to Spiro—'

'Christos – was that his name?'

'Spiro tells me that Christos, who is a cleaner, can speak only about ten words of English and certainly can't read it. He thought the idea comic. Of course, I didn't tell him why I wanted to know; I talked about the staff on the island in general.'

Liz tried to think her way through that. 'But Christos might just have liked looking at the pictures. I imagine there were other pictures besides snakes?'

'That I can't say. I didn't have time to look at anything else. However, one thing is certain: we won't be able to ask Christos what he was looking at the magazine for – or even if he ever looked at it at all – because Christos was sent to the mainland early this morning to be a cleaner at Niki's office. A promotion, Spiro said – quite unexpected.'

They had reached their cabin. They went inside, sat down, and looked at each other.

'Greg,' said Liz, 'I find that rather scary.'

Four

The promised folk dancing for that evening turned out to be nothing like the tourist-café version. No crockery was smashed; the dancers who appeared wore correct costume, the men in white shirts and rather baggy black trousers, the women in rich-looking brocade skirts and tight velvet jackets. But at about eleven o'clock some informality emerged: the audience were invited to join the circle dances and the chains.

Rather to Gregory's surprise, Elissa Paroskolos joined the dancers. She was already at the party when he and Liz arrived, sitting with Niki and a group of his friends from the financial world, drinking mineral water and taking a fairly lively part in the conversation. Dr Donati was present but at the other side of the gathering, apparently unconcerned at what his patient might be up to.

Gregory and Liz had been rather late in coming to the pavilion. They'd had a long discussion about future action. When Liz had said she felt uneasy, Gregory had suggested it would be better if she joined one of the boats going to the mainland early next morning to fetch the mail. 'And do what when I get there?' she demanded.

'Find a nice hotel in Athens and stay there a few days to do some sightseeing.'

'And you'd come too?'

'No-o.'

'You want to stay on Kerouli and find out what's going on.'

'If anything is.'

'If you stay, I stay.'

'But that's not necessary, Liz. I feel a sort of obligation to stick it out until the birthday celebrations are over, because in a way I represent my family here. But that doesn't apply to you . . .'

'Whatever applies to you applies to me,' she said stoutly, and no amount of logic would convince her otherwise.

So when they got to the pavilion, the little orchestra of fiddle, zither and mandolin were well launched into their programme and the dancers were in the middle of a pattern dance.

'There's Elissa,' Liz murmured.

One glance at her made them doubt the anxieties they'd been feeling. She was smiling and nodding at something one of the men was saying.

'Now I think that's a Betty Jackson she's wearing,' murmured Liz. 'We did a copy of that for the Zeira shops and it went well.'

He could see why. The dress was a simple shirt-waister, but made in the most beautiful soft coral silk. With it she wore low-heeled sandals with straps of the same colour. When, a moment later, Elissa got up and was drawn into the folk dance along with other guests, Liz understood the choice of dress. This was a dance in which the performers held on to each other's belts while they did little swaying steps.

Elissa had come prepared to take part, which certainly didn't seem like the behaviour of someone whom they'd been thinking of as rather ill; and since Niki was dancing with her, it seemed her husband thought her fit enough to do so.

The two observers went off to find some food. When they returned with well-filled plates, they sat at a table some distance from the dance floor. Mr Crowne was relatively interested in Greek folk music, but Liz would have preferred something a little more modern. All the same, she accepted the invitation from the dancers to join them, so of course he had to follow.

At one point in the pattern he found himself crossing hands and turning with Elissa. She was flushed and smiling, but he thought her eyes were rather red, as if from an allergy. Perhaps a side effect of her medication.

By and by the orchestra signalled an interval by a long trill on the zither. Elissa made her way back to the long table at which she'd been sitting, followed by Liz and Gregory.

Niki went off to speak to a servant about refreshments for the dancers.

'Are you enjoying the programme, Gregory?' Elissa asked, motioning him to a chair at her side.

'Very much,' he said. He was straightening a chair for Liz, so they sat down around one of the corners of the table. 'Although Liz is always keener on dancing than I am.'

'It's not difficult to catch on,' said Liz: 'just follow what your next-door neighbour is doing.'

Elissa drank some mineral water, which by now must have been tepid. 'It's kind of tame,' she said with a shrug. 'I like something with a little more excitement in it.'

'Really?' Gregory said in surprise. He knew nothing about Elissa's life as a grown-up, but as a child she'd never been keen on anything requiring much physical output. 'Such as what? That stuff Liz does – all jerky arms and shrugs?'

Liz gave him a punitive dig of the elbow. 'Jerky?' she said. 'My every movement is poetry in motion.'

Elissa wasn't really listening: her ears seemed to be attuned to some remembered music. 'What I was thinking of was the dances we used to go to on weekends, when we had plenty of time to catch up with essays and things. We'd get up late and do some work on class projects, but in the evening we could really let go. There was something so eager and free about the Cajuns. And the music was good too – mostly just an accordion, but it was irresistible; it set your foot tapping as soon as you heard it . . .'

'An accordion,' said Gregory, interested at once 'That's an instrument you almost never hear except in folk-music clubs; but then of course Richard Galliano – he uses some *bal musette* and there's often an echo of Argentine tango.'

'Oh, don't,' Liz begged. 'The hydraulic is enough of an oddity, don't let's get into accordions.'

'It's a *hydraulis*, not a hydraulic.'

'But what is it?' Elissa asked, laughing.

'Some ancient musical instrument he wants to get a look at. We're going to Athens tomorrow to look at it.'

'Athens,' murmured Elissa. There was something wistful in her tone.

Niki returned at that point, bringing with him a servant carrying fresh wine and sweetmeats. The conversation turned from music to the television programmes earlier that evening on satellite. Since Gregory and Liz had been too busy to switch on, they soon ceased to take part and, at about one in the morning, drifted towards their cabin.

It seemed to her that he was very silent as they picked their way along the winding path under the glow of a half-moon. As they were going indoors, he remarked, 'That was an odd thing Elissa said about going to Cajun dances.'

'Was it?' Liz said, yawning. 'What's Cajun, anyhow?'

'It's a folk area in the United States – mostly Louisiana, I think.'

'Uh-huh?' she said, hopping about as she took off her evening shoes. Greek dancing was quite hard on the feet.

'Elissa seemed to be saying she went to Cajun evenings while she was at university.'

'Did she?'

'Yes – something about doing classwork in the daytime on weekends but in the evening going to dance to Cajun music.'

She put her shoes on the floor of the wardrobe. 'I seem to remember that,' she agreed. 'So what's your point?'

'Cajun music is played in Cajun districts, which are in Louisiana. Elissa went to university in Boston.'

Liz had set her shoes on the shoe rack. 'But . . . couldn't there be a Cajun café in Boston? I know I've eaten German and North Chinese and Ukrainian when I've been in New York.'

He nodded, emptying the pockets of his evening jacket before hanging it up. 'Of course.'

'But?' she said, seeing that he was deep in thought.

'But . . . There's been something bothering me about the way Elissa speaks.'

Whatever she'd expected, it wasn't that. 'What d'you mean, they way she speaks? She speaks very nicely – faultless English with an American accent. So does Niki.'

'Yes.'

'Well, what are you getting at?'

'She was educated at Smith College and Harvard Business

School. I'm almost sure that's the background. So she learned her English in Massachusetts.'

'Greg. Is there a point to this?' she said. She was tired and not in the mood for puzzles.

'Elissa doesn't speak with a New England accent.'

'Oh, come on! You're not telling me you can pick out regional accents?'

He looked surprised. 'Yes, of course. Not always, but quite often. For instance, it's quite clear to me that Niki learned his English in New York. After all, Liz, I'm in the music business. It's part of my training to hear intonation and inflection.'

Now she was quite cross. It was after one in the morning and they were having a conversation about intonation. 'I'm sure that's all very interesting,' she said in a manner that plainly said it was not. Then she went into the bathroom, closing the door rather noisily.

The little disagreement was forgotten next morning. Outside, the bright beauty of an April Monday beckoned them to set off on their outing. They made a quick breakfast at the pavilion, learning there that a boat was due to leave for the mainland at around ten thirty. Some of the other guests were already on their way to the little quay. Gregory and Liz drank up their coffee and hurried after.

As they rounded one of the bends in the winding path, an extraordinary sight met their eyes. Elissa Paroskolos was a few yards ahead of them, having what looked like a wrestling match with her nurse.

'But, madame, you know it is not allowed,' Trudi was crying as she held on to her patient with one arm around her waist and one around her shoulders.

'But the others are going. I want to go too!'

'No, no; it is out of the question, madame!' Trudi, much stronger than Elissa, was actually dragging her off balance.

The prince strode forward. 'What on earth is going on?' he demanded in a tone that made the nurse almost come to attention.

Elissa staggered. Liz dashed to her side; she took the hand Elissa threw out for support.

51

'I want to go to Athens like everybody else!' Elissa cried, with an almost childlike plaintiveness.

'So you shall, dear,' soothed Liz.

'No, Miss Blair; you must not say that. It is absolutely forbidden . . .'

'By whom?'

'By Dr Donati, sir. He wishes Mrs Paroskolos to remain on the island in safety until her health is completely restored.'

'But why should it be less safe if she goes to Athens?'

'Sir, she is not fit to face the turmoil of Athens. Noise and excitement are very bad for her.'

'She was doing all right last night at the dance,' Liz said. 'Weren't you, love?'

'I want to go on the boat,' Elissa repeated. 'I'm fine. I promise not to do anything too energetic. I want to go, Trudi. It's so long since I was anywhere except round and round Kerouli!'

'No, Dr Donati's orders—'

'I think you may tell Dr Donati that we have undertaken to look after his patient today,' Prince Gregory von Hirtenstein said in tones that brooked no argument. He offered his arm to Elissa, Liz took the other, and together they went on down the track.

'But, madame, your medication . . . !'

'I'll take it when I get back,' Elissa called over her shoulder.

Luckily the boatman was waiting to cast off. In moments the motor cruiser was heading away from the cliffs and towards the sea lane for Athens. Trudi was left staring after it.

'Thank you,' breathed Elissa. 'I thought I'd get on board before she realized I'd gone, but she's so attentive . . .'

'So it seems. Have you really never left the island in all these months?'

'No, and hardly anyone comes to visit. It gets very dull. But Dr Donati says it's part of the regime, and I feel guilty at slipping away against his orders, but you know . . . I get so *weary* of Trudi at my elbow all the time.'

'She certainly doesn't seem to be lively company,' Liz remarked.

The other passengers were leaning forward in their seats to

nod greetings at Elissa and thank her for last night's party. Conversation became general. Elissa held her end up well, speaking Greek to those of her guests who preferred it and English to the rest.

There was a quiet quay in one of the lesser harbours where private passengers could alight. A line of taxis waited for these lucrative clients. Elissa, Liz and Gregory were whisked away through the noisy streets of Piraeus, past suburban areas only a little quieter, and finally into the pressure of Athens and the steep approach to the Acropolis.

Soon it became necessary to pay off the driver and go on on foot, because cars were parked so closely in the narrow lanes that the taxi couldn't make progress. Gregory led the way across a busy road, along the splendid honey-coloured front of the Odeon of Herodes Atticus, and then off again down a turning with old houses on either side. At a heavy old oak door with its panels outlined in dust, he pressed an entry phone and identified himself. A series of squeaks came in response; the old door made a buzzing sound and, when pushed hard by Gregory, inched open to reveal a narrow stone hall and a stone staircase.

'Up here!' called a feminine voice. They went up the stairs. On the first landing stood a plump lady in a black dress and a plastic apron. In the dimness she peered at them through owlish glasses. 'Mr Crowne? How nice to meet you in person.'

Liz cast a grin of understanding at Gregory. There was no mistaking where the professor had learned her English. She spoke in the ringing tones of Oxbridge.

'Professor Tzelili? I hope you don't mind – I brought two friends with me.'

'Anyone who is interested in the *hydraulis* is welcome,' she replied, clasping his hand with both of hers and nodding at the two women. 'Come in, come in; you would like coffee, of course.'

She led the way into a long room with a stone floor. Large windows let in the bright light of late morning. Around the walls were tables and trestles, on which lay what appeared to be several large metal basins – brass perhaps, varying in size and shape. Alongside there were pipes of varying lengths. Here and there on the floor were large plastic storage boxes, out of which poked all kinds of planks of wood and thin sheets of bronze and aluminium.

At the far end of the room was a dais on which stood something that Liz sort of recognized. It looked like a harmonium, of the kind that had accompanied the hymns in the Baptist chapel of her childhood. Yet it wasn't a harmonium: it was narrower and its base was round, and out of it stuck about four rows of uneven pipes, like the array that might come out of a small church organ. On what was apparently its front there was a short keyboard.

The professor led the way past it. 'This is the one I am making for Costas Emilios,' she said over her shoulder to Gregory. 'It is for the most part finished. I was just about to fill it with water when you arrived.'

Water? Oh, of course – *hydraulis*, thought Liz. She suppressed a grin. But the idea of a musical instrument powered by water seemed inherently comic. It reminded her of a plaything she'd found once in her Christmas stocking, a pipe which, when you blew into it, gave forth a single burbling birdlike call.

They went through a doorway into a room that might have been described as an office. It had a desk, a filing cabinet, a chair or two and a table supplied with the means of preparing drinks and snacks; but there were papers and books piled on everything, all of them touched with a slight film of the honey-coloured dust that seemed to be everywhere in this part of Athens.

Professor Tzelili found the kettle under some mechanical drawings. 'We'll have Greek coffee,' she announced. 'I find it excellent for clearing the head, and I need my head cleared: I've been working on the pumps of that instrument since six this morning.'

'Something wrong?' Gregory said, with quick sympathy. He retreated towards the door, looking back out at the *hydraulis*. The professor, meanwhile, got down on hands and knees to plug in the kettle, muttering about the inadequacy of her electricity supply.

'Do you work on your own?' Liz inquired, to make conversation.

'Oh, dear me, no. I have assistants, volunteers from the University, of course, and a couple of technicians who do the metalwork. But Mondays are not good – people never seem so keen to start work after a weekend, and besides . . . Now where is the coffee jar? I had it earlier. I put it – let me see – did I take it out to the workroom? No, of course not.'

'Let me help,' said Elissa, and set about lifting books and plans until at last she found the jar on a shelf above the desk. She brought it to the professor, who then couldn't find the coffee pot. It was unearthed at last behind a potted plant with very aggressive leaves, which might have meant the plant had been moved in front of it during a search for something else: a devoted but disordered researcher.

Mr Crowne, meanwhile, had moved back into the workroom and was touching the keys of the *hydraulis* with an exploratory finger. By the time the womenfolk had found little cups and filled them with steaming black coffee, he was kneeling at the back of the instrument, where the tank for the water was housed. There was some sort of gauge there, which he was trying to read.

'There's only about one litre in it,' he observed as he got to his feet, dusting the knees of his jeans.

'Yes, and of course I must fill it to test the mechanism,' said the professor, handing him his coffee; 'but it must be done with care and I use a measuring jug to ensure that the level is absolutely right.' Liz would almost have taken a bet on her next words. 'Now where did I put the measuring jug?'

It turned out that the measuring jug was at the sink on the back landing where the professor obtained her water supply. She swallowed her coffee in a gulp, leapt up and began to hurry to and fro with jugs of water. Though it seemed an inefficient method, in a surprisingly short time the cylinder of the *hydraulis* was sufficiently topped up to allow the production of a note when one of the keys was pressed.

The sound was soft and plaintive. 'B flat,' murmured Gregory. 'But an impure tone, though it's asking too much to have it in any key we'd recognize today. If the bellows are pumped, do you get a clearer note?'

'Stronger, and to some extent clearer, but of course overtones within the harmonic vibration . . .'

She and Gregory became involved in a technical discussion for which the professor's English wasn't quite adequate. They switched to Greek from time to time. This made it even more boring to Liz and Elissa, who drifted off to look out of the window. There they got a glimpse of the trees on the path leading up to the Parthenon. Elissa leaned her elbows on the sill and gazed longingly out.

After some moments it dawned on Gregory that his two companions were suffering from ennui. He wrenched himself away from the pleasures of the *hydraulis* and, with an apologetic glance at the professor, went to join the two women.

'Not having much fun,' he suggested. 'I'm sorry; I should have realized it wouldn't be your kind of thing. Why don't the pair of you go and have a look at the Parthenon or something?'

'And leave you here?'

'I'd like to stay a bit. I want to hear what the *hydraulis* sounds like when the bellows are pumped and you try to play a tune on it.'

'Try "Chopsticks",' Liz suggested.

'Or "Yankee Doodle",' Elissa put in.

'Show some respect. An instrument much like that was played at the court of the Emperor Nero . . .'

'And look what happened to Rome: it got burnt,' said Liz.

'You go and do something more interesting. We can meet up for lunch.'

'How about it, Elissa? Would you like to?'

'I'd like that.'

'Okay, off you go then.' Gregory was already turning back towards his new love when Liz poked him hard in the shoulder with an outstretched finger.

'Where and when?'

'What? Oh, to meet . . .' He hesitated. 'What, actually, are you going to do? Look at the Parthenon?'

'Well that, of course. But we don't want to spend all morning on it.' Liz had the grace to look a little ashamed. '*I'd* like to look at the dress shops.'

'Oh, so would I,' Elissa burst out.

The prince tried not to smile. Everyone, it seemed, had their obsessions – his was music, and the two women had just declared theirs.

'In that case, flag down a cab, ask the driver to take you to Demokritou or nearby, a sort of Bond Street area; and when you've tired yourselves out, look for a hotel called the Korinthe. It's on a corner near the Gennadios Library, with a good restaurant and a nice quiet bar where you can sit reviving yourself with a drink until I get there.'

'That sounds all right. You won't get carried away with your rendition of the "Moonlight" Sonata and forget to come?'

'I'll be there by about two o'clock,' he promised.

They hurried away. Liz felt they must pay some tribute to the Parthenon but, as she said, 'We can come back another day.' They were quickly in Akropoli Square, hailing a taxi.

The shops on the slopes of Likavittos were a surprise: Cartier, Laura Ashley, La Perla . . . Liz and Elissa strolled at random, got lost, accepted free facials at a cosmetics counter, were seduced into paying for expensive creams, bought new earrings and some DKNY jeans, and thoroughly exhausted themselves.

At length, as they were trudging rather wearily uphill in the unexpected warmth of early afternoon, they sighted the Library almost by chance and, by visiting every nearby street corner, found the Korinthe Hotel.

A bijou establishment, it had topiarized bay trees at its doors and a very welcome shade within. They straggled into the bar, threw down their parcels, and ordered long, cool drinks.

'I've got to wash my face,' Elissa exclaimed. 'That goo that I let them put on feels as if it's running down in streams.'

They went to the cloakroom, as bijou as the hotel's exterior, with gold-rimmed mirrors and washbasins embellished with roses. Elissa ran hot water into a basin, leaned over and gave her face a refreshing splash or two with her hand. Liz, meanwhile, was running cold water over her wrists to cool off.

'Oh, damn!' cried Elissa.

'What?'

'I've lost a contact lens.' Leaning over the basin, she was feeling about gently with her hands.

At the cry of a lost lens, Liz leapt to her aid. 'Are you sure it went in the basin?' she asked.

'Yes, I threw the water up and blinked and I felt it go.' She was bending over, her hair falling forward across her cheeks to dangle in the water.

Just in case she was mistaken, Liz stood about a yard away and examined the carpet for the tell-tale gleam. 'Can you feel it in the basin?' she asked.

'No, as a matter of fact I can't, but I'm sure it's here.'

'You're short-sighted or something?'

'Strong light is harmful to me, you see. So I wear these special lenses to filter out the harmful rays.'

'I see.' Liz had given up on finding the lens on the floor. Elissa must be right; it must be in the basin. She moved closer to help find it and saw it almost at once – caught in the thick, long tresses drooping forward into the water.

'Hold still,' she said. 'I've got it.' With the tip of a finger she picked it off the wet strands of hair. 'There!'

Elissa straightened. 'Thank goodness!' She turned to Liz, accepted the lens, and once more leaned forward to watch in the mirror as she restored it to its place.

Liz, meanwhile, was staring at her in surprise. Elissa, concentrating on her task, was unaware of the scrutiny. She settled the lens, blinked at herself two or three times, then turned her attention to washing her face free of the cream.

'Right, let's see if our drinks have come,' she said, and led the way back to the bar.

There were only one or two other customers, too intent on their own affairs to notice two young women shoppers. Elissa sat down, took a long swallow of sweet Martini and lemonade, then began opening the handsome carrier bags. 'Do you think I should have bought the charcoal jeans?' she inquired.

'No, you seemed to like the dark blue.' Liz, usually avid in any discussion about fashion, was hardly paying attention. Elissa was too pleased with her shopping to be concerned at her lack of interest. She was studying the package of cosmetic cream when Mr Crowne arrived.

He was clearly delighted with his morning and dying to talk about it; but good manners demanded that he first ask if they'd enjoyed themselves and, when invited, pass judgement on the new earrings. Then Elissa declared she was famished, so they asked for the menu, ordered, and were almost at once shown to a table in the restaurant.

Liz's surprise was put aside. They had an enjoyable long lunch, which, having begun rather late, took them up to almost four in the afternoon. It was time to head back to Piraeus for the return to Kerouli.

The other guests who had made the morning trip were already waiting on the quay, so they embarked and were motored back to the island. Now Liz began to feel some apprehension, for they had stolen Dr Donati's patient from him that morning.

Dr Donati, however, although waiting on the island jetty, was full of bonhomie. 'Well, my dear,' he said as he helped Elissa ashore, 'how do you feel? Not too exhausted?'

'I feel fine,' she said, with perhaps too much conviction. 'I had a marvellous time!'

A marvellous time. Daughter to a multi-millionaire, heiress to a vast fortune, and an afternoon among the fashion shops of Athens was a marvellous time. Liz shook her head to herself, following in Elissa's wake along the jetty. Little electric carts whisked her away with her doctor, and then some of the guests. Liz and Gregory elected to walk up the steep winding path.

He was carrying her parcels. 'Estée Lauder,' he remarked, examining one of the carriers. 'Aren't you the girl who wouldn't let me buy her "Madame Rochas" on the plane because it was too expensive?'

'Don't ask,' she groaned. 'I let myself get carried away.'

'I hope you got Elissa to pay for it.'

'Huh! We dragged her off without checking she had her handbag with her, didn't we though? I paid for everything on my credit card.'

'Never mind. It was all in a good cause. You gave her a day she enjoyed.'

'Greg . . .' She stopped on the path, gripped his arm with an anxious hand. 'Greg, something weird happened.'

He gazed down at her. The deep-set hazel eyes were filled with concern. 'What is it, Liz?'

'Elissa was washing her face in the cloakroom. She lost a contact lens, but we found it.'

'A contact lens?' He recalled the occasions when her eyes had seemed red. 'Oh yes.'

'Greg . . . The lenses she wears are tinted brown. She says they filter out harmful rays.'

'Well, I suppose that's—'

'She looked straight at me before she put the lens back in. Her eyes are blue, Greg. The natural colour of Elissa's eyes is blue.'

Five

G regory said nothing. After a moment he turned away and resumed his progress up the path. Liz went along at his side.

'Greg?'

'I'm thinking.'

'Thinking what?'

'That I never knew her very well. I've no idea if she was wearing contact lenses as a child; she was a nine-year-old brat and I steered clear of her as much as I could.'

'But a child, Greg? If a child had some eye condition, wouldn't she be more likely to wear glasses of some kind?'

'Not if she had a mother as vain as hers. From what Grossmutti said, everything had to be perfect, even the baby.'

They walked on in silence until they reached their cabin. Liz went into the bedroom, threw her shopping on the bed, then sat down in an armchair. 'Did either of her parents have blue eyes?'

'How do I know?' he replied in irritation. 'I never met them.' After a pause he added, 'Grossmutti would know. But then, she's off on one of her safaris for fabrics to use in a redecoration scheme. So I can't ring her.'

'Hasn't she got a cellphone?'

'Yes, but she despises it and keeps it switched off in the car "for emergencies", such as a breakdown on a motorway. She'll have pinned up a list of places she's going, but who knows where? In the kitchen? In the office? Papa won't have a clue.'

They looked at each other in uncertainty. Liz had been surprised – even shocked – to find that the girl she'd thought of as a typical Mediterranean beauty had northern blue eyes. But did it mean anything? Did it matter?

61

'The old family doctor,' Greg murmured. 'If she has an eye condition, he's sure to know.' He went to the bureau, searched among the debris in a drawer and came up with the scrap of paper on which he'd scribbled Dr Dragorasie's number on Spetses. He used the room telephone to place the call. Liz watched him. After a moment she could faintly hear a voice replying.

'Answering machine,' he said, frowning in disappointment. He listened, shrugged, then replaced the receiver. 'He's gone away on a family visit,' he reported. 'Any messages will be attended to when he returns. Doesn't say when.'

Liz muttered under her breath.

He sighed. 'There's nothing we can do unless we want to ask outright. We could go to Dr Donati and say, "Does Elissa have light sensitivity?"'

'And he'd say, "Drop dead".'

'More likely, he'd say it's a matter of patient confidentiality.'

'I suppose he would or could. If it matters. *Does* it matter, Greg?'

He thought about it, running his hand back and forth through his hair as if to stir up his brains. 'Yes. No. I don't know. If you come to think of it, Elissa Paroskolos is entitled to wear tinted contact lenses if she wants to, for whatever reason. It's just odd, that's all.'

They could see no further use in discussion. They began to change for the evening, which was to have a sixties theme with an appropriate band and singer. The sky above was perfectly clear with the moon more than half full, but there was a cool April breeze, which meant that food would be served inside the pavilion.

They found a few new faces among the assembled guests, some of them elderly ladies in clothes that more or less matched the theme of the evening out of sheer necessity. These were yet another group of the poor cousins and aunts and step-relations who had had to be invited but would be ferried away next morning to their unglamorous homes.

Elissa was there, listening to an aged gentleman who seemed to be trying to flirt with her. Her head was bent, she was smiling, but she seemed distant – weary perhaps, and certainly uninterested.

Niki buttonholed Mr Crowne as he and Liz were about to join a group already seated at a table and well into heaped platefuls of food. 'I hear you took my wife out on quite an adventure this morning,' he remarked, jovially but with a glint of something else in his eye.

'An adventure? Hardly. We went to look at a reconstruction of an ancient Greek musical instrument. Do you know Professor Tzelili? She's attached to the Music Department of the University.'

Niki said he didn't know Professor Tzelili. 'But Elissa bought some clothes?' he continued.

'Oh yes, of course she wasn't interested in the *hydraulis* and neither was Liz, so they went off to try on dresses. You know, Liz is a fashion buyer; she's madly interested in clothes.'

'Oh, of course.' Niki gave a smile of understanding at Liz and seemed to hesitate. Then he said, 'Gregory, I don't want to sound tyrannical, but Elissa is under medical care and it would really be best if you didn't interfere—'

'Interfere? Oh, I'm sorry. I didn't think of it like that. It was just that we were there and she said she'd like to go . . .'

'Yes, well, she's getting tired of being cooped up – I can see that; but Dr Donati wants her to have complete rest until after the big celebration on Thursday. And that outing really did tire her out. So please . . . ?'

'I understand.' Greg was longing to ask, 'What colour are your wife's eyes really?' but couldn't think how to say it without sounding absolutely crazy and very impolite.

Niki nodded, as if satisfied: nothing to worry about in a pre-Christian musical device or a few goodies from expensive shops. He strolled away to act host to other guests.

Liz was already heading for the buffet table to choose ingredients for her meal. She murmured, 'What was that about?'

'He was telling us not to do anything against doctor's orders.'

'Oh, what a fuss about nothing!'

'But she does seem tired, Liz. Perhaps we were wrong to spirit her away like that.'

63

She turned to look at Elissa, who was now chatting with the relative on her other side, or at least the relative was talking to Elissa and Elissa was nodding to show she was listening.

'She's having no fun,' Liz said. 'There's a place at that table; I'm going to sit there and talk to her about Levi's and Gucci shoes and things like that.'

He nodded agreement. He, for his part, went now to a table where three elderly ladies in outmoded black were sitting, beaming at the scene around them. They looked up as he joined them, delighted to have a tall young man as the fourth at their feast.

They preferred to speak Greek, although two of them had a fair knowledge of English. They began on a panegyric: what a beautiful island, how well designed the pavilion, how plentiful and delicious the food, how good and kind of Niki and Elissa to bring them here as part of the celebration. Their gentle old voices flowed on; he agreed with all they said, and went in search of dessert for them when they'd eaten their main courses. 'What a delightful man,' they said to each other.

As he returned towards them with a waiter bearing a tray of cream cakes, he crossed the path of Liz and Elissa, who were walking towards the moonlit path outside. 'Elissa's beat, so we're going back to the house. She wants to show me a couple of dresses she had delivered a few days ago, and then she's going to bed.'

'I'm sorry, Elissa,' he said. 'We let you do too much.'

'Not at all,' she said, her tone languid yet tinged with bravado. 'I enjoyed it. See you tomorrow, Gregory.'

'Goodnight, Elissa.'

The two young women walked off, rather slowly, arms linked. His cargo of sweet things had been carried to his old ladies, and for a moment he thought about finding more entertaining company; but they turned towards him with smiles of gratitude for the cakes, waving at him to come and share them. He felt compelled to go back.

The music so far had been from tapes, but now the musicians arrived. They set up at the far end of the pavilion: four young men and a girl. The prince, who knew nothing about pop music, listened with moderate interest, but the old ladies were enthralled. Quite soon they were singing along, for this was the music of their youth and early womanhood, bringing back memories of stolen kisses when Mama wasn't looking, of vinyl records, of heart-throb vocalists.

Quite clearly they were longing to dance. The prince, duty bound, took Cousin Natalya up on the little dance floor. There she proceeded to do a watered-down version of the twist, while he performed two of the three all-purpose dance steps Liz had taught him.

By the time he'd taken the third of his fellow diners for a sedate exhibition, Liz was back. He excused himself from the family relatives on the grounds that he ought to dance with Liz. They let him go with reluctance, sending hand-kisses after him as he joined her.

She seemed very pleased with herself.

'Enjoyed looking through Elissa's wardrobe?' he enquired.

'Oh, you've no idea of the lovely things she's got. The dress for the birthday party is an absolute winner. And you know, Greg, everything is the very latest! It must be great to be able to buy something almost straight from the catwalk.'

'So that faint green tinge that's come over you is envy.'

'You'd be envious too if you were in my shoes. And speaking of shoes, she's got almost as many as Imelda Marcos – well, no, that's not quite true, but she's got about fifty pairs.'

'You didn't by any chance come away with a pair of her evening slippers tucked about your person?'

'If you look at this dress, you'll see there isn't anywhere to tuck even one slipper.' This was true. Against the chill evening, she was wearing a long-sleeved dark blue jersey dress that clung to every curve. 'However, I did come away with *something*.'

'A good idea for your next chain-store presentation?'

'I'll show you later.' She gave him a mischievous wink. 'Not a pair of shoes, I assure you, because hers are all flatties – not as glitzy as she used to be, but I suppose her sense of balance has been affected by her illness.'

They were dancing at that moment to a slow number, once a hit for the Kinks. It came to an end and Liz whirled away laughing, making a little curtsey before she went in search of a drink.

Greg was waylaid by yet another elderly relative, who, having seen him chatting with others, inquired almost blatantly what gossip, new or old, they'd been passing on. Great-aunt Irene wanted him to know that she was the acknowledged expert on the Dimitriouso family, far more reliable than Cousin Natalya or Aunt Ariadne. Head bent, he listened, trying to keep track of Liz and longing to get away.

To his surprise, Liz was ready to leave the party quite early. 'We want to be up in time to take an early boat to Piraeus,' she said as they walked back to their cabin.

'We do? Why is that?'

'We have things to accomplish there.'

'In Piraeus? Are we going out on a boat trip from there?'

'No, we're going to find an optician.'

They had reached their door and unlocked it with the smart card. The light came on automatically. Inside, they paused. The prince was still trying to catch up with the logic of Liz's remark.

'There's something wrong with your eyesight?' he enquired.

'No, with Elissa's.'

His brows came together in a frown of confusion. 'We won't find out anything about Elissa's eye condition just by going into an optician, Liz.'

'Yes we will.'

'No, we'd need to know who had prescribed—'

'Not at all. I'd think any good optician would know what the ailment was, if you gave him the lenses.'

A silence.

Then he said, 'Liz, you didn't!'

'Yes I did.' From the bosom of her dress she produced a tiny box of ivory plastic. She held it out.

Greg turned, carefully closed the open door of the cabin, then took the box from her. Opening it, he saw two gleaming little lenses lying on a special blue anti-static cushion. In haste he closed it.

'This is crazy, Liz. She'll miss them.'

'No she won't. She's got about half a dozen different sets in her bathroom cabinet. And I'll put these back next time I go to have a girlie session about her clothes – tomorrow afternoon when we get back from the mainland, for instance. I'll buy her something and take it to the house, if she's not circulating among the guests.'

He sat down, setting the lens case on a nearby table.

Liz studied him. 'What's wrong?'

'I'm trying to think this through. We're going to make inquiries about Elissa's medical condition . . .'

'But we did that already, when we went to see Dr Thingummy on Spetses.'

'Yes, we did. But we didn't steal something beforehand.'

'Oh, come on. I didn't take any of her jewellery! It's just a pair of contact lenses.'

'But it implies we suspect . . . I don't know what we suspect.'

'We suspect that Elissa isn't well enough to be in control of her father's financial empire. That's why we went to see the old family doctor.'

'Who has now suddenly decided to make himself scarce . . .'

'What?' Her voice was sharp with something like alarm.

'Well, it struck me as rather a coincidence that he went on a visit to relatives almost the minute we waved him goodbye.'

'You never said so.' She was staring at him in the beginnings of alarm.

He shrugged. 'Liz, Elissa's father Yanni casts a long shadow, even though he's dead. The Dimitriouso money has power, and if anybody does anything to annoy the present owner of that money, life could be very uncomfortable. Dr Dragorasie is getting old and he's not too well. If he got a phone call from Niki saying they'd prefer he didn't make waves, he probably decided a visit to his cousins would be good for him – that's all.'

She eyed the little ivory-coloured case she'd so blithely purloined a few hours earlier. 'Are you saying I've done something silly?'

His troubled expression gave way to a grin. 'You've always had criminal tendencies,' he said. 'You go to fashion shows with the ulterior motive of stealing ideas for your chain stores.'

'So now I've moved into the big time: it's contact lenses now!' Her spirits had revived after her moment of apprehension.

They felt her career of crime deserved a toast, so they opened one of the bottles in the kitchenette's fridge. Liz lost her sense of alarm, which was Gregory's intention. He hadn't meant to scare her, but he had some understanding of the power of Niki Paroskolos and his ailing wife.

Putting that aside, they went to bed and later to sleep, rising in good time next morning to drink a cup of coffee before catching an early boat.

There were a few homegoing guests on the boat. Anxious to extend the pleasure of the visit with their rich relatives, they called up memories of the previous evening and, as they disembarked, exchanged addresses and telephone numbers with Greg and Liz.

'Why do we do this?' Liz wondered, as they were taken by taxi into the shopping centre of Piraeus. 'At the end of a holiday I always seem to end up with names and addresses and, of course, I never do a thing with them.'

'We-ell . . . In this case you never know.'

The pharmacies, surgeries and opticians were opening as they were set down. After strolling about for a while, they chose an optician not far from the State Theatre. Its window showed not only a few pairs of expensive designer frames, but an eye-testing chart and the information that the doctor and the optometrist were available on the premises that day.

They went in. A pretty assistant came to greet them. It had been decided that Greg would do all the talking in case the conversation had to be in Greek.

'Good morning,' he began. 'I wonder if I could ask you to take a look at these lenses.' He produced the case from his suit jacket. 'My friend had them prescribed in London recently for an eye complaint, but they've given her nothing but trouble ever since.'

'Certainly, sir.' The assistant liked the look of him – not some tourist type in jeans and sweatshirt wanting cheap sunglasses, but in a good suit and with a quiet tie. 'It so happens we have both an oculist and an optometrist on duty this morning. May I see the lenses?' She took them, opened the case, nodded to herself and half-turned towards the interior of the shop. 'I may show them to our technician?'

'Of course.'

'Please take a seat.' Indicating some magazines on a low table, she went away.

'What did she say?' Liz enquired.

'The expert is going to take a look at them.'

'What expert?'

'I don't know.' He translated the sign about the doctor and optician on duty.

'Oh, right.'

After about fifteen minutes the assistant returned accompanied by a man of about forty, wearing a starched white cotton jacket. He came to them with something between a frown and a smile.

'These were prescribed for you, *keiria?*'

'He's asking if they were prescribed for you, Liz.'

She gave him a dig in the ribs. 'Tell him yes, of course.'

'Oh, we may speak English,' said the optometrist at once. 'For an eye defect, I was told?'

'Yes.'

'What defect was that?'

She gazed at him, completely at a loss.

'For sensitivity to . . . er . . . ultra-violet rays,' said Gregory, inventing wildly.

'Photophobia, you mean, perhaps?'

'Yes, that's it,' Liz agreed.

'And who prescribed them?'

'Well . . . er . . . an optician. In London.'

'You attended the eye department of a hospital, whose ophthalmologist provided these?'

'No, no, it was an optician's shop.' The name of a commercial enterprise occurred, but she thought she'd better not suggest it, because these lenses belonged to a millionairess who certainly wouldn't have gone to a place like that.

'Madame, I am at a loss. Are you sure these are the lenses that were prescribed? Do you have the prescription with you?'

'No . . . I never thought to bring it on holiday.'

'No, of course not.' He weighed the little ivory case in his hand, shaking his head. 'Well, madame, I think a mistake has occurred. You must have been given lenses prescribed for someone else. These are not appropriate protection for a sufferer from photophobia. No wonder they have been giving you discomfort. They are purely cosmetic in purpose.'

'Cosmetic?'

'To change the colour of your eyes from . . .' he sought for the English term . . . 'greenish-brown? I think there is some other word but I don't know it. To change your eye colour to dark brown. They certainly serve no medical purpose.' He handed them back to Liz.

They were held silent by surprise. This was a technically suitable response for the story they'd given in the first place, but it wasn't quite what they'd expected. The optometrist watched them sympathetically. 'If you wish, our ophthal-mologist will see you later,' he suggested. 'I had a word with him, and he could fit you in about one this afternoon?'

'Er . . . no . . . I'm afraid we have to be . . . Perhaps I could telephone later and arrange something . . .'

'Very well.' He turned to a desk, where he picked up a card. 'Here is the number. But in the meantime, madame, you should have protection from the glare.'

'Sunglasses, you mean?' said Mr Crowne. He understood that the technician didn't want to see them leave without earning some profit from them. 'Of course.' He glanced around. 'I see you have some very attractive styles . . .'

Liz agreed, although she had a perfectly good pair of sunglasses in her bag. The technician shook hands, saying he looked forward to hearing from her later. The assistant took over. By and by, having spent the equivalent of sixty pounds on glasses she didn't need, they left.

They found a bench under a turkey oak. 'Well,' said Liz, 'what do you make of that?' She took the lens case out of her bag, opened it, and stared at the contents.

'Could it possibly be that you picked up a non-medical pair? I mean, she has a lot of these, you said. Could she have tried to wear ordinary lenses at some time – but why in heaven's name should she?' he ended, slapping himself on the forehead in castigation. 'That's nonsense. She has half a dozen sets of lenses because none of them suit her – she has red-rimmed eyes, and that's the kind of thing you see among friends who are trying to get accustomed to contact lenses.'

'You're right,' she agreed, thinking of half a dozen fashion models she knew.

'Wait. She's trying to get accustomed to wearing contact lenses.'

'Yes, I think so.'

'So . . . she hasn't been wearing them all her life. I tried to remember if she had blue eyes or brown when she was a little girl. If she had brown, it certainly wasn't because she was wearing brown lenses. They're a relatively recent improvement.'

'Perhaps after her illness? She's light-sensitive now; could that come from a bout of meningitis?'

'So until last year she had blue eyes?'

'What?'

'She was laid low with meningitis on a skiing holiday last year. If she's only had to have brown lenses to protect her eyes from the light since her illness, she's had *blue* eyes up till then.'

'Greg! Stop! I'm in a daze!'

'But the brown lenses she's wearing aren't for photophobia. They're just to make her eyes look brown.'

'I can't bear any more. I don't know what you're saying.'

'Neither do I, damn it.' He jumped to his feet. 'We have to find out more about Elissa Paroskolos. Somebody is in some way doing something – perhaps she's doing it herself, perhaps someone is doing it *to* her. But we've got to find out or I'll go mad!'

They found one of the few Macdonalds, where they ordered coffee and muffins: they'd skipped breakfast and were hungry. Liz swallowed a reviving gulp or two, hoping it would make her brain work better. She felt totally bewildered. She took out the little lens case again, set it on the table between them and stared at it.

'It seems she's got to have brown eyes,' Gregory said.

'Does it?'

'Why else is she wearing them?'

'I don't know. You said you had to find out more. Where can we do that?'

'In the newspaper files, I suppose. They'd have them in the public library, perhaps. But I don't know where the public library is in Piraeus.'

'Should we go into Athens then?'

'The University would have a library. But . . .'

'What?'

'Better still, I know people there. And one of them is sure to have a computer.'

'Not Professor Tzelili,' she said, smiling.

'No, she only has the *hydraulis*. But the great thing about music, Liz, is that you meet a lot of people at concerts and recitals and theatres, and you get to know them, and send them tickets you can't use yourself, or discs you want them to listen to . . . So I think I'll just ring around and see if I can hunt somebody up – preferably somebody who's got an Internet service I can use my password on. Lend me your mobile.'

It took him some time. He didn't have his address book or organizer with him so he had to rely on memory for the numbers, some of which proved incorrect. Liz watched and listened, and ate not only her muffin but the remains of his as well. At length he had a conversation in Greek, longer than the forerunners and clearly giving good results. He said *'Adeio'* then looked at Liz, smiling.

'My friend Stratis Lonagidas. He lives in Sina Street, so we'll take the Metro to Panepistimo and be there in about twenty minutes. Come on.'

'Aren't you going to eat?'

'I see you've done that for me,' he replied, and pulled her to her feet. 'Come *on!*'

They took the Metro from Piraeus and changed at Omonia. True enough, they were soon crossing a busy road and hurrying up a rather steep side street, to a low-rise apartment building where the outer door opened at a push. Stratis Lonagidas opened his door as they entered the hallway. 'This way,' he

72

said, and ushered them into the most cluttered room Liz had ever seen.

It held two keyboards, a synthesizer, several amplifiers, electric guitars of various designs, a xylophone, a drum kit, an ether wave player, several hi-fi players with wires attaching them to other machines, and a bulky tape recorder. On a separate table were two computers, one of which seemed to be showing sound waves.

'Liz, this is Stratis; he's into advanced electronic music,' said Mr Crowne. 'His "Chordiasko" was performed in Berlin last year.'

'Not well performed,' put in Stratis, who was small and thin and bearded. 'Nobody seems able to make the right sounds on an ether wave machine, you know.'

'I expect it's very difficult,' Liz ventured.

'Difficult, of course it's difficult; there's no point in composing something *simple*,' said Stratis. 'Well, you want to use a computer. I've protected my software on that one so you can't harm anything, and you'll see the service providers on the desktop, so help yourself.'

'Thank you, Stratis.'

'Do you need any help? If not, I'll push off; I've got a group of students rehearsing Schönberg in half an hour. Might not be back before you go, so just bang the door hard; it'll lock itself.'

'Thank you.'

He hurried out, causing a faint discordant sound wave on one of the guitars. Greg switched on the computer indicated by their host, then found two folding chairs, which he opened out and set by the computer. With the xylophone poking into their backs, they sat down to find out what they could about Elissa Paroskolos.

'Magazines and newspapers,' suggested Greg. 'The British Library Automated thing – that's the first step. You said you knew about Elissa's clothes by reading about them in magazines. Give me a few titles while I log on.'

'Well, *Vogue* and *Harper's* . . . But they're about *fashion*, Greg, not about her life.'

'So what, then? *Hello*? Some gossip magazine?'

73

'Perhaps we should try the newspapers. There'd be something about her at the time of her father's death, and then her marriage – wouldn't you think?'

He paused, thought about it, and decided that since Elissa had been educated and had spent quite a large part of her life in the United States, the American database for the on-line library service would be the best starting point for anything about her family. He then called up the *New York Times*, hesitated, and decided to start with the death of Yanni Dimitriouso. He entered 'Obituaries' and then 'Dimitriouso'.

The obituary for Yanni provided an account of the family, its wealth and influence, together with some speculation about what would happen to that huge financial empire now that its ruler had gone. Some views from those who knew family members formed part of the obit. Links to the financial page were given. Elissa Paroskolos was mentioned, with an advice to go to page 16.

The article on page 16 was by a woman reporter describing the jet-set life of Elissa Paroskolos, who would now have to settle down to being the head of the Dimitriouso empire. It appeared she'd had an interview with Elissa; she explained she'd been granted this exclusive because she herself had Greek forebears and so could understand Elissa's problems.

It was Nancy Lanan's view that the recently wed Elissa Paroskolos wouldn't be found wanting. 'Contrary to common opinion, Greek women understand the use of power, though they sometimes have to use it very discreetly. Now Mrs Paroskolos will be able to wield it with more openness. Her husband Niki is prepared for the change in their life style, she told me. "Niki is a businessman in his own right," she pointed out. "He and I may very well develop some mutual projects in the future. I'm looking forward to it."'

'She seems to have met Elissa face to face,' Gregory mused. 'Let's look her up and see what else she might have written about her.' He typed in the name Nancy Lanan, but the *New York Times* had nothing further to say about the reporter; it seemed the piece about Elissa had been a one-off.

After a search he left the *Times* then tried for a web page headed with the reporter's name. It turned out Nancy Lanan didn't have a web page. He was a little surprised at that, for most journalists were on-line somewhere. He went back to the library database. He had researched among music journals for information, so he used the same tactics: he typed in the name Nancy Lanan, in hopes of a list of her published pieces.

There was a pause; then followed a screen containing the journalist's name and a fairly long list of work together with the names and dates of the magazines in which it appeared. He was about to type in a request for any feature about Elissa when he stopped dead.

'What?' demanded Liz as he stared at the screen.

'Look.' He brought the cursor to a paragraph about halfway down. It read: '*Gung Ho!*' and the date of the publication; then 'Subject: *snake venom*. Title: *Poisonous Pets* Length 2800 words, illustrated, intended for backpackers and off-track travellers. See also *Urgent Antidote!* in KANSAS MEDICAL WORLD and *Handle with Care!* in CAREERS OUTLOOK.'

Liz stared at the item. Then she said, with a tremor in her voice: 'Wasn't *Poisonous Pets* the article you found on the table in the pavilion?'

Mr Crowne was slowly nodding his head.

Six

The cursor winked at the beginning of the paragraph.

'When Dr Donati explained about that magazine – the day after Elissa had the dream about snakes – you said it was too big a coincidence,' whispered Liz.

'Yes.'

'But this isn't a coincidence, Greg. We actually found this on our own.'

'Yes, we did.' He paused. 'And this time I think we ought to read it. If you recall, Dr Donati walked off with the magazine last time.'

'Can we get it up on the screen?'

'I think so.' He called up the link, the screen cleared and reshaped itself, then up came the reproduction of a magazine page. There was a headline: POISONOUS PETS, then a byline for Nancy Lanan and her photograph, postage-stamp size. The lead-in read: 'How would you like to stare a venomous snake in the eye? Nancy Lanan tells you how it feels.'

The article was written in a non-scientific, humorous style. It began: 'The fangs were twelve inches from my nose. Did I flinch? You bet I did!' It went on to explain that the writer, in the course of a journalistic trip to Brazil, had been invited to join a tour of the Butanta Institute. 'They "farm" the snakes just as we would a herd of cows, but what they get from them is venom. From this, precious serums are made to save lives.'

The body of the piece conveyed information, with names and descriptions of the deadliest snakes and a warning not to be careless when off the beaten track. 'For instance, don't dangle your hand in the water if you're on a river trip. You'd probably see a croc if it was looking for lunch, but you might not see a water snake.'

The wind-up was written so as to instil vigilance. 'So you thrill at bungee jumping and you love fast cars? Okay, but death from snakebite is a thrill you should avoid. Drive, don't run to the nearest hospital.'

Before the wind-up the writer allowed herself a few personal notes. She explained she'd become interested in snakes during a year at Louisiana State University.

'Louisiana!' breathed Liz, pointing.

Greg nodded, and stopped scrolling down the page so that they could read more attentively. 'I went one Sunday to a snake-handling ceremony held in a country barn,' he read. 'Since I was doing a year on camera technique at the Art Department, I thought I'd come up with some great pictures. But I can tell you, when the preacher urged the congregation to dip into the basket for a pit viper, I got so dizzy I nearly dropped my Nikon. Offered the tour of the Butanta, I felt I had to go, just to prove I wasn't a wimp. But if you detect a slight camera shake in some of the photographs, you know why!'

The article was profusely illustrated with photographs taken at the Butanta Institute. The quality was excellent. Miss Lanan might say she was scared, but she hadn't allowed it to interfere with her professionalism.

When he came to the end of the article, Gregory hesitated for a moment, then switched on Stratis's printer and printed it out.

'Are you going to show that to . . . I don't know – who would you show it to?' Liz enquired.

'I don't know what I want it for. I just feel that it's something solid in this collection of nothingness. Elissa *did* speak about the Butanta Institute and here's a printed piece about it.'

'You said the article in the *New York Times* proved that this reporter woman had met Elissa. Perhaps that's where they met – at the Butanta.'

He shook his head. 'I can't believe Elissa was ever in Sao Paulo. And if by some miracle she was, I can't imagine her ever going to look at snakes having their venom extracted.'

'Then . . . Louisiana? Elissa talked about that folk music – what was it?'

'Cajun.'

'Yes.'

'Well, that's where they met. And Nancy Lanan went to this snake-holding thing, and her photographs were in the college magazine, perhaps.'

'Yes, perhaps.'

'So Elissa showed an interest, so she told her about her visit to the Butanta . . .'

'No.'

'What d'you mean, no?'

'In her article she specifically says that the visit to the Institute came *after* her year at Louisiana University.'

'No she doesn't!'

He flicked through the pages he had printed out. Liz read the paragraph that mentioned the snake-handling ceremony. Sure enough, the implication was clear: the journalist had gone later to the Butanta to prove that she could overcome the feelings she'd experienced earlier that Sunday in Louisiana.

'Oh,' groaned Liz. 'I thought I'd found a sort of explanation.'

Mr Crowne gave her a little hug. 'Good try,' he said.

He moved out of the database for periodicals and logged on to directories. An hour spent bringing up items from various financial and biographical sources failed to turn up any mention of Elissa ever being at a university in Louisiana.

The session was brought to an end by the reappearance of Stratis Lagonidas, in a very bad mood.

'How did the rehearsal go?' Gregory asked in a rather careful tone.

'It was a fiasco! A travesty! Musicians? They call themselves musicians?' He threw his fists in the air, accompanying the act with a stream of Greek that Liz took to be oaths. His small, neat body was vibrating with rage. It was so intimidating that she got up and went round the other side of some of the musical equipment, just to be on the safe side.

Gregory closed down the computer in haste. Their host looked as if he might smash something at any moment and might choose the computer if his attention were drawn to it. 'We'll get out of your hair, then,' he said. 'Thanks a million for letting us use your set-up.'

78

'It's not as if we have much time to get it right,' exclaimed Stratis. 'The performance is next week, but do they care? No, of course not! I'll string them all up by their thumbs!'

'Well, I'm sure you'll sort it out, Strat,' Gregory murmured, urging Liz towards the door. 'See you again some time.'

'If I haven't killed myself in despair!' returned Stratis. Their last glimpse of him was as he opened a bottle and dashed something intoxicating into a pottery mug.

'He gets like that,' Greg said in apology as they went out to the pavement. 'Nobody really likes his stuff, so that makes him angry in the first place; and then, when he tries to put on a concert of somebody else's work, he chooses something that's too difficult for his students.'

Liz didn't want to discuss difficult music. 'What are we going to do now?' she asked.

'Get something to eat. If you remember, you gobbled up my breakfast muffin.'

It was early afternoon. The day was growing warm. Liz chiefly felt in need of a long, cool drink and, despite the muffins, was ready to eat. They found a little shopping arcade off Panepistimiou, where a vegetarian restaurant was tucked in between a gift shop and a pharmacy. They ordered cold beer to begin with. The food, when it came, was excellent and plentiful: layers of aubergine in rich cheese sauce with a salad arranged like a circular picture on its plate.

Once they'd satisfied their thirst and had a few mouthfuls of food, they plunged into a discussion of the morning's events.

'I can't believe Elissa was ever at Louisiana State University,' said Mr Crowne in a firm voice. 'Even if for some reason she'd wanted to go there, her father would never have allowed it. Only the very best was good enough for his child. I don't know anything about LSU, but I feel sure Yanni would have hit the roof if Elissa had ever suggested it.'

'Maybe she went in for a bit of teenage rebellion?'

'Well, maybe. But if she was rebelling, why not California? That would be a lot more to her taste than steamy old Louisiana. Not that I've ever been to Louisiana, but I always imagine it as hot and humid.'

'What subjects did she take? Anything Louisiana might specialize in?'

'She was being groomed to take over the family business, I imagine. Her father had no real trust in the ability of women, so since she was going to be his heir, he'd make her take business studies, economics, stuff like that.' He spooned up some of the luscious sauce, then paused, spoon in hand. 'I suppose Louisiana does offer those courses. But it seems to me that Elissa would rather have been on the eastern seaboard, where she could get to New York for the theatre and the glossy fashion shows, and places like Hyannis Port for recreation among the influential types.'

Liz was nodding, though rather doubtfully. 'You're thinking about the obnoxious child you used to know. Maybe she turned out less horrible as she grew up, so those things wouldn't be so important.'

'Do you think so?'

'Well, meeting her now, she seems nice enough to me.'

'Ye-es. But don't forget, that's after a long illness that seems to have made a change in her. From what my father and grandmother said, she was just as horrid as ever when they met her – but of course that was a while ago, before the meningitis.'

They ate in silence for a while. The waitress came to take their empty plates and to ask if they'd like dessert. They opted for coffee but made sure they would get French style.

'You know,' Liz said with hesitation, 'about that magazine article . . .'

'Yes?'

'It's come back to me that the servant – what was his name, Jesus?'

'What? Oh, you mean Christos. Yes, he was banished to the mainland before we could get a chance to speak to him.'

'What I was thinking was . . . It seems we were prevented from finding out about the article. I mean, we were shown it but then it was whisked away.'

'It was indeed,' Mr Crowne agreed, remembering the dexterity with which Donati had removed it.

'So . . . always supposing there's something strange going on . . . the magazine article is important.'

He nodded. He was trying to work out what the magazine article contained. 'It's about snakes. Elissa is afraid of snakes.'

'Freudian in the male sense,' she quoted.

'It's about being at the Butanta Institute.'

'But Niki said she'd never been there.'

'And I believe him.'

'It mentions Louisiana University and Elissa talked about Cajun dances.'

'But we've more or less agreed that Elissa never went to Louisiana.'

'But we don't *know* that, Greg.'

His mouth turned into a straight line. 'We do, Liz. We're so sure it's not the kind of place Elissa would want to go to, we accept it.'

'*You* accept it.'

'Liz, if we're going to make any sense out of this, we've got to make a few assumptions.' He gave her a sudden smile. 'I'm assuming, for instance, that you would never willingly sit through a Wagner opera?'

'And you couldn't be more right.'

'So I'm also assuming that Elissa Paroskolos would prefer Smith College and Boston to Louisiana, and would never have any interest in snakes – unless it was a snakeskin handbag.'

'We-ell . . . okay.'

'So what else is in the article? What haven't we covered?'

He got the printout from his jacket pocket, unfolded it, and they pored over it together. But it was just an informally composed warning against snakes in South America based on a visit to a snake-venom laboratory. The prince shuffled the pages together and was about to refold them and put them away when he paused. He gazed at the first page. Then he brought it up close to his eye.

'What?' demanded Liz.

He leapt up. 'Wait there,' he said.

Before she could say anything he was heading for the door of the taverna and had vanished.

81

The waitress approached. 'Is anything wrong?' she enquired, and then, seeing Liz didn't understand, repeated it in English.

'Oh, no, He's gone to . . . get cigarettes.'

The waitress remained by the table. It came to Liz that she was worried about being paid. Liz produced her wallet and took out her credit card, because she had only a small supply of euros. She was signing the slip when Gregory reappeared, bearing a small carrier bag that seemed to contain a flat cardboard box.

He sat down beside her. The waitress came up to deal with the receipt. He ordered more coffee, then took out the package from the carrier bag. The labelling was in Greek, Liz could make nothing of it. He undid the cardboard packet and produced – a magnifying glass.

Liz burst out laughing. 'What's this, Sherlock?'

He grinned. 'The pharmacy didn't have one but I got it in the gift shop. It's probably not very good. But let's see.'

She watched in amazement as he smoothed out the first page of the printout so as to look closely at the postage-stamp photograph of Nancy Lanan alongside the strapline. For perhaps a full minute he stared through the glass. Then he handed paper and magnifying glass to Liz.

'Take a look.'

Certain that he was playing some weird joke, she obeyed. The lens in the magnifying glass was poor – in fact, she'd have said it was perspex rather than glass: she had trouble getting the range; but, after manoeuvring, she got the little photograph into focus.

She saw an oval face with short, thick, dark hair coming down on the brow; neat ears close to the head, a wide smile showing fine white teeth; blue eyes.

She looked up at Gregory.

'What? What am I to see?'

He pulled the page so that it lay between them, produced a pen from his pocket, and began to draw. She leaned against him to see what he was doing. He was shaping in a cloud of dark hair around the head and cheeks.

He was turning it into a photograph of Elissa Paroskolos.

Seven

Liz folded the sheet of paper with unnecessary vigour and pushed it away. 'No, Greg!' she said. 'No, no no!'

The waitress came with the coffee. A lover's tiff, she thought, and tactfully made herself scarce.

'You just did that by a trick,' Liz insisted. 'There's no resemblance.'

'There is,' said Greg.

'No!'

'Why else do you think I wanted to get a close look at the colour of her eyes? There she was in the photograph, looking out at us, and I saw *Elissa.*'

'No you didn't!'

'You can close your mind to it if you want to, Liz, but I think Nancy Lanan would look very much like Elissa Paroskolos, if she wore brown contact lenses and had her hair grown long.'

Liz sat in silence. She was shaking her head. 'It's not possible, Greg.'

'It's possible. Somewhere in what we read on Strat's computer, Nancy Lanan said she had Greek forebears. And then . . . think about it: Elissa suddenly changed her dressmaker.'

She gave him a glare of angry surprise. 'Well, what about it?'

'She couldn't have her clothes made by the same dressmaker. She's thinner than Elissa.'

'But Elissa lost weight because of her illness.'

'But she's *taller* than Elissa. That's why she's wearing flat heels.'

She frowned. 'But . . . but that's because her sense of balance—'

'That's how you accounted for it to yourself. But look at it this way: that girl couldn't have her clothes made by Elissa's couturier because she's about two inches taller. Loss of weight, yes. That could be due to her illness. But nobody grows taller when they're ill, *chérie*.'

'I don't want to hear this! You're building something out of nothing . . .'

'It's not nothing. Her voice is wrong. I said so before. She doesn't have a New England accent when she speaks English.'

'So if you're so clever, where does she come from? Louisiana?'

He hesitated. 'No, she doesn't have a Southern accent. I don't know what the accent is, Liz. I'm not really an expert in United States regional speech. All I know is that the girl at Kerouli doesn't talk as I'd expect Elissa to.'

'That's just what *you* say. You're basing this on things that nobody else would bother about or believe in.'

'What about the snake-handling? We agreed, didn't we, that Elissa was unlikely to have gone to Louisiana for any understandable reason, and even more unlikely to have been interested in snakes.'

'Nobody likes snakes, Greg. You can't make anything out of that.'

'But Elissa was so scared of them it gave her nightmares. And Dr Donati was very eager to explain it all away by letting us have a glimpse of an article about the Butanta Institute.' He paused, working it out as he went along. 'And then he twitched it away from us, and now it turns out to have been *written* by Nancy Lanan.'

'That's just a coincidence.'

He made no response. He picked up his cup for a mouthful of coffee.

She avoided looking at him. She was determined not to let him convince her. He was telling her something that might have come out of Grimms' fairy tales. She didn't want to hear it, didn't want to think about it.

What she wanted was to be back in London in her own flat, listening to Britney Spears on her hi-fi and working up some

84

of the sketches she'd made of Elissa's clothes ready to use as fashion indicators for next autumn.

But what if the clothes weren't Elissa's?

No, she wasn't going to think that. With determination she eyed the faux-marble table top.

'Okay then,' Greg said, understanding her reluctance. He moved his wrist so she knew he was looking at his watch. 'Time's getting on. We should be heading for Piraeus to get the boat back to Kerouli.' He finished his coffee and made as if to beckon the waitress to pay her.

She found herself putting a hand on his arm. 'Wait,' she said.

He waited.

The thought of returning to the island with this still unresolved between them was impossible. 'Let's go over it again, Greg. What you're suggesting is so . . . so . . .'

He put an arm round her shoulders. 'Yes it is. I know it is.'

'But you really think . . . ?'

He made a pause before he replied. 'That little photograph is of someone who's awfully like Elissa Paroskolos. And Elissa Paroskolos has been acting awfully unlike herself since we've met her.'

'Well, you keep on saying she's selfish and bad-tempered, and that girl certainly isn't. But that could be—'

'Because of the long illness. Yes, that accounts for so much, doesn't it? It *has* to account for so much. She's wearing different clothes, different shoes; she has nightmares about snakes, she talks about dancing to Cajun music, she speaks with an American accent but it isn't a New England accent, *she has blue eyes hidden behind brown lenses—*'

'Stop, stop, I'm suffering from overload!' Now she took a big swallow of coffee to get her brain in order again. 'What you're saying, of course, is that someone is playing the part of Elissa.'

'Yes.'

'But Greg! That's such a . . . a strange – an unheard-of thing to do . . .'

'Well, there's a tremendous amount of money involved.'

'Oh.'

'Don't you remember, that first evening? We said to each other that she didn't seem fit to have control of her father's financial empire.'

'I remember that.'

'She seemed so uncertain, didn't she? And no wonder, if she was only playing the part of Elissa.'

'No, wait, Greg. That's where it all falls down. Let's agree that perhaps this Nancy Lanan has enough resemblance to Elissa to make it possible. But why would she do it?' She gave the table a little thump with her fist. 'If anybody asked me to impersonate another woman, I'd be horrified! She wouldn't do it.'

'She might – if she was offered enough money.'

'No, no . . .'

'Yes, why not? Clearly this Lanan woman is a freelance journalist. If you think about it, she's not been at it very long, because she must be about the same age as Elissa – that's to say, twenty-five-ish. Someone comes along and says, "Ms Lanan, here's a cheque for fifty thousand dollars. Just play the part of a sick millionairess for a few days so as to reassure her board of directors and you can put it in your bank account." She could certainly use the money. And . . .' He paused. 'It would be an *adventure*, Liz. This was a girl who forced herself to go to the Butanta Institute to prove she wasn't – what was the word she used?'

'A wimp.'

'A wimp. So she's taken it on, but it's proved harder than she imagined, so she's having nightmares and getting tired of having to stay on that tiny island.'

'And when you look back,' Liz put in, 'it almost looks as if that nurse . . .'

'Trudi.'

'Is acting like a minder.'

'A minder. That means guard, watcher?' he enquired, because although he spoke excellent English, certain nuances of slang eluded him.

'Yes, it does.'

'So Trudi is her minder. Not because she's ill, but because she's got to be kept under control and playing her part.'

86

They fell silent. What they were suspecting was too alarming to talk about any more for the moment.

After a long silence Liz said, 'It can't be true. Nancy Lanan is alive and well and living in New York, writing articles for *Gung Ho*.'

'No she's not.'

'She is, Greg. All this that you've said is . . . it's supposition, speculation. Nancy Lanan isn't the girl on Kerouli; she's home in the US.'

'It wouldn't be difficult to find out.'

'Find out what?'

'If she's in the US. We could phone around, find her if she's there.'

'We don't have her phone number.'

'We could ask International Directory.'

'Come on, Greg. Be sensible. You've no idea whether she's in New York or Los Angeles or Louisiana!'

He had to admit the truth of that. He mused over it for a few minutes, then said, 'Well, we could ask the magazine for her telephone number.'

'Which magazine? You mean *Gung Ho*?'

'Yes, why not?'

'But you don't know how to get in touch with *Gung Ho*. And besides, I don't think they'd give it out to a stranger.'

'Well, she's probably got an e-mail address – they'd give me that, wouldn't you think?'

'But what good would that do? We haven't got a computer. And don't suggest we go back to your friend Stratis!'

He leaned back in his chair, half-closing his eyes. Liz waited, more perturbed than she would have cared to admit. Greg was so level-headed, so dependable. The small business he ran needed reliability, because some of the musicians he dealt with could be so volatile. If he genuinely believed there was something wrong on Kerouli, it was because he had reason enough to convince him.

'Here's what I think,' he said: 'It's time for us to go to the boat jetty if we're going back to Kerouli this evening.' He looked at her, waiting.

'N-no, Greg. I . . . I don't think I could go back to Kerouli and talk to Elissa – not with all this hanging on my mind.'

'Right. So I think we should go to a hotel for the night. In a hotel we can get the use of a telephone and an up-to-date PC.'

'And use it to try and find Nancy Lanan?'

'Yes, that and other things.'

Somehow it seemed a very big decision. It wasn't just the idea of absenting themselves from that evening's festivity on the island; it was as if they'd be taking up the position of turning themselves into sneaks, fault-finders, judges . . . But she couldn't go back to Kerouli tonight. She would have to look at Elissa Paroskolos with different eyes.

'All right, let's go to a hotel.'

He smiled at her. He had expected that decision. One of the reasons he found her so compatible was her open-mindedness. He took her hand and squeezed it.

'It'll be all right,' he said.

'Yes.'

'So let's go and buy a few things we'll need for overnight. Then I think we'll head for the Ariston – that's at Akropoli, where we were yesterday – not far on the Metro; but I'll ring first and tell them we're coming. Lend me your mobile.'

He called the hotel, and from the conversation she gathered he'd stayed there before on some musical jaunt. When he handed back the phone, he was already putting down money for the coffee. They went out into the arcade.

'Toothbrushes, toothpaste, throwaway razors for me – what else?'

'Clean undies,' she said.

'Of course. Well, let's split up. I'll go into the pharmacy, you go on the hunt for a lingerie boutique, and we'll meet at the entrance to the arcade. Collect a lot of carrier bags,' he added. 'I told the hotel receptionist we'd got exhausted doing a lot of shopping and decided to stay in Athens overnight.'

'No problem,' she said, feeling more cheerful at the thought.

He suppressed a grin. Any chance of shopping always had a good effect on Liz. He dropped a kiss on her brow then set off in search of his own purchases.

The desk clerk clearly didn't mind whether they had carrier bags or not. He greeted Gregory as Mr Crowne, but clearly knew he had another identity. The room was ready, he told them, and an IBM Thinkpad was already installed in their room – also, if he might add, some wine and fruit, and if there was anything else, Mr Crowne need only mention it.

'For the moment, that's all,' Gregory said in a tone Liz called his 'I'm-incognito' manner. It made hotel staff and airport officials feel they were somehow in the secret of his true identity as against the rest of the world, and doing something special for the ex-Crown Prince of Hirtenstein.

The room was charming, softly lit with downlights trained on photographs of the Parthenon, the Agora, and other beauties of Athens. The television set had been switched on to the visitor programme, displaying 'Welcome to the Ariston Hotel, Mr Crowne,' and advising him to touch various buttons on the remote for further services.

'This is très posh,' Liz observed. 'Whose credit card is this going on?'

'Mine, of course, but don't worry about it.'

'You mean they give you a special rate, you rat!'

He had the grace to blush. 'Well, yes, they do. But then they can put in their brochure that they're patronized by bank presidents, diplomats, and royalty.'

'Well, thank goodness for that, because I spent a lot more than I intended to in that lingerie shop.' She delved into a carrier bag, to produce a very skimpy set of bikini undies in blue silk and lace. 'What do you think?'

'I'll tell you later,' said the prince. 'Business first.'

He pressed buttons on the remote control to bring up a 'What's On' programme on the screen. It was in Greek, and he pressed other buttons until he found what he wanted.

'Right,' he said. 'There's a show on at the Rodon Club that'll do.' He found the smart card for their cabin on Kerouli, which gave the telephone number of the island office. Then he used the room telephone to get through to it. 'This is Gregory von Hirtenstein,' he said. 'Von Hirtenstein. Yes. Ms Blair and I have decided to stay over in Athens to hear Tania Tsanaklidou . . . yes . . . yes . . . no, we'll be back around lunchtime tomorrow, I think. Please let Mr Paroskolos – yes, thank you. *Kalispera.*'

'Well,' said Liz in admiration. 'You think of everything, don't you?'

'There's no point in having them wondering what on earth has happened to us and sending out alarm calls.'

'I'm with you on that.' She'd switched on the Thinkpad and, though it was different from the computer she used at home, she had no trouble handling it. When Greg drew up a chair to sit beside her at the handsome little bureau, she'd already logged on and was repeating the process for the US Library database.

She typed in 'Nancy Lanan'. Once again the list of journalism was presented. But there was no e-mail address for the writer, which seemed strange. Most journalists, they muttered to each other, would supply some means of getting in touch, in case you wanted to hire their services.

So they had to find some other way of getting an address. 'Well, we were going to ask at *Gung Ho.*'

'I don't think they'd give out addresses or phone numbers to strangers.'

'Not to me: they'd think I was a stalker. You can ring the magazines. They'll feel more kindly towards a woman. And you can say you want Ms Lanan to write a piece for you about . . . I leave that to you. Get going, *amore mio*; it's midday in New York and they'll all go out to lunch.'

'Right you are.' She scribbled down some of the names and telephone numbers on the hotel's scratch-pad. Rising to go to the phone, she said, 'Oh, can I use this while we're on-line?' But the Thinkpad was plugged into another socket. 'Very efficient,' she commented.

'A lot of business types come here, and the hotel has conference facilities and all that kind of thing.' He said this over his shoulder while he continued to hunt through the data system, looking for possible addresses by which to find Ms Lanan. Liz began pushing buttons to get the overseas exchange.

She began with the *New York Times*, because the article in

those pages had been about Elissa; she felt she might glean something about a possible relationship between the two. The obituaries editor said in snooty tones that Ms Lanan wasn't a staff writer and although they perhaps had her telephone number, it was not available. Liz transferred to the features department and got more or less the same brush-off.

So she went on to *Gung Ho*, which had its being in Chicago. She asked for the features editor, was put through, asked for anyone who might have edited the feature about eighteen months ago dealing with the Butanta Institute, and was put on hold. Finally, a blithe and rather booming voice said, 'Ludo Perkowitz, how may I help you?'

'Ah . . . Mr Perkowitz . . . I'm calling from Athens about your article on the Butanta Institute in Sao Paulo.'

'From Athens? Well, what d'you know! And what, if I may be so bold, does Athens want to know about Sao Paulo?'

'It's not about the city; it's about the writer of the piece.' She paused, but when Perkowitz said nothing, she prompted, 'Nancy Lanan.'

'Who? Oh, our Nancy! Yeah, yeah, what about her?'

'I was thinking of hiring her to do a section for a one-shot fashion brochure I'm putting together.'

'Fashion? Nancy? He sounded puzzled. 'You sure you've got the right name?'

'Yes, the writer of the piece about the snakes.'

'Well . . . That was Nancy, all-righty. It made her go pale even to remember it. Yeah, our Nancy. Ready for anything . . .' He seemed to consider the verdict before going on, 'She's written quite a few things for me. But fashion . . . ? Are you doing a brochure about blue jeans? Trainers? Because otherwise, y'see . . .' He stopped in puzzlement.

'Yes, casual clothes, vacation clothes,' Liz improvised. 'She was recommended to me.'

'By who?'

'I forget.'

Mr Perkowitz seemed to pull himself together. 'Well, who am I to rain on her parade? If you want her to do it, she can do it. But she's not on staff here, y'see; we've no contract. You're okay to hire her if you want to.'

91

'That's good. Do you have an address or a telephone number where I can reach her?'

'Oh, I thought you meant you'd been in touch already. Nancy? No, I don't have anything on her at present.'

'But she's been a contributor. You'd have her on your files.'

'Sure, got an address and an e-mail, but that wouldn't find her at the moment, y'see. She's off on her own somewhere, getting material for an exclusive book – a biography, I think she said.'

'She hasn't been in touch recently?'

'No – wouldn't say where she was going or who she was going to write about. Dead secret, the whole kit and caboodle.'

'Oh.' Liz was dashed, but rallied. 'Could I have her e-mail address?'

'Take five while I check it out.' There was a pause. She heard the click of keys as he called up something on his desk computer. Then he said, 'Take another five; it's noted here as "inactive". I'll ask.' A hiatus while Liz could hear a muffled conversation, then he came back on the line. 'No, got nothing here. Seems her e-mail went inactive because she either didn't pay the bill or cancelled. Got an address and phone for her where she lives in Bloomington, but Gerda says she rented it out on a long lease before she left on this book-research thing—'

'A long lease?'

'Oh, yeah, this book, y'see – she said it would take about a year or more. According to her it was gonna be *big*!' He gave a gusty sigh. 'But journalists are always gonna write *big* books – heard it a hundred times.'

'She didn't leave any forwarding address or anything?'

'Gerda says no. Hey, Gerda, pick up on line two.'

Liz heard clicks and then a throaty voice said, 'This is Gerda Blundall. Who's this I'm speaking to?'

'I'm Lizbeth Legrand,' said Liz, using a name not unknown in the wholesale fashion world. 'I just wanted to get Ms Lanan for a one-shot fashion spread. Is there any way I can contact her?'

'We had her e-mail for a couple of months, but I sent her something that came in for her here – an offer for a yacht-race piece – and it was refused as "undeliverable".'
Gerda made a huffing sound. 'Gone into seclusion, to write her magnum opus.'
'She's probably come to her senses by now – might be glad of the fashion brochure bit,' Perkowitz put in, 'but I can't help you. Try Ma Bell at Bloomington. She might be back but, of course, she can't get into her old apartment so she'd have a new phone number.'
'Thanks a lot,' said Liz.
'Athens, eh? You sure speak good English for a Greek lady.'
She laughed. 'I'm English.' She had a sudden thought. 'Does Ms Lanan have an interest in Greek matters? She did a piece about Yanni Dimitriouso when he died.'
'She did? Well, she's been in Greece a few times – tried to sell me pieces about backpacking in Macedonia, or wherever it is. But that's not really rugged enough for us.'
'Does she speak Greek then?' Elissa spoke it fluently.
'Oh, sure. I thought that's why you wanted her, for a fashion spread in Greek.'
'She has Greek grandparents or something,' supplied Gerda. 'Doesn't speak it too good, you know, but gets by okay. I'd bet she could write about clothes in Greek if you had a good editor. Hope you catch up with her, Ms Legrand.'
They said friendly goodbyes.
Greg had turned from the bureau to watch as she held the telephone conversation. 'You got an address?'
She shook her head. 'She has an apartment in Bloomington, but she's rented it out while she's off somewhere writing a book. Where's Bloomington?'
'There's more than one, I think, but we're probably talking about the one in Illinois. They have a good choir there – at Illinois Wesleyan University.'
Liz was calling up International Directory to be put through to Information at Bloomington, Illinois. After a few transfers she was talking to a telephonist in Bloomington, who within about ten seconds told her that they had no customer called Nancy Lanan.

'Anywhere nearby in the neighbourhood?' she asked hope-fully.

'I'm afraid not, ma'am.'

She replaced the receiver, downcast. 'So,' she murmured, 'it seems Nancy Lanan is alive and well but not living in Bloomington writing articles for *Gung Ho*.'

'No, but she might be in any other city in America,' he said to comfort her. 'She's off somewhere writing a book, you said.'

'Yes, but Greg . . . she speaks *Greek*, she's got *Greek roots* – grandparents or something.'

He nodded in understanding. 'Clearly if you were Niki Paroskolos and you wanted someone to play the part of your wife for a few days, it's better to choose someone who looks quite like her and speaks the language.' He gave it some thought. 'Nancy Lanan met Elissa,' he recalled. 'There was that interview in the *New York Times*.'

'And that's how Niki knew she existed,' Liz said.

'Yes, Elissa perhaps spoke about it – "Hey, guess what: she's got Greek blood; she even looks quite like me" – quite an interesting thing to happen, even in a crowded life like Elissa's.'

Liz went to the bowl of fruit on the coffee table, where she picked off a few grapes as a refreshment after her session on the telephone. 'That piece in the *New York Times*, about Elissa's plans on her father's death,' she murmured.

With a nod of agreement he turned back to the Thinkpad. She leaned over his shoulder to read the interview; but it was a straightforward question-and-answer piece about Elissa's plans. It told them nothing about her that they didn't already know.

Gregory spent another half-hour trying the search engines that provided links with specified names. All the pages about Elissa gave her parentage, date of birth and marriage and her succession to the Dimitriouso fortune on the death of Yanni. One or two provided some information about her business activity afterwards, and the part she'd played in financing some charity events. None of it seemed helpful, it was all too impersonal.

'It's all very objective. What we need is some insight into

her family, her private life . . .' All of a sudden he threw his fists into the air. 'Great-aunt Irene!'

'Who?'

'At the sixties party last night, with all the old relatives! Great-aunt Irene, of course – she'll know everything about everybody.'

'But we don't know how to get in touch with her.'

'Yes we do. We exchanged addresses on the dock this morning.' He went to his jacket, hanging over the back of a chair, and felt in the pockets for his diary. 'Here they are: Ariadne Hipodati, Natalya – no, no, that's not . . . here she is! Irene Empodomai, with an address in Kipseli and a telephone number.'

'Kipseli? Is that far? Can we ring her?'

'It's just outside Athens, if I remember rightly.' He stopped, diary in hand, half-turned towards the telephone. 'We can do better than ring her. We can invite her here for dinner.'

'For dinner? But Greg – it's well past eight now. By the time she gets here, it would be quite late.'

He patted her on the shoulder. 'Darling, this is Athens. People don't eat till late in Athens.'

'But she's an old lady. It's asking a lot to drag her across the city . . .'

'Nonsense, she'll be delighted!' He was sure he was right. Great-aunt Irene had struck him as the kind who would rise to any challenge, and for her a trip across Athens in the evening would seem like a romantic adventure. 'We'll get a taxi to pick her up and bring her here; she'll be pleased as Pancho to be invited and be one better than Natalya and Ariadne and the others last night.'

'Pleased as Punch,' Liz said.

'What?'

'Not Pancho – Punch.'

'Oh. Of course. I should have wondered why Pancho Villa came into it.' He paused. 'Why is Punch pleased?'

'Who knows? Fashion's my thing, Greg, not puppetry.'

'Punch is a puppet? *Comme c'est étrange!* How can a puppet be pleased or otherwise?'

'Greg, you're wandering. Ring that old lady,' Liz said with

severity in which there was some weariness. It had been a long day and looked like going on longer.

Great-aunt Irene was thrilled to be asked to dinner by an ex-crown prince. She put out feelers to learn whether any other relations from last night's party had been invited. When she discovered she was the sole guest, she couldn't hide her satisfaction. 'I'll be ready to leave in fifteen minutes,' she assured Gregory. 'I'll just change my dress.'

'Oh, please don't bother. Liz and I have been in the city all day; we're in casual clothes.'

But when the taxi delivered her to the Ariston about forty minutes later, she was clad in the black silk frock that denoted her long widowhood, and pearls that advertised her status. Liz and Greg, who were waiting for her in the vestibule, felt quite outclassed, although they'd spent the interval showering and trying to make themselves look presentable.

Great-aunt Irene was interested in the gold and dove-grey decor of the dining room. 'I remember when this used to be quite a humble place,' she told them. 'My dear husband used to come here sometimes for trade exhibitions. He sold leather goods, you know, suitcases and satchels . . . But with the coming of modern materials and the wish for lightweight luggage . . .'

In politeness to Liz she tried to speak English, but she had learned it in schooldays of long ago. Often she had to resort to her native tongue. Although she wouldn't have admitted it, she had to be guided through the menu, which was strong on French cuisine.

But once the hors d'oeuvres were gone and she'd had three-quarters of a glass of wine, she was launched into gossip and reminiscence. Yanni's funeral – she'd sent lilies from her own little garden, only to witness them obliterated under a heap of hothouse flowers. She remembered Greg's father there, had chatted to him; they'd agreed that Yanni would be sorely missed. Elissa's wedding – she'd had no invitation and was just as glad, because she couldn't have afforded a suitable wedding present.

'Of course, I wouldn't have gone anyway. Paris – why should she get married in the Greek Orthodox church in Paris?

Just to show off, that's all. Katya went – she fixed it up so she got an invitation and she stayed in Montmartre, which I hear is *not* a respectable area, though inexpensive; but she was determined to go, utterly determined. She told me the wedding was all very ostentatious.'

'My grandmother was one of the guests,' said the prince. 'She didn't enjoy it.'

'No, I gather Elissa rather overdid everything – too much lace on the wedding dress, too many tiers on the cake, too many people at the wedding party. She's learned some sense now, hasn't she? That party last night was really quite nice.'

'Did you have a chance to chat with Elissa? How do you think she looked?'

'Oh, very attractive. She's always very attractive, you know. The Dimitriouso girls have always been attractive.' She gave them a wink. 'Too attractive for their own good, sometimes,' she added, and took another large sip of her Sancerre.

A waiter took away their plates; another came with the fish course. Sancerre was replaced by Chateau Bonnet. Great-aunt Irene scarcely noticed, but drank with enjoyment. Liz looked in anxiety at Greg. The poor old thing was getting drunk.

Greg merely shrugged. He'd chosen the food and wine so as to give Great-aunt Irene a good time; too late now to change things. Besides, the wine was loosening her tongue. She was talking now about Elissa's mother.

'Ran away! Simply packed her bags and ran away! With an estate agent. If she'd chosen someone with more money than Yanni, or someone with a title' – here she gave a beaming smile at the prince – 'you could have seen some sense in it. Mind you, her divorce settlement was enormous. That was because Yanni wanted to keep his beloved daughter, and he thought, poor man, that Arietta wanted her. He would have agreed to anything to keep Elissa with him.'

'It must have been sad for Elissa,' Liz remarked.

'What was that?' demanded the old lady, not quite catching the meaning. 'It didn't make Elissa sad; it made her angry. Everybody says she became even more impossible. She ate like a sea monster, and when they tried to put her on a diet, she flew into terrible rages . . .'

97

'But she's quite thin now,' Liz prompted.

'Oh yes, the ailment – what is it? – mentilosis . . . menstruensis . . .' She stopped, blushing. She felt she'd said something indelicate but didn't quite know what.

'Meningitis,' Gregory supplied.

'Oh yes, a terrible blow. I gather she's greatly changed, greatly changed. For the better,' she added with emphasis, and cut into her sole meunière.

When the Beef Wellington came, Margaux was poured. Liz made a move as if to prevent it, but too late. Great-aunt Irene took a mouthful or two then launched out again. This time she was trying to get hold of some gossip about Gregory's grandmother, the ex-Queen Nicoletta, who, in her time, had been a beauty and the subject of many tales.

Gregory had no objection. Most of the stories about Grossmutti were only too well known. He nodded and shook his head and added a few comments to Irene's discourse. It seemed only fair to give her something in exchange for all her information.

It took some time to get the conversation back to Elissa. Irene said it was evident that Niki had done all the arranging for the birthday celebrations. 'He's trying to give everyone a chance to take part,' she reflected. 'A good idea, because most of us were really keen to see how she'd got over the . . . men . . . menil . . .'

'Meningitis.'

'Yes, it's a very serious thing, I'm told, and Cousin Natalya thought she'd have turned into a simpleton, you know, because of brain damage or something. But no, she's all right, isn't she? And nobody can say she isn't. It would have been such a disgrace for the Dimitriousos if one of their girls had gone crazy, would it not?' She ate some food, then added, 'One of the Dimitriouso girls was more than a bit odd, you know. Aunt Merope – she married Panaghis Gabranis, if I remember rightly. And then there was Despina – she wasn't a Dimitriouso, but she *should* have been, but a wild girl, yes she was, Despina Plestriso. But she couldn't get Stelios Dimitriouso to marry her, poor soul. Of course he couldn't; he was already engaged to Elissa's great-grandmother Cornelia Mattemno, so he couldn't have married Despina if he'd wanted to, which he didn't, of course, because you know it would have been unsuitable, and she'd *proved* herself to be unsuitable, otherwise why would she have been in that state in the first place?'

Great-aunt Irene had slipped into Greek somewhere in the long journey into things past. Now she came back to find that her host and hostess were no longer paying attention. Although, to her, it was all fresh and as if it had happened yesterday, to them it was a pointless list of names.

So she said, in good English but rather hastily, 'In any case, that was the family history when I was a little girl and what does it matter now? People don't care about morals in the same way these days.' She couldn't help adding, in defence of her own outlook, 'I think they handled Despina very well, the Dimitriousos. A very decent sum of money and a ticket to the New World – very tidy. Now in the case of Arietta and the divorce, it was all over the front page of the newspapers! Shocking!'

'You were saying that Niki wanted all the family members to see Elissa and be reassured,' said Gregory. 'On other evenings, there have been business friends, people from the Bourse, for instance?'

'Oh, I've no doubt. Niki is very well known for his acumen.'

'But Liz was saying that she thought it a great strain on Elissa.'

'Yes, we were told it was her re-entry into society,' Liz agreed. 'I just thought that five days of parties was a lot for someone who'd been an invalid so long.'

'Well, if you have to re-introduce her to a lot of people, you can't do it in one day, can you?' asked Great-aunt Irene, with considerable discernment.

'But why the hurry? It could have been done over months instead of days.'

'But that wouldn't do, my dear,' said Great-aunt Irene, looking wise. 'Of course Elissa wants to be in good form for her birthday on Friday.'

'But it's only a twenty-fifth birthday, after all. There's nothing special about it.'

'Of course there is,' said the old lady with an arch lift of the eyebrows. 'That's the day she comes into the main inheritance.'

'But I thought she—'

'Oh, she's only had a small part of it! Much though Yanni loved her, he'd always say that women had no head for business. So he put most of his fortune into a trust for her, and her twenty-fifth birthday is the day it matures.'

Eight

It was a very subdued pair who rose next morning. Even the lacy bikini went unadmired. They went down to breakfast at nine, after a night spent curled around each other, sleeping in exhaustion.

Great-aunt Irene had departed somewhere between midnight and one o'clock, still quite bright and willing to chat. For their part, Liz and Greg had been almost reeling with fatigue. Greg had taken the old lady's hand, intending to please her by raising it to his lips and kissing it in farewell; but to his consternation she had forestalled him, dropping a neat curtsey in her black dress and lace-up shoes.

'Goodnight, Your Highness,' she'd murmured, and had been helped somewhat unsteadily into the taxi by the driver.

He had already tipped the man well to see her safely to her door and into her home. He and Liz had waved as she was driven away, then tottered to the lift. They had been too tired to discuss what they'd just heard.

There was still a reluctance in the morning. Mr Crowne felt as if his head were stuffed with ticker tape, although he'd drunk only moderately at dinner. Ms Blair was in something of a state of shock, and certainly very unhappy.

Fresh orange juice and good coffee did a lot to revive the prince. Still, he felt in need of something more. Had he been at home in Geneva, he'd have sat down at the piano to handle something fairly difficult – something by Liszt, perhaps the Sonata in B minor. It would have made him concentrate, cleared the thought processes and made the neurones spark.

Here, though, that was impossible. There was a piano in the ballroom of the hotel, of course, but he felt he'd stretched goodwill far enough by asking for the Thinkpad.

So the next best thing was a walk and some fresh air –
or air as fresh as one could hope for in the Athens rush
hour.

When Liz had eaten her fruit and rolls, they went out. After
several waits for the lights to change, they crossed to the
ruins of the Temple of Olympian Zeus. They strolled for a
few minutes, saying little.

By and by they found a slab of fallen marble in the shade
of an arch. They sat down.

'Last night was a bit of a shock, Greg,' ventured Liz.

He nodded agreement. 'I always felt we needed a reason,' he
said. 'If there was an imposture going on, I felt that just trying
to reassure the board of directors wasn't enough to justify it. I
mean, in the normal course of business, Niki must have been
granted power of attorney, because meningitis is a very serious
illness and her signature would be needed just in the ordinary
run of things. I'm sure he has temporary control of her business
routines.'

'And we said that, if she was going to be so unsure of
herself, perhaps that wasn't enough to reassure the directors
of the company.'

'I think it's "companies", in the plural: Dimitriouso Finance
Corporation, or something like that – a conglomerate. I wish
I knew more about high finance . . .'

'Darling, even a man who knows about accordion music
for folk songs and the *hydraulis* can't be expected to know
everything.' She was trying for lightness, and he rewarded her
with a faint grin.

He said, 'At least I know when I don't know something:
Niki's reason for putting on that charade didn't seem strong
enough.'

'And now Great-aunt Irene's given us the reason. Elissa has
to be there in full control of herself tomorrow to sign papers,
taking over control of the trust.'

'So some very important people have to be convinced that
Elissa is fit to take over.'

For a moment she was a loss. 'What important people?'

'The trustees, Liz. They're probably lawyers and lead-
ers of the community – old friends of Yanni Dimitriouso,

102

hard-headed types.' The prince thought it over. 'I see how it's supposed to work. The trustees would, of course, hear from friends and acquaintances how Elissa's handled the last few days and are satisfied she's doing all right It's a very important thing because of the trust maturing, almost like a coming of age.'

'So Niki hires a stand-in for the few days before the birthday, to let everyone see she's okay.'

'A first-class stand-in. Did you catch what Great-aunt Irene said about family history?'

'Ah . . . No, I think she'd drifted off into Greek at that point.'

'She said that decades ago – when Great-aunt Irene was little – some girl was shipped to America. I wasn't paying much attention, so I forget the girl's name; but Great-aunt Irene said the poor thing couldn't get Stelios Dimitriouso to marry her, so that means she was expecting his baby – don't you think?' He looked at her for her agreement.

'Oh, so that's why the old thing was nodding and winking at you! A local girl gone to the bad – was that it?'

'A great disgrace, in those days. Even now,' he added, thinking about it, 'I don't believe it would be treated lightly here. But in those days it was a terrible blow to family pride, so off she went to the New World.'

'Where she had her baby and probably passed herself off as a respectable widow . . .'

'And made a respectable marriage and raised her baby, who in turn married and had children . . .'

'Where are you going with this, Greg?'

'Until in the end we find Nancy Lanan,' he went on, ignoring her interjection, 'who looks like Elissa Paroskolos, because one of her great-grandparents was actually Stelios Dimitriouso, who was also the great-grandfather of Elissa. What we've seen is a family resemblance.'

Liz was dumbfounded.

'Don't you think that's the kind of thing that happened?' he asked, needing her support.

'You're saying they're sort of second cousins, twice removed?'

He hesitated. 'If that means they're distantly related, yes.'

'And somewhere between then and now, one of her grand-parents or parents had blue eyes.'

'Yes.'

Liz considered this. 'Do you suppose either of those two knew about frisky old Great-granddaddy Stelios?'

'Elissa would know, almost certainly. You saw how Irene could give chapter and verse last night. I think they're pretty keen on family history in these parts.' He himself had been born into circles where a careful account was kept of every-body's peccadilloes, because even in minor royal families inheritance mattered.

'And perhaps Nancy Lanan knew. Perhaps that's how she persuaded Elissa to give her that interview, which seems to have been quite a coup.'

He was shaking his head. 'I don't think so. This poor girl was packed off with a little bit of cash and her steamer ticket to America. You were supposing a little while ago that she passed herself off as a respectable widow. She wouldn't be likely to talk much about Stelios Dimitriouso, would she?'

'Perhaps not,' Liz allowed. She was silent for a while as she considered the possibilities. She'd come to like the 'Elissa' with whom she'd spent a day shopping. 'Perhaps when Elissa saw Nancy, and realized they resembled each other, she might have told her they came from the same stock . . .'

'No, it's not likely. Elissa would see herself as a better class of person than Nancy Lanan, who, after all, is a mere hack journalist.' He paused, guessing that Liz had a sense of friendship for the young woman she'd come to know. 'I see what you're hoping: that Nancy took on this charade out of family feeling – is that it?'

'We-ell . . . I'd rather she didn't do it just for the money,' Liz confessed. 'She seems to me to be too nice for that.'

'Perhaps *Niki* told her,' he said, thinking it over. 'He might have been there when the interview took place and noticed the resemblance. Or Elissa talked to him about it, said the girl might actually be – what did you call it? A second cousin . . . ?

'Twice removed. You guessed it right; it's a saying that means somebody related by the very weakest of ties.'

'I see. Well, one way or another Niki might have quite naturally got to know about the relationship, and then, when Elissa later fell ill and became for the present – I think the phrase is "legally incompetent" – he called on Nancy to help him.'

'That could be how it happened,' Liz said, much cheered. 'He'd say to Elissa, "Look, sweetie, you're still a bit under the weather and your birthday is coming up, so what about asking your American cousin to lend a hand?"'

'And Elissa, who's no fool, realizes that if she's a bit wavery in front of all her friends and relatives, it won't look good. So she's got Nancy's address through that interview they did . . . Is that how it happened?'

'Well, if I'd seen someone who looked a lot like me and was probably a relation, I'd get an address or a telephone number,' said Liz, adding as a rebuke, 'even if I thought she was "a different class of person".'

'So what sort of a deal would Niki have put to Nancy? Come to Kerouli and play the part in the run-up to the birthday . . . ?'

'Ah!' She held up a finger. 'That girl on the phone from the magazine – she said Nancy spoke Greek "well enough to get by".'

'And so?'

'Well, Mr Sensitive-Ears, does the Elissa we know speak Greek only "well enough to get by"?'

He was taken aback. It was a point he hadn't even thought of.

'She speaks it well,' he said slowly. 'I can't detect any difference between the way she speaks and the way Great-aunt Irene speaks. But then,' he added, 'my sensitive ears aren't so sensitive about Greek. English and a few American accents, French accents – I can distinguish between those. And the Swiss cantons – there are differences there. But I don't know if I could tell whether someone speaking Greek was native born or not.'

Liz was pleased with herself. It was seldom she caught him out. 'But nobody else seems to have noticed anything wrong with the way "Elissa" speaks,' she went on in a schoolteacher voice.

'Not that I've heard.' He was waiting for her to explain herself, still somewhat at sea.

'So that means, if originally she spoke it only fairly well, she's had to brush up on it.'

He gave her a glance of admiration. She was no fool, his darling Liz. 'Which means she's been learning the part, so to speak. Which could take quite a time.' Now he'd got her drift. 'Not only fluent Greek, but she'd have to learn about family relationships, how as a child she watched her father remodelling the island – things like that.'

'They told me on the phone that she'd taken a year off to write a book.'

'A year,' he echoed. 'Liz . . . could Niki have called her in soon after Elissa fell ill?'

They were silent together. She found a daisy among the tough grass by their seat, picked it, and twirled it in her fingers.

'Do you think Dr Donati told Niki his wife was perhaps going to take *years* to be really well again?' he ventured at length.

'Dr Donati . . . He'd have to be in the know. Wouldn't he? I mean, he must know that that isn't Elissa out there on the island.'

'Yes, certainly. He must be playing a major role.' He held up a finger. 'He kept poor old Dr Dragorasie from visiting.'

'Oh, that nice old man . . . If he hadn't taken off on a family visit, we could have asked him about all this.'

Greg made no reply. His silence surprised her. After a moment she repeated, 'We could have asked him, couldn't we?'

'Well, Liz . . . The point is . . . Have we any right to ask anybody anything?'

'Of course we have! There's something funny going on!'

He was shaking his head. 'Somebody is taking Elissa's place for the moment. That's not so unheard-of among famous people, people with money. Howard Hughes is supposed to have had – what do you call them? – stand-ins who led reporters away from his real activities. Film stars, pop stars – they have look-alikes who help them elude their overeager fans. I think I

106

read that one of the British generals in World War Two had a double to mislead the Nazis while he planned the Normandy landing or some other big manoeuvre. If Elissa has agreed to have someone play her part for a few days – or even longer – she has a perfect right to.'

Liz was thunderstruck. 'You mean it isn't illegal?'

'Not unless Nancy were actually to sign those papers tomorrow. Then it would be fraud. But there's no reason to think she'd do a thing like that.'

'No, of course she wouldn't,' she said with conviction. 'She's a nice girl, not a swindler.'

He nodded agreement. They rose. Liz set down the daisy flower on the slab as an offering to the Temple of Zeus, and they began to walk back towards the hotel. 'We ought to pack up our things and go to Piraeus for the boat,' she resumed. 'Didn't you tell them we'd probably be back for lunch?'

'Yes, and moreover you've got to get those contact lenses back into Elissa's bathroom!'

She stopped, gave a little shiver and a suppressed giggle. 'I can't think of her as Elissa,' she muttered. 'I think of her as Nancy now.'

'Well, for heaven's sake don't let her know that!'

'I suppose not. It sort of means we've entered the conspiracy, haven't we?' She had taken his arm, and she pressed herself against it in search of reassurance.

He shrugged. They walked on. 'I feel funny about it,' Liz maintained. 'I mean, you said there's nothing wrong in it, but it seems . . . like helping with a lie.'

He made no rejoinder. He didn't find it as unsettling as Liz. From all he had heard from his grandmother, life in even the lesser royal circles had meant dealing to some extent in lies.

They had the same long wait for traffic lights on their way back to the Ariston. Although the hotel was only across the main road, it took them almost fifteen minutes to reach it. They went into the lift, in which they were alone. Liz took the opportunity to nuzzle the prince's ear, thinking that when they got to their room they might not hurry straight into packing up to leave. They stepped out, and he was about to open their room door with the smart card when he stopped short.

107

'What?' said Liz in surprise, staring at him.

'There's one thing we haven't thought of,' he said, feeling rather strange.

'What's that?'

'Where is Elissa in all this?'

'What?'

'Where is she? She's not in that house in Kerouli.'

'Of course she is.'

'No, it's only two storeys, and when Nancy had that fainting fit after she saw the picture of snakes on the computer, you had free access to the upper floor. Isn't that right?'

'Well . . . yes.'

'They couldn't have permitted that if you were likely to walk into the real Elissa upstairs.'

'Well . . . she's in one of the cabanas . . .'

'You don't really believe that.'

'No, I suppose I don't,' she admitted. 'Well then, she's probably in their place in Athens, then. The place where the servant was transferred to – the biblical one.'

'Christos.' He put the card in the lock, opened the door, and they went in. Liz sank down on a chair, for to tell the truth she had had the wind knocked out of her by his question.

Once in, he closed the door then walked to the window. He stood staring out. 'I don't think she's at their apartment in Athens,' he said. 'If Christos can be sent there at short notice, there's nobody there to be noticed and wondered about. I don't think Elissa is there.'

'Greg.' Her voice had a quiver in it. He turned from the window to face her. 'Greg, what are you saying?'

'We've been taking it for granted that Elissa is agreeing to all this. But Liz . . . how do we know that's true?'

Nine

Neither of them made any attempt to answer the question for the moment. Liz rose on rather shaky legs to gather up the pretty carrier bag, which now held discarded clothing. The prince watched her.

She said, 'You can't mean Niki would do a thing like this without asking Elissa.'

He shrugged.

She went on, 'Of *course* he would ask Elissa.'

'But how if Elissa's mental condition is . . .'

'You mean if she's gaga?'

'I'm not sure what gaga means, *mon amie*. That's to say, I know it means mentally at sea, but I don't know how *far* at sea. Let's suppose that Elissa has been affected by her illness. Let's say that Donati – and he's an expert, don't forget – let's say he told Niki that she was never going to be up to the strain of managing the corporation.'

'But he told us he was helping her improve – didn't want us upsetting her . . .'

'Liz,' he said gently, 'he was talking about Nancy at that point.'

'What?'

'He didn't want us interfering in the plot – getting to know Nancy so that we realized she was *not* Elissa.'

'Oh God!' She threw down the carrier bag, snatched a tissue from the ornate box on the bedside table, and began to sniffle into it.

He came to put an arm round her. He hated to see her upset. He held her close, murmuring comforting words.

They sank down on the bed together, and for a time, in the reassurance of their embrace, they forgot the frightening world of deceit and pretence. But quite soon they had to return to it. They sat up; Liz made pushing motions at her hair; the prince stared at his shoes.

'Even if Elissa doesn't know,' she said, 'that doesn't make it wrong.'

'Say that again?'

'Even if Niki hasn't told Elissa he's involved Nancy in a scam, it doesn't mean he's doing it for a bad reason.'

'How do you come to that conclusion?'

'Well, you said it yourself: if somebody acts as a fill-in for somebody else, it's not illegal.'

He listened to her, and realized she was too good-hearted to think ill of Niki Paroskolos or Nancy Lanan. She'd met them, talked to them, shared meals with them; she couldn't see either of them as criminals. He gave her a hug, but he was shaking his head.

'Listen, my angel; we're going on supposition here. So just let's suppose that Niki is doing this because his wife is . . . let's say, not up to it and perhaps never likely to be. Another supposition we made was that, on the big day, Elissa would at last be brought onstage to sign the trust deeds.'

'Yes, right.'

'But what if she's not up to it at all? What if, all this time, she's been far away in Dr Donati's clinic in the Bernese Oberland, being treated for serious after-effects of meningitis?'

'Greg! Greg, don't.' She beat on his chest with her fists. 'Don't say things like that!'

He held her close so that he smothered the attack. 'Liz, it could be happening. Nancy Lanan may be going to sign those papers tomorrow.'

'No, you're off on a totally wrong track. Niki would never do such a thing.'

'Why wouldn't he?'

'Well, because he could never bring it off . . .'

'He's doing all right so far, don't you think? Nobody else seems to have suspected that the young woman acting hostess on Kerouli isn't Elissa.'

'But letting it go beyond that – letting her sign the documents – it would be an enormous risk, Greg.'

110

'It's an enormous amount of money. Not just millions: billions.'

'But . . . but . . . Niki doesn't need to do that. He's got money of his own.'

That made him pause. He let go of Liz, stood for a moment staring over her head, then shrugged. 'Well, in the first place,' he said, 'people always seem to like having *more* money. Niki's got power of attorney, I'm sure, so if those documents are signed he will also get control of the funds they've been guarding. Which is a lot. In the second place . . .'

'What?'

'In the second place, do we know how much money Niki actually has?'

'Of course we do. He's into air transport – freight carriers, I think I was told, and perhaps one of the smaller passenger airlines. I forget.'

He held up a finger, like a teacher making a point. 'How well have airlines been doing recently, Liz?'

She gave a little gasp. He saw tears welling again in her eyes, and felt a brute; but the fact was, a very ugly case seemed to be developing against Niki. There wasn't any use trying to shield her from it.

She blinked, swallowed, then turned to the Thinkpad still plugged in on the bureau. 'Let's see if his business is doing well or badly,' she said, switching it on.

Liz was accustomed to looking up financial information, because the fortunes of the high-street stores were important to her. She summoned up tables and lists, selected out transport and then air transport, then paused. 'What's the name of Niki's firm?'

'I've no idea,' Mr Crowne confessed.

'I'll try Paroskolos.' There wasn't anything under that title. She tried various versions of the name but came up with nothing. She gave up on the screens of air transport and tried FTSE quotations, but the list was enormous. 'This is hopeless,' she groaned. 'It might take for ever.'

He switched off without consulting her, put his arms round her waist and drew her to her feet. 'Technology is baffling,' he murmured. 'Let's do it on the old boys' network.'

'And which old boy do you have in mind?' She was smiling a little now.

'A comparatively young old boy on the Bourse.'

'The *Bourse*? You mean the stock exchange? There's a stock exchange in Athens?'

'It's a capital city, my darling. Of course there's a stock exchange.'

He looked in the drawer of the bedside table, came out with the phone book, looked up the number. After a few minutes he was chatting amiably with someone at the other end of the line.

Now it was Liz's turn to listen to one end of a conversation, and she was even worse off because it was in Greek. However, it didn't last long. 'He'll meet us for a drink,' Greg informed her. 'But not until about noon. So we can either go out and you can do more shopping, or we could find some other way to fill in the time.'

She smiled. She knew just what he had in mind.

By and by they packed up their few belongings and went down to the hall. While Liz waited for their taxi, Greg had a friendly conversation with the desk clerk that ended in much handshaking and expressions of goodwill. The taxi bore them off to a neat little alley off Stadiou, Greg pointing out the stock exchange as they went by. There was a bar with lots of chrome and glass, with a name above it, which, while Greg paid the driver, Liz deciphered as 'Chreemata', meaning 'Cash', she thought. They went in. A very handsome young man in a business suit of charcoal-grey wild silk waved to them from a glass table at the back of the bar.

'Hi, Grego, *pos eeste*?'

'Hi, Sevi, good of you to meet us,' Greg replied in English. 'Liz, this is Severo Konialidis, lead tenor in the stock exchange barber-shop quartet.'

Liz laughed aloud as she shook hands. 'Barber shop! Are you going to burst into song?'

'No, alas, since there are only three of us and I can only sing when we are four.'

'I didn't know you were interested in barber-shop quartets?' she said to Greg.

112

'I'm not. I hate them – all that syrupy smooth harmony, but if you can get Sevi to sing alone, he can give you quite a good "Nessun dorma" or "O sole mio". What are you drinking, *feelos*?'

'This is Pimm's. It's the fashion at the moment.'

Greg waved at the waiter for three more of the same.

'So, you want to talk business,' Sevi said, glancing at his watch. 'Let's do it, because Frankfurt is giving us trouble at the moment and I need to get back soon.'

'It's very good of you to spare us your time,' Liz said, giving him her nicest smile.

At once he seemed to forget about Frankfurt. 'What's on your mind, dear lady?'

'Could you tell me something about Nikolas Paroskolos and his standing in business at the moment?'

'Ah?' Sevi's heavy eyebrows went up in surmise. 'Heard something?'

'No, no, on the contrary; we know nothing,' Greg intervened. 'We've come to you for basic information. Niki Paroskolos is our host at the moment . . .'

'Oh, for the birthday *yortee*? You were invited to that? I thought it was only old crones from the backwoods of family estates who were asked.'

'No, no, quite a lot of business types have been there.'

'Oh, Niki's bosom friends, I suppose. Yes, that makes sense; it reassures them all that, even if he's going down the tubes, his wife's money is still there.'

'Going down the tubes?' Greg said in alarm.

The waiter brought their drinks. Sevi was given a chance to rethink the remark. 'Well, no, perhaps not,' he allowed. 'I shouldn't have gone that far. But you know how things have been in the air business recently, Grego. Everybody's hurting, and Niki's business isn't even a front-line concern.' He finished what was in his old glass and stirred the mint on the top of the new one.

'So are things very bad for him?' Liz prompted.

'Has he been asking you to invest? If so . . . well . . .' He sipped, pursed his lips, then shrugged. 'Long term, it may be okay. But it's not a holding that leaps to mind for the small investor.' He smiled. 'Sorry if that makes it embarrassing for you. You should tell him you haven't any cash that needs a new home just at present.'

'That's only too true,' said the prince, who certainly didn't make a fortune from his concert arranging.

'He didn't actually suggest any investment,' Liz said, understanding that they had to give some reason for their interest in Niki's affairs. 'But one of the guests the other night said he was going to put in some money, because when Mrs Paroskolos came into her inheritance, she'd probably make funds available to him.'

'Well that's possible.' Sevi agreed. 'But then you know, Elissa Paroskolos is no fool. Her dad might not have had much confidence in her business sense, but she's better than he believed. She and Niki haven't always seen eye to eye on matters financial – and she's generally been more in the right than him. At least, so the gossip goes.'

'You're saying that she's not likely to advance Niki much cash.'

'Well, Grego, if it were me that was asked to undo the purse strings, I'd think twice and even three times,' Sevi said. 'And Elissa is at least as sensible as I am. I may say, reluctantly, maybe even more so, because she's got more to lose.'

'Um,' said the prince, thinking that in the past twenty-four hours everything they'd found out had made him feel less optimistic.

Sevi went on to mention a few healthy places for any money that they might think of investing. He seemed to be imagining they had marriage in mind, and neither of them troubled to disabuse him. He rose, with a glance at a very bulky Girard Perregaux watch, to say he must get back; Frankfurt was probably giving out Wagnerian howls by now. He beckoned the waiter, paid for the drinks, shook hands all round, and hurried away.

'Barber-shop quartet,' said Liz with a giggle. 'Everybody you know is connected with music, aren't they!'

'Except you, *mein Schatz*. You're connected with clothes shops. And besides, barber-shop isn't music; it's the equivalent of a Knickerbocker Glory.'

114

'Well, your pal Sevi is no strawberry sundae, that's for sure. You asked me, "How well have airlines been doing?" And he gave us the answer.'

'"Everybody's hurting",' quoted Greg. 'And it's been an ongoing thing. After the long spell of alarm brought on by the terrorists, there's been a slump that hasn't corrected itself. So you see, Liz . . .'

She nodded in understanding. 'It might be a great temptation to ensure that Elissa's money became available. And it certainly wouldn't become available if the trustees thought she was a cent or two short of a euro.' She took a strengthening draft of her Pimm's. 'It's not good, love.'

'No, it isn't.'

'So what are we going to do?'

'*We* aren't going to do anything. *You* are going back to the hotel where you'll stay overnight again, and I am going to Kerouli to talk to Nancy Lanan.'

'Ha!' she said. 'We went through all that before. Where you go, I go. Besides, that room was only made available because you are who you are. They're not going to give it back to me on my own.'

'Well, in fact, I mentioned to the receptionist that you might be back—'

'You rat! So that's what all the backslapping was about! Well, I'm not going back to the Ariston, so there! I've been with you so far and I'm going to Kerouli now.'

'But Liz, it's different now. Before, you were just a bit anxious about the servant being sent away so fast, over that magazine business. Now there's a whole body of . . . I can't call it evidence, but there are facts that make things on the island look very odd.'

'Because for one thing,' she said, as if he hadn't spoken, 'Nancy is far more likely to talk to me than to you. Don't forget: we shared the same changing room in the designer-jeans shop.'

'*Liz!*'

'And moreover, all my clothes are in the cabana, and I can't afford to go shopping for replacements with my credit card – you know how easily I get carried away.'

115

'But it could get very unpleasant on the island if we're right in what we think—'

'And besides, I've got to get that little box of contact lenses back into Elissa's bathroom – and if you think you can take on that job, just think what they're going to say if you try to go into her bathroom.'

'But I want to use the contact lenses as evidence, so that doesn't arise.'

'Evidence of what?' she said, condescending at length to hear him. 'They're brown lenses. She's perfectly entitled to wear brown lenses if she wants to – you said so yourself. And besides, if Dr Donati's anywhere around, he'll blind you with science.'

'Well, if you're there, he'll only blind you too. What good does that do?'

'It does *me* good. I'll be there, in the know, instead of biting my expensively manicured nails in Athens.'

'Liz, truly, I'd be happier if you'd just—'

'I know you would, darling, but the only way you'll stop me going back on the boat with you is to push me into the water.'

He understood it was useless. He felt responsible, because it was he who'd brought her here. He felt anxious, uncertain, outsmarted, frustrated; but he also felt foolishly pleased that she should want to be with him in what might turn out to be a very disagreeable situation.

They were close by a Metro station, so they used that to get to Piraeus. At the special jetty where they would board the private ferry boat, there was a gang of men with heavy camera bags. 'Guests going to Kerouli?' asked one in Greek.

'Yes – you?' Mr Crowne replied.

'We're the press – the lowly photographers. The TV people get to go on the helicopter,' was the envious reply.

'But they've got a lot more gear, Basi.'

Greg translated for Liz. 'But there's nowhere for a helicopter to land,' she protested.

'Yes, the tennis court.'

'Oh yes.'

116

'Anybody famous?' asked the other photographer, nodding at Liz.

'No, no; we're a pair of nobodies.'

The photographer looked as if he didn't entirely believe that. Guests of the Paroskolos family couldn't be nobodies. But the motor cruiser came in and tied up at the quay; a satchel of mail was carried to the port's post office; one or two cases of stores, were loaded; then they boarded and, within minutes, were off.

True enough, they saw a helicopter parked on the tennis court as they went by on their way to their cabana. Men in jeans and T-shirts were loading aluminium cases and equipment on to one of the little electric carts for transport down the narrow island paths. Pausing a moment to watch them, Liz touched Greg's arm.

'I wouldn't have thought Niki would allow so much publicity,' she said in a puzzled voice, 'if what we're imagining is true.'

'The camera never lies?' he said with irony. 'Well, it depends how much lighting Niki – or more correctly Dr Donati – permits. Don't forget, Nancy told you some yarn about an eye condition brought on by the meningitis.'

She nodded as they walked on. 'The illness makes a wonderful excuse for almost anything, doesn't it?'

In the cabin they stowed away their purchases, showered and changed, then went in search of lunch. Most people at the pavilion were in the latter stages of the meal. They nodded to one or two now-familiar faces; then, after choosing food from the buffet made their way outdoors to find a quiet spot under a rhododaphne in bud.

'There don't seem to be so many guests,' Liz remarked, glancing about.

'You're right.' After a moment's thought, he added, 'I suppose they had to empty some of the cabins to house the press people.'

'Surely Niki isn't going to allow a huge gang of them?'

'I suppose not.' He addressed himself to his risotto. 'Well, some of the guests have gone home.' He thought about that for a moment. 'You know, there's been a succession of them,

117

hasn't there? Financial types, business friends, local bigwigs, and then, the other night, all the ancient relatives. Most of them have only stayed over one night and then gone home.' He nodded at the guests enjoying an after-lunch liqueur. 'This perhaps, is the final sifting, leaving room for those who'll take part tomorrow – the legal eagles, the trustees, and enough of an assemblage to look good for the cameras.'

Liz said angrily, 'You mean Niki's using us as extras in his crime film!'

'I'm afraid so. However, perhaps we'll manage to change the plot.'

'What, actually, are we going to do, Greg?'

'We're going to talk to Nancy this evening. She generally shows up for part of the fun and games. If she denies there's a deception going on, we'll produce the box with the brown lenses and demand an explanation.'

'Uh-huh,' she said, sounding dubious. 'And if she says, "I admit it, guv, it's a fair cop", what do we do then?'

'We find out what's intended for tomorrow. If Elissa is going to be flown in by helicopter at the last minute to take her proper place in the trust ceremony, well and good.'

'Even if she's not a hundred per cent fit? Even if she's a bit muddled in the head?'

The prince understood her anxiety. 'Liz, sweetheart, Yanni wanted his daughter to inherit. For all his anti-feminism and the setting up of a rather insulting set of conditions, he wanted Elissa to get his fortune. If we ensure that happens, we've done all we can.'

'But just suppose, Greg – just suppose – Nancy Lanan tells us to go fly a kite?'

'Then things get serious. We have to go to Niki, demand to know where Elissa is. A lot depends on what he says.' Greg was frowning now, still trying to see his way through the maze of suspicions in which he felt trapped. 'I'm worried about Elissa,' he admitted. 'It seems he's got her hidden away somewhere under wraps. And you know, Liz, that seems to mean that she's certainly not herself, because the Elissa my family knows, and everybody else seems to know, would never let herself be treated like that.'

118

'But she's probably somewhere like a posh nursing home, somewhere nearby where she can be brought in for tomorrow.'

'Ye-es.'

'What does that mean? You sound dubious about it.'

'If she's "nearby" in a nursing home, that would mean involving somebody else in this deception. I'd think Niki would play this close to his chest. And I keep on thinking that Dr Donati's got a residential clinic in the countryside near Mürren.'

'Oh, Greg, she's not there! Don't be silly! Even if she's *been* there, Niki must have brought her somewhere nearby for the ceremony.'

They'd both forgotten their food. They were leaning towards each other, speaking in low voices even though their table was sheltered from the others.

'Liz,' he said, 'what if Niki intends to let Nancy sign the papers?'

She stared, drew in a breath. 'Nancy wouldn't *do* that!' she riposted.

'You like her. She seems a nice girl. But just suppose . . .'

'I refuse to suppose any such thing.'

'But she *is* playing the part of Elissa Paroskolos. We're sure she is. We tried to talk ourselves into believing she's doing it for family feeling but . . . Do you remember the morning we met her on the path with Trudi?'

'Yes, of course. She said she wanted to go to Athens and we took her with us.'

'Yes, but look back. Try to recall what we saw as we came round the bend in the path. Trudi was *restraining* her.'

'But that was because Dr Donati said it wasn't good for her to go into the hubbub of Athens.'

'Liz,' he said, in a very calm, even tone, 'that was *Nancy Lanan* on the path. Nancy Lanan wouldn't be upset by the hubbub of Athens.'

'Oh!'

'It's just becoming clear to me: she's under some sort of duress.'

'Nancy is?'

'Yes. You said Trudi is her minder. Well, perhaps that's more true than we suspected. Think about it: Nancy isn't ill, she doesn't need a nurse – so what really is Trudi's role? I think it's to keep her in order. And that seems to imply that perhaps she got talked into all this, and now wants to get out of it, or at least isn't as happy as she was at first.'

Ten

L iz listened to all this with growing alarm. It seemed too much to wrestle with.

'Now, wait, Greg,' she said. 'Remember? Elissa – I mean Nancy – came back to Kerouli with us, no problem. If she'd got mixed up in something that scared her, wouldn't she just have taken off for the airport?'

'Oh damn. That's true.' He pushed the food on his plate around with a fork. 'But, Liz – Trudi *does* shadow her. For some reason Niki has to keep Nancy under surveillance until this ceremony tomorrow is over.'

'Well, perhaps it's just to ensure she doesn't make any mistakes. After all, meeting and greeting all these people – she must need someone to prompt her about who's who.'

'I can't help wondering if perhaps Nancy realizes things aren't right with Elissa – if she feels Elissa is being bullied, neglected, something like that.'

A couple with whom Liz and Greg had chatted in the past and knew only on first-name terms came up now. They were aglow with the after-effects of Grand Marnier and the excitement of the helicopter's presence. 'Isn't it thrilling?' said Panighis with a broad gesture of his arm. 'Never been so close to a helicopter before!'

'Pani wants to ask for a trip aboard the thing, but I'm not keen,' said his wife. 'They've been buzzing about all morning, so terribly noisy!' She smiled at the prince. 'You didn't come to last night's party?'

'No, we stayed over in Athens to hear Tsanaklidou.'

'Oh, she's so wonderful! Pani, shall we go to her show when we get back to Athens?'

'If you like, dearest, if you like.' They were about to move

121

on when he thought of something. 'By the way, sir, the birthday presents are to be on display tomorrow in the house. I think it's so the cameramen can take shots of them at the same time as they film the ceremony. If you weren't here last night, you probably don't know about it.'

'I'm not sure I follow?'

'It means they have to be given to the housekeeper today so he can unwrap them and lay them out on the table with the right card attached – get the idea?'

'Oh, I see. Thanks for the tip.'

'Elissa would probably have mentioned it to us this evening,' said Liz.

'Oh, she won't be with us this evening. She was with us earlier for lunch, but Niki says Dr Donati recommends an early night,' said Mrs Panighis. 'And of course tomorrow morning she'll have her hairdresser over from Athens, and perhaps last fittings to her dress, which I hear is really something special.'

'Yes, it's from Lagerfeld Gallery; she let me have a look at it the other evening,' Liz agreed.

'I'm so looking forward to it,' gushed Mrs Panighis. 'Such an occasion for the family! I only wish we'd kept in closer touch, but you know . . .'

Her husband nodded in solemn agreement. 'Well, the breach is healed, and we were invited.'

Smiling in their delight, they left.

'Well,' said Liz with an angry little flick of the fingers, 'that kind of puts a spoke in our wheel. We're not going to be able to get at Nancy; she's being sent to bed early like a naughty child.'

'Perhaps we should confront Niki.' But even as he said it, he was shaking his head. 'He'd have us thrown off the island.'

'He wouldn't throw you out. You're a Serene Highness.'

'That wouldn't matter. This is his home and he's got a lot of prestige here. By the time we'd managed to get back with a lawyer or somebody, the trust deeds would be signed and sealed.'

'Perhaps we should have gone to the police, Greg.'

'And said what? That one of their respected citizens was

mixed up in something shady, for which the only evidence was a hunch on our part?'

'Well, no . . . Perhaps not.'

Soon afterwards, they gave up trying to eat. 'I think I ought to find Niki and have it out with him,' said Greg. 'We can't go on like this.'

'I'm coming too—'

'Liz, stay and finish your meal.'

She was already on her feet, however, and picking up her shoulder bag. 'I'll go with you as far as the helicopter,' she said. 'It seems to be the big sensation of today.' She intended, of course, to stick with him no matter where he went.

A thought occurred to him: if Niki intended to bring his wife to the island at short notice, just in time for the signing, what better method than a helicopter? The crews manning the motor cruisers were too much in the know about island life, too fond of gossip; but helicopter pilots might be more discreet, or perhaps just less interested in the affairs of the Paroskolos family. So might Elissa have flown in on any of the machines 'buzzing about'?

They made their way to the tennis court. Sure enough, there sat a helicopter, its blades gently rotating, like some sort of genetically improved grasshopper.

A group of guests was sitting around on steamer chairs outside the wire netting of the courts, idly watching. Mr Crowne reflected that it would be very difficult to smuggle a woman off and away from the helicopter in front of an audience. But then . . . hadn't Mrs Panighis said Elissa's hairdresser had come? Could Elissa have been brought in as some part of the staff?

Elissa Paroskolos, daughter of Yanni Dimitriouso, would never have consented to such a thing – unless, of course, she was a cent or two short of a euro, as Liz had put it.

He and Liz took seats on an extended chaise longue. Alongside was yet another couple whom he recalled only by first names. Alexis – that was the man's name; and his wife, or partner, was Thérèse, a pretty Frenchwoman of a certain age.

'I heard Elissa's hairdresser was coming to see to her hair

for tomorrow,' Gregory remarked. He felt Liz give him a stare of amazement at this sudden interest in beauty treatment.

'Oh yes, Giulio; he's coming, but not until early tomorrow – after all, he has his salon and his clients in Athens, *n'est-ce pas?*'

'He's coming early on the helicopter?'

'I think not. He comes on the boat. From what I hear, tomorrow only the lawyers will be using *cette belle bête.*'

'A lovely animal, as you say, Thérèse; and a great accomplishment, to organize all this traffic. Niki, of course, is well known for his understanding of transport.'

'That is so. But the major-domo also is very effective in this matter. He tells me it is like managing Charles de Gaulle airport, and I believe him; but mainly the pretty animal has been transporting *spécialités*, such as the birthday cake, which is enormous and in three tiers, and also vintage champagne, and vast flower arrangements. More recently the press corps and people who record events of this kind are arriving, for I hear Niki wishes to have it filmed as a part of family history.'

It was easy to guess that Thérèse had been taking a keen interest in the comings and goings of the helicopter. She and Alexis were tennis players. So what else was there to do, now that their battleground was being used by an interloper, but watch its comings and goings?

It seemed unlikely that Elissa could have been brought by helicopter without being spotted by the attentive Thérèse. Yet there was still time for it to happen. Under cover of night, perhaps?

The prince was very hopeful that Elissa would be brought to the island – because if she were not . . . It meant a gigantic fraud would take place, and he, Gregory von Hirtenstein, was somehow honour-bound not to let it happen.

Just at that moment a little bustle took place round the far side of the helicopter. The obstruction of the wire netting on both sides of the court made it difficult to make out exactly what was happening, but then it became clear that a group of passengers was embarking. Some pieces of luggage were loaded aboard, then came people.

Among them was Niki Paroskolos. At first Greg thought

he was just seeing them off, but he climbed aboard with them.

'He's going?' exclaimed Liz.

'Yes, the *châtelain* told me he's giving a big dinner in Athens tonight for the members of the law firm who are responsible for the legal side,' said Thérèse, who seemed to be tuned in to all the gossip. '*Très généreux*! Then I understand he stays overnight, for such things go on very late, and he returns together with the trustees, who I hear are flying into Athens from various points tomorrow.'

Liz put a hand on Greg's arm. That ended any prospect of an immediate confrontation. They sat in silence, watching the rotor blades increase their speed until the great contraption, so unattractive on the ground, rose into the air like a dragonfly.

His Serene Highness didn't know whether to laugh or cry. Nothing, absolutely nothing, was working out as he expected. It seemed a diabolical plot against his efforts to find out the truth – and yet it was all so innocent, so perfectly in harmony with what a busy and thoughtful host might do.

Thérèse chatted on. She was delighted to display insider knowledge. He began to find her extremely tiresome and rose to his feet. 'Let's go for a walk,' he said to Liz.

She knew he was feeling miserable. She hurried, unprotesting, beside him as his long legs covered the slopes to the top of the island. They stood for a long time, staring over the waters, watching the helicopter fade out of sight en route for the mainland.

Soon it was time to think about returning to the cabana to change for the cocktail hour and the evening's entertainment, which they learned was to be dancing to music by a trio of musicians specializing in 'Melody Memories' – in other words, said Liz, 'Grandma's favourites.'

Mention of grandma reminded Greg to produce from his suitcase the birthday present for Elissa Paroskolos. Grossmutti had provided it – an antique silver photograph frame that she'd bought for one of her Biedermeyer-style interiors but had been rejected by the client. 'I'm glad to get rid of it,' she'd confided to her grandson as she handed it over.

He'd had it professionally gift-wrapped at Mövenpick in

Geneva. It seemed entirely eerie to him, to be taking this unwanted frippery as a gesture of congratulation to a young woman whom he suspected of fraud.

He sighed. 'We ought to take this up to the house and hand it over to the major-domo.'

'You seem really fed up, sweetheart.'

'I wish we could hand it over to Elissa in person; but Niki seems to have put her into seclusion.'

'Ah,' said Liz. 'One moment.' She delved in among the pretty shopping bags she'd brought back from Athens to produce a tiny carrier of clear plastic with dinky handles of silver cord. In this reposed a single bottle of nail polish by an élite maker of cosmetics. 'It so happens I've invested a huge sum in a present for Elissa,' she pronounced.

'You mean you bought that for her?'

'Yes, and when I discovered we couldn't get at her, I was chuffed at the idea of keeping it for myself. But now let's go back to Plan A. We'll go up to the house and I'll charm my way into Elissa's presence to give this to her. Take a look – it matches one of the colours in her dress exactly.'

The polish was a soft pink, something like crushed strawberry. Greg, who, of course, hadn't seen the dress, could only nod in approval. 'But they won't let you see her,' he prophesied.

In this he was wrong. After presenting the photo frame to the *châtelain*, and watching it being unwrapped and placed on the long table, he explained that Liz would like to see Elissa. She at once held up the tiny, glistening carrier. 'It's for her to put on her nails tomorrow,' she explained. 'It's a perfect match for her dress.'

'Ah . . . well, Ms Blair, let me just check . . .' He went swiftly to a house phone, spoke for a few moments, then returned to bow in acquiescence. 'Mrs Paroskolos is resting upstairs,' he said. 'Do you know the way?'

'Yes, thank you; I was in her boudoir when she showed me the dress.'

'Of course.' He waved her towards the staircase.

On the way to the house they'd agreed that she should try for this opportunity – probably the last – to talk Nancy out of going on with the deception. Greg watched her go with misgiving; he didn't really like having her out of his sight in this strange household. He passed the time making a tour of the long table on which the birthday gifts were displayed. Grossmutti had estimated theirs with perfect judgement: not as opulent as those from Niki's business friends; not as trivial as those from minor family members.

He'd only just completed the tour when Liz reappeared. He could tell by her expression that things hadn't gone well. They bade farewell to the housekeeper and went out into the cool evening.

'That confounded nurse was sitting there doing her confounded crochet,' she said. 'I couldn't say a word about anything.'

'But who was it she was guarding, Liz?' he demanded. 'Was it Nancy? Or was it Elissa?'

'It was Nancy, of course,' she said in surprise. 'What made you think it might be Elissa?'

'It was just a sort of last hope – that Niki might have somehow brought Elissa to the island for the actual signing. The helicopter trips, you know?'

'Oh, it would have been so *good* if that had happened.' She walked on, shaking her head. 'No, it was Nancy. She was delighted with the nail polish – said she guessed I'd bought it because it would go with the dress. She mentioned the evening when she let me go through her clothes – I mean Elissa's clothes. No, I don't – because, they all fit Nancy . . .'

He was depressed, yet tried for optimism. 'There's always tomorrow,' he said. 'Niki might bring Elissa tomorrow when he comes back with the trustees.'

'Oh, come on, Greg; how would he explain it to them?'

'Well, how do we know they haven't been in on it all the time? A very important person in the financial world is very ill, needs absolute peace and quiet to recuperate. But news of so severe an illness would bother the stock markets. So they agree to hire someone to act the part of Elissa for a while.'

She gazed at him in disbelief. 'Do trustees and lawyers do that kind of thing?' She sighed. 'It would be nice if it were true, however strange. But Nancy's definitely going to be at

127

the ceremony tomorrow. I can't remember exactly what she said, but it was something about putting on the polish – how she hoped her hands wouldn't be too shaky from nerves to put it on, and Madame Defarge said she'd put it on for her.'

'Madame Defarge? – Oh, *la tricoteuse*, I see, from the book by your Charles Dickens.' He stifled a groan. 'So it does really sound as if Nancy means to go through with it.'

'The only good thing,' said Liz, ' is that I hopped up and put the new nail polish in Elissa's bathroom before anyone could say not to, and at the same time I put the box of contact lenses back.'

He felt such a blaze of anger that he nearly shouted at her. Didn't she understand that the brown contact lenses were the only halfway decent evidence of anything underhand? But it was no use reproaching her. They were gone now, and there was no chance of confronting Niki until tomorrow.

If Liz thought he was unusually quiet that evening, she put it down to natural apprehension about the next day's events. He, for his part, was trying to recover his equanimity, telling himself not to blame Liz for putting back the lenses. He hadn't contradicted her when she had said that morning that Dr Donati could explain them away. He even admitted to himself that she was probably right.

His problem was to think out what he could say to Niki tomorrow. Scare him – that was the best tactic: walk up to him point-blank and say, 'I know what you're up to!'

It didn't matter that he actually didn't quite know what Niki was up to: all he wanted was to put a stop to the signing of the documents. If there was an explanation, if it could be settled quietly, without a scandal – any solution, so long as he was satisfied that Elissa was all right and that no fraud was in progress . . .

Neither of them slept well, with the result that they were rather late for breakfast. It was clear that the staff at the pavilion were eager to finish the service, and they soon saw why: the little electric carriages were quickly on their way between the pavilion and the house, carrying tables and chairs. The big open-plan ground floor was being made ready for the great event.

The programme in their cabana informed them that there would be drinks at midday, that at one lunch would be served, and that at two thirty the ceremony of the trust documents would take place. Having started the day in rather casual clothes, Liz and Greg changed into something more formal, Greg into a Savile Row suit and sober tie, Liz into her all-purpose black dress with a white-and-silver silk scarf as embellishment. They packed the rest of their clothes. They'd be going to Piraeus along with the remaining guests at some time in the late afternoon. Or perhaps not, depending on what happened when Mr Crowne challenged Niki Paroskolos.

There were less than a hundred guests now, probably to make room for the considerable number of newcomers – some press people, the gang of television operators, and some business types who might be juniors from the law firm.

The equipment and lights of the television crew took up a lot of room. The part of the big ground floor alongside the staircase had the table with the birthday presents on show with, at its centre, a huge floral display of lilac, carnations, Peruvian lilies, and acanthus. Glass tables and metal chairs from the pavilion had been set out for lunch, each table laid for eight, with snow-white linen, glistening crystal, a bright array of silver cutlery and a low centrepiece of flowers. Bars of sunlight streamed in through the louvred windows, allowing glimpses of the sea but keeping out the glare.

At the back of the room a special table was arranged where the signing ceremony would take place. On it stood yet another gargantuan floral display, a blotter with a pristine sheet of blue blotting paper, with three Mont Blanc pens laid alongside. Three chairs were arranged ready. Of the chief participants, the trustees and heads of the law firm, there was as yet no sign. The helicopter bringing the Athens party hadn't yet arrived.

Nor had Elissa made an appearance. The island guests were kept sufficiently entertained, however. Waiters scurried about with trays of drinks, reporters found willing victims for interview; the group from last night consisting of two violins and a pianist was playing – as far as Mr Crowne could make out above the hubbub – Boccherini's minuet from the E major Quintet.

He moved about restlessly, trying to stay close to the door so as to buttonhole Niki the moment he appeared. When fellow guests tried to engage him in conversation, they found him inattentive. Liz had to do all the socializing, but she had had more than one glass of champagne and so was quite relaxed about it.

They heard the helicopter. The prince braced himself for action by the door.

Foiled: the party, when it came in, arrived through some side entrance, where they'd been deposited by the little electric carts. With the three lawyers and the four elderly male trustees in expensive tailoring he saw, to his dismay, a Greek Orthodox priest in cap and gown. This assemblage made their way to the two main tables, distinguished by being set a little apart from the rest. There they stood in expectation. All the guests followed suit. There was a short pause, and then down the staircase came their hostess, with Dr Donati at one side and Trudi at the other.

She looked so lovely there was an impromptu burst of applause. Her dress was of soft silk jersey woven so that the colour changed from a rich rosy pink at the rolled collar round her throat to almost maroon at the knee. Her hair was arranged in loose, deep waves with a ruby clasp holding it back above one ear. Her only other jewellery was her wedding ring.

She almost stopped at the applause, but the doctor gently urged her on. Niki turned from his place at the table to greet her, taking both her hands in his and kissing her on both cheeks. The applause died away, everyone stood waiting. Greg noticed that Dr Donati had been placed at the same table as Nancy, with Niki and the four trustees. Trudi was at the next table, from which she could keep an eye on her charge.

The priest said grace in Greek, some of the guests repeating his last few words with him. They took their seats. Liz whispered to Greg, 'I'm really impressed!'

'He's got not only the Law but the Church on his side.' He added a few imprecations under his breath. He felt he'd been outfought, although his adversary didn't even know an attack had been intended.

The meal commenced. Course after course of superb food

was served; wine was poured generously; many toasts were drunk. Greg noted that the press corps was being as lavishly entertained as the guests. In his suspicious frame of mind he felt sure this was to keep them from being too critical of the occasion.

The flow of dishes at last came to an end. Coffee was served, liqueurs were offered; those who wished to freshen up had the chance to do so; acquaintances moved to other tables to chat. Greg took the opportunity to thread his way among the tables, but he couldn't get at Niki, who was deep in conversation with the television crew. He seemed to be laying down rules for the next stage in the proceedings.

Nancy Lanan had also got up and was being shepherded by Trudi towards the table where the pens awaited. One of the lawyers had laid a briefcase on the table and was taking out documents in coloured leather covers.

Niki spoke over his shoulder to Trudi. The nurse left Nancy's side to listen to his instructions. For the moment Nancy was almost alone, a few paces from the lawyer at the table. She reached out a hand to the back of a chair, to draw it out so as to sit at the table.

No more time for dithering, for pondering. This girl whom he'd grown to like might be about to commit a serious crime. His Serene Highness Prince Gregory of Hirtenstein had to do something, and do it now.

He stepped close behind her.

'Nancy Lanan,' he said in her ear.

He heard her give a gasp. She swung round to face him, eyes wide, face pale.

She fainted dead away at his feet.

Eleven

The prince's first thought was to kneel beside her. The lawyer with the briefcase was, however, a control freak.

'Stand back, give her air!' he commanded, elbowing Mr Crowne aside. 'Dr Donati! Quickly!'

The doctor was already hurrying up with Trudi springing to his side. Others crowded round, held back by the outspread arms of the lawyer. 'Please! Please! Give the doctor room.'

Somewhat appalled at what he'd done but quite glad not to be involved, Mr Crowne backed away. Guests eagerly took his place. The TV crew, aghast at having missed the drama, were shoving people about so as to get through, the man with the camera on his shoulder causing some damage to the shoulders and hair of others as he went by.

Liz struggled through the group. 'What happened?'

'I'll tell you later.'

'Is she ill, Greg?'

'Seems so.'

They allowed themselves to be forced back to the rim of the group. They were now close to the table where Niki and the distinguished guests had sat. Greg drifted alongside, found Nancy's place, and picked up a half-filled glass by its rim. He emptied its contents into a neighbouring glass, folded it into the handkerchief from his breast pocket, and gave it to Liz. 'Put it in your handbag.'

'Why?' she said in astonishment.

'Fingerprints.'

She gave a champagne-inspired giggle, but did as he bade her. She took the arm he offered, and they went out of the house totally unnoticed by all the rest, who were agog over the scene at the back of the big room.

They walked to their cabin, where Greg took back the glass, carefully stowing it away in his suitcase in a nest of clothes to protect it. Liz, sobered by the fresh air and the walk, watched him. She made a sound, half-laugh and half-snort, as if to say, 'What good is that going to do?'

'Nancy Lanan's fingerprints might be on record somewhere,' he said defensively.

'Only if she's been arrested – and you'll never convince me she's a professional criminal. Anyhow, how are you going to get hold of them?'

'I'll think about that.'

'Somebody in Washington who sings in a barber-shop quartet?'

'Why are you so cross?' he asked, because her tone was acerbic.

'It was you,' she accused him. 'Something you did caused Nancy's collapse.'

He couldn't deny it. 'I didn't expect it to have such a dramatic effect,' he said.

'But what did you *do*?'

'I just called her by her real name.'

Liz sank down on a nearby chair. Head bent, she thought it over. 'You seem to have given her a hell of a shock.'

'Yes.' He sighed. 'I don't think I took into account the strain she's been under over the recent past. I see now it was a mistake.'

'And how!'

'But I had to prevent her from signing those papers, Liz. I don't know what the sentence is for a fraud as big as that, but she might have been condemning herself to at least ten years in prison.'

Liz looked up suddenly. The hazel eyes had gone wide. She drew in a slow breath. 'Greg . . . I don't think I . . . I never really thought about that . . . I somehow thought it wouldn't happen, wasn't real, would all work out somehow. I never thought about prison, or anything like that.' She rose, reached up to smooth back his hair in a loving gesture. 'You were right to do it,' she said. 'I'm sorry I was being so rotten to you.'

He put his arms around her waist and they stood for a time, drawing comfort from each other.

'What happens now?' she asked.

'No idea. Let's go back and find out.'

Rather reluctantly she followed his lead. When they walked into the house again, they found the priest intoning a prayer while the guests stood around with heads bent. 'What's he saying?' she whispered.

'He's asking for Elissa to be restored to full health, asking the others to pray for her.'

A little chorus of *Amin* brought the session to an end. This seemed to be the signal for dispersal. The guests began to filter towards the door. Greg glanced about until he caught sight of one of the trustees; he'd learned from fellow guests at their lunch table that this was Michel Augard, from Luxembourg.

With Liz at his side, he worked his way into the path of M. Augard. 'Excuse me, monsieur, I wonder if you could tell me what happened and how Madame Paroskolos is now?'

Augard gave him a slight dismissive bow. 'I have no particular knowledge, I fear. Excuse me.'

'Please, monsieur, my friend Ms Blair has become very friendly with Madame Paroskolos and is very anxious.'

Augard turned to Liz. His gaze softened a little. 'Madamoiselle Blair,' he said with a little bow.

'Monsieur,' said Liz with a smile. Her French was just good enough to have followed this so far.

'And you are . . . ?' Augard said, turning back to Greg.

'Gregory von Hirtenstein.'

'Ah!' exclaimed Augard. 'Excuse me! We had unfortunately not been introduced.' He gave another bow, much less dismissive. 'Madame Paroskolos is recovering now but is much shaken by what occurred. Her husband is with her but sent a message that she is resting quietly. He mentioned that the doctor said perhaps Madame had taken some champagne, which reacts unfavourably with her medication.'

'A great pity that the big event could not take place.'

'Indeed, Your Highness. And now, of course, it cannot take place for some days, perhaps weeks. I for one have to be in Madrid tomorrow on business, and I know Leskowski is expected in Miami for one of his confounded charity golf events that begins on Monday.'

'But surely the trustees could sign the papers and leave them for Madame to sign later?'

Augard looked just the slightest bit put out by this curiosity, but then reconsidered – after all, this was royalty, no matter how passé. 'That is not permissible under the terms of the trust,' he confided. 'All must sign in the presence of the others. The trustees must be in agreement that Madame is capable of handling the corporation. If not, I regret to say that my dear old friend Yanni, who, alas, was a male chauvinist, insists the trust be continued for another five years, until the thirtieth birthday of Madame.'

'*Bon Dieu*,' murmured the prince. He was thinking of Niki's problems. If his friend from the stock exchange was right, Niki needed the money now, not in five years' time.

The trustee thought he was exclaiming at the misogynistic outlook of his late friend and nodded in understanding. 'However, we can arrange another meeting for next week or more probably the week after, and by then Madame Paroskolos will be well. And, to speak truth, it will be better if we meet without that great audience staring at us. Most unnerving for her.'

They were making their way outdoors as they spoke. The scene reminded Greg of breaking-up day at school, with everybody heading to the dormitories after the leave-taking service. M. Augard, who looked to be in his fifties and whose girth was evidence that he was devoted to good food, grunted as he addressed the downward slope of the path. 'My knees,' he groaned. 'Why would anyone wish to live in a place with so many ups and downs?'

Greg gave him his arm. 'Those little electric carriages are available – probably at the side door where you came in.'

'I want to smoke a cigar; I'm looking for a quiet spot to enjoy it in peace.'

'But to get to the tennis courts – perhaps when you've finished you'd better go back through the house and board the transport.'

'Ah yes, the tennis courts. Quite capacious as a landing stage. Good for the helicopter, noisy beast though it is. I should not favour the idea of a boat crossing after such a rich meal. You also will be travelling by helicopter?'

'Well, no . . . Liz and I have been travelling by boat.'

'My dear fellow, that's absurd. Why not take to the air? It's much quicker. Unless, of course, you have a particular need to go to Piraeus?'

'Not at all.'

'The helicopter will take us to the airport, where I shall be boarding my plane for Madrid. If you need to go into the city, there are plenty of taxis.'

'No, Liz and I will be flying to Paris.'

'Have you anything to pack? For my part, my overnight bag is in safe keeping at the airport.'

'We are packed and ready to go, monsieur. I must, however, write a note of thanks and regrets to our host.'

'Understood. Well, then, in half an hour the first landward trip will take off. I shall speak to the pilot to tell him you and Madamoiselle Blair are joining us.'

'But will that disarrange the passenger list, perhaps . . . ?'

'My dear fellow,' said M. Augard with a wave of a podgy hand, 'there is a certain amount of disorder now in Niki's splendid arrangements. The impression I received, which came via the *châtelain*, was that the family would be glad to see the back of us and as soon as possible.'

'In that case, Liz and I will be at the tennis courts in half an hour.' They exchanged little bows, and M. Argaud took out his cigar case while the prince shepherded Liz away towards the cabana.

'Did I gather he's taking us on the helicopter?'

'Yes, so let's get a move on. I need to write a polite something to Niki.'

This was done in short order, with Liz looking on. As he finished, she placed a hand on his shoulder.

'But should we be leaving?' she asked.

'We have to. The guests were always expected to take their leave at the end of the ceremony.'

'But I feel . . . as if I'm chickening out . . . What about Nancy?'

'Yes, what about Nancy?' he rejoined, putting the note

in an envelope and writing Niki's name on it. He turned to face her. 'She was about to sit down and sign those documents when she fainted. What do you think will happen if she tells her confederates that I called her by her real name?'

'What?'

'Up until now Niki Paroskolos has had no idea we know Nancy's identity. Would you like to be here on this little island, after everybody else is gone, if Niki and his friend the doctor know we know?'

Liz went nearly as pale as Nancy had when she'd fainted. 'Oh . . .' she breathed. Then, gathering herself together, 'Come on, Greg! You're not saying they'd do anything to us?'

'*Chérie*, billions of dollars are involved. People will do very bad things for money.'

'Such as what!'

'We take a walk round the island and accidentally slip off one of the steep paths. Or we have a boating accident. *Quelle dommage!* Everybody is very sympathetic – poor Niki, coping with a sick wife and then his guests die on him.'

She gave him a soft blow on the arm with her fist. 'Nonsense; you're only trying to scare me.'

'Yes, and I hope I'm succeeding. Come on, let's catch that helicopter.'

He left the note in the middle of the bureau for the chambermaid to take to Niki. Rather than wait for an electric cart they walked to the landing ground, carrying their luggage. The television people were there already, to be joined presently by Michel Augard and another trustee, a Finnish banker.

The flight was too noisy for conversation, but it was short. At the airport the big machine landed in a section reserved for private aircraft. Here M. Augard shook hands and said farewell, to be driven away in a smart little car to an executive jet. The Finn also took his leave, summoning up a limousine to take him to Athens.

The TV crew were hurrying off to deliver film to their headquarters. Greg and Liz were left to their own devices. Two men in jackets with the name of the helicopter firm

137

were unloading their luggage and other packages from the aircraft. Liz said she'd go in search of a cloakroom. The prince, as was his wont, fell into conversation with the porters.

'That's a far faster way to get to the mainland than by boat,' he remarked.

'Oh yes, *keirie*, but not nearly so pleasant.'

'Rubbish, Dari; boats belong to the old days. Helicopters are modern,' said his companion.

Dari, an elderly man with a great bristling moustache of grey and a matching fringe around a bald head, gave a snort of derision. 'Can't fly when the wind's too strong; can't fly when there's thunder – there's not a boat skipper at Piraeus who'd be put off by any of that.'

'But you're pleased enough to work for Elikoptero Synchrono, aren't you?' The younger man gave Greg a shrug of amusement. 'Worked here since the firm started up, but never says a good word about it.'

'This helicopter has been flying back and forth from Kerouli all yesterday and today,' mentioned Greg.

'Oh yeah, we know all that! Big day for the *keiria*, though I heard on the radio something's gone wrong.'

Greg said neither yes nor no to that. 'Were either of you working here a year ago when Mrs Paroskolos was brought home from Switzerland?'

'Sure, I was. Poor little thing!' mourned Dari. 'I remember it well – all wrapped up in red blankets on a stretcher . . . So you see, Homer, you shouldn't be so anxious to win the lottery; money doesn't always bring you happiness.'

'Dry up, old man,' said Homer affectionately. 'You know the saying: even if Mrs Paroskolos is sick, she can be sick in great comfort.'

'Ah, but you didn't see her that day: pale as ivory, and all that beautiful hair cut off—'

'You were close enough to see that?' asked the prince, startled.

'You bet. Helped carry the stretcher from the jet to the ambulance and stayed with it to load it on the 'copter.'

'She had short hair? You're sure?'

'I expect they had to cut it off because of her illness,' Homer put in. 'When my cousin Katerina had scarlet fever, they cut hers.'

'Be quiet, boy,' said Dari, becoming disturbed. 'Complete confidentiality – that's what the boss guarantees.' He glared at Greg. 'You a reporter? Don't you go printing anything or we'll be in trouble.'

'I won't print a word,' promised Mr Crowne, and went with them as they pushed the cargo handcart to the small building that served as staging post for high-class travellers. Here Liz rejoined him. They and their luggage were taken to the main building by yet another smart little car.

They had return tickets, because they'd been expecting to leave Greece at about this time today. There were a couple of hours to wait for the flight after they checked in, so they went to the self-service café. They found a reasonably quiet corner in which to drink their coffee.

Liz was still unhappy at leaving Nancy on Kerouli. 'Say what you like, Greg, I think she's been tricked into all this somehow. And she's probably going to sign those papers tomorrow, anyhow, so we're just letting it happen.'

'No, no. Two of the trustees were on the helicopter with us, now weren't they?'

'So what?'

'Didn't you catch what Augard was saying? The trust documents have to be signed in the presence of all of them. I gathered it would be at least a week, probably longer, before they could all get together again.'

Some of the tension and anxiety went out of Liz's attitude. 'Ah,' she said. And then, on thinking about it, 'So where does that leave us?'

'It gives us leeway. There are people I can contact, enquiries I can make . . .'

'What sort of enquiries?'

'Well, about Elissa, for instance.' He held up his finger in the teacher-like gesture. 'Where is Elissa?'

'We went through this before—'

'But I learned something this afternoon that narrows things down. One of those porters at the heliport remembers the day

Elissa was flown in from Switzerland. He told me she had short hair.'

Liz raised her eyebrows as he paused. 'Are you going to explain that?'

He reached across to pat her hand. 'Remember the photograph of Nancy Lanan? Short hair, blue eyes. The girl who was flown in from Switzerland had short hair. I think that was Nancy Lanan. I don't think Elissa ever left Mürren.'

She put her hands over her ears. 'Don't say things like that, Greg! That's horrific! You're saying she's been there all these months?'

'It's not good,' he agreed.

'Not good? It's like that bit in *Jane Eyre* with the mad wife shut up in the garret.'

'Now, now. It's nothing like that. She's ill; she's being looked after in an excellent clinic – that's the truth of it. And meanwhile Niki, who's in desperate need of money, puts on this performance with a look-alike so he can get at the trust funds.'

'Then what, after he's got the money? Does he bring Elissa back? And if he does, what does she say?'

'It depends if she's fully restored to what she used to be. The old Elissa would probably hit him over the head and take control of her money. But I think we have to face the fact that perhaps she's not the woman she used to be.'

'So when you say you're going to make enquiries . . .'

'The first place I'll go is Mürren.'

'And if she's there and we know that a fraud is going on . . . ?'

'I'm afraid I'll have to go to the police. But it will be the Swiss police, because our Financial Crimes Department knows how to handle big-scale fraud.' And, he added internally, you'll be safe in London and I'll be safe in Geneva, not at the mercy of a criminal on his own little island.

'Yes,' she sighed. 'I can see that's the only thing to do.' Some remains of affection for Nancy made her unhappy, but she was resigned to the fact that there was a serious crime here and that Nancy must face the consequences.

The flight to Paris was called. Once in the air, their conversation turned to more workaday matters. Liz would soon be busy seeing the summer clothes into the stores with which she had contracts. Greg told her that he was going to arrange a recital in New York for the *hydraulis*, which made her smile at last.

In Paris they had to go their separate ways – Liz to London, Greg to Geneva. They kissed farewell. She suddenly grasped him by the shoulders and said, 'Greg, if you go to Donati's clinic – be careful!'

'Oh, don't worry, I'll take care.'

She kissed him again, with more passion, and with a tired wave of her hand headed for her departure gate.

He went more slowly towards his. He was busy with a thought that he had been careful not to share with Liz, and it was this: M. Augard had told him the four trustees must all be satisfied that Elissa was fit to take care of the financial corporation she was about to inherit. That must mean that she was fully recovered from her illness. Therefore there was no need for her husband to have power of attorney, and the lawyers involved in finalizing the trust would ensure that it was terminated.

Mr Crowne had been supposing that Niki would get the use of Elissa's money after the trust matured because the power of attorney would still be in force. If that were at an end, how would he get his wife to lend him the sums he needed to prop up his airline?

There were two possibilities: either Elissa was so incapacitated that she would sign whatever he placed before her, or he might inherit it.

As he himself had said to Liz, it would be very easy to arrange a fatal accident on Kerouli.

141

Twelve

M r Crowne flew in and out of Cointrin Airport so often
that he'd evolved a system for calling up a taxi. While
he waited in Baggage Reclamation he telephoned Riri; by the
time he walked out of the door with his case, the car would
be there.

Riri was about sixty, devoted in a romantic fashion to the
ex-royals who lived at Bredoux. Generally he was full of
conversation about the fortunes of the local football team,
the skiing conditions, and so forth; but tonight he could see
that his aristocratic passenger was weary and disheartened. So
they made the trip up to Bredoux almost in silence.

There were no visible lights in the house. Mr Crowne stood
for a moment after the taxi had gone, staring up at the stars.
They always seemed clearer and brighter here, and tonight they
gleamed down at him with that age-old message: 'What do you
matter, you mortals? We were here before you and will be here
when you have passed away.'

From round the back of the house came the comforting
sound of something mortal waiting to welcome him. His red
setter, Rousseau, was whining with his nose against the door
of the old stable where he spent his nights.

Smiling, he went round to let him out. Rousseau put his fore-
paws on his chest and gave him a nuzzle. He then ran to sit on
guard by his master's luggage so that no night wanderer should
steal it away. With a grin the prince followed him, opened the
front door, and brought in his case. Rousseau sat obediently,
waiting for a sign that he could follow him in. Greg's grandmother had strict rules about letting Rousseau into the house.

'*Viens, mon ami*,' said Greg. After all, they hadn't seen each
other for a week.

He made himself a cup of instant coffee with Rousseau sitting with his nose against his knee. Then he went to the window, to see if there was a light in the little office attached to the new stables. His father was still up.

He found ex-King Anton asleep in a chair, his spectacles falling off his nose and a magazine in his lap. He gave the outstretched feet a gentle push with a shoe, and the king woke up, blinking.

'Ah, my boy, you're back,' he said. 'Had a good trip?' For the moment he'd forgotten where his son had been.

'No travel problems, sir. Is Grossmutti back?'

'No, not yet,' said his father on a yawn. 'What time is it? Good heavens, I must get to bed; I've a pupil coming early.' Anton von Hirtenstein taught equestrianship and dressage to beginners who had dreams of one day reaching the Olympics. He rose, and the magazine slipped to the floor. As he bent to retrieve it, he said, 'Extraordinary article in here, Grego, about the new plastic horseshoes.'

'Plastic?' his son said in astonishment.

'Yes, and it seems they come in funny colours. Yellow, green – can you imagine putting a horse through a cabriole when it's wearing yellow shoes?' Laughing to himself, he made his way to the door, waiting for his son and the dog to follow so that he could put out the light. Rousseau, sighing, allowed himself to be closed into his quarters next door for the rest of the night.

As father and son walked through the little passage leading to the main part of the house, Greg asked, 'Is Madame due home soon?' because he longed to talk to his grandmother about what was going on in the Paroskolos household. Ex-Queen Mother Nicoletta wouldn't be overcome with astonishment and horror at his suspicions. In her seventy years she'd seen strange things and heard of more. She didn't shock easily.

When at last he hunted down the message she'd left – it was slipped into the frame of the mirror in her bedroom – he learned she wouldn't be back until at least the following Tuesday. There was a house telephone number where she could be reached, but he didn't like the idea of trying that.

Presumably it was in the home of the client who was having her drawing room redecorated by Grossmutti.

After his father had gone upstairs Greg found he was hungry. He made himself a sandwich in the kitchen to eat with the remains of a bottle of white wine from the fridge. He felt in need of someone to hear his story before he left for Mürren the following day. Not that he really feared any dire consequence from the trip, but all the same, he might crash the old Mercedes, or slip and break his neck on an icy path in the mountains. *Someone* besides himself needed to be informed.

Grossmutti wasn't here. His father would be amazed and upset. At length he went into the living room to leave voice-mail for the family lawyer. M. Soumier received scant business from the Hirtensteins, who weren't a litigious tribe, but he had handled occasional difficulties over business contracts for each member of the family since they were all more or less gainfully employed.

He asked Marcel Soumier if he might call on him at his home early next morning, and begged for a reply before nine. He knew this was asking a great deal because next day was Saturday, a day of rest for most Genevois; but he repeated before signing off that it was extremely important. It had the desired effect because around eight next morning, when he was still trying to get himself awake, the lawyer telephoned.

'What's the matter, my friend?' asked Marcel. 'One of your clients suing you?'

'Nothing like that, Marcel. May I come?'

'Of course. I've nothing important today until lunchtime – the in-laws always share Saturday, you know.'

'I'll be with you in an hour, if that's convenient.'

'Shall I give you breakfast?' inquired Marcel with a smile in his voice.

'No, thanks; I'll be off to the Oberland as soon as you and I finish.'

'Good Lord,' said his friend, and hung up without another word.

The Soumier family lived in an apartment easily reached from Bredoux. Mr Crowne was there within the hour he'd

144

stated, the setter at his side, with his nose pointed at the crack where fresh air came in at the window. 'Stay,' Greg told him as he got out. Rousseau looked disgusted. An underground car park wasn't his idea of a good outing. His master went up to the Soumiers' flat, and was led at once to the room Marcel used as his study. Greg held up a tape recorder.

'Do you mind if we tape this?'

'Good heavens, are you going to make a verbal will?'

'No, no; this is something I've got involved in and it's not finished yet, and I don't know how it's going to turn out. So I think it ought to go on record, and then you can keep the tape somewhere safe.'

Alarmed, the lawyer gestured him to set the recorder on a low table where he did his reading in a comfortable chair. He pulled up another chair for Greg. 'Go ahead,' he said, dying to know what this could be about and, to tell the truth, rather amused. He was sure it was going to be about some temperamental soprano trying to marry herself into the Hirtenstein family.

He grew progressively less amused as he listened.

'Are you seriously saying that Nikolas Paroskolos has been passing someone else off as his wife?'

'Absolutely.'

'And that the real Elissa Paroskolos may be . . . incarcerated . . . in a nursing home somewhere on the slopes of the Schilthorn?'

'Yes, I am.'

'That's crazy, Grego.'

Greg sighed. 'Perhaps it is. That's why I have to go there, to find out if Elissa is there or, if not, where she is.'

'She's with her husband on Kerouli.'

'No, she really isn't. But it doesn't matter whether you believe me or not.' He switched off the recorder and ejected the tape. 'Just have this in safe keeping, Marcel. And can I ask one more thing?'

'What now?'

'Will you telephone the clinic and ask if it will be convenient for M. Couronne to visit this afternoon? Say I'm thinking of bringing my sister as a patient.'

145

'Grego!'

'Go on, Marcel; it'll only take you a minute.'

'Why should I involve myself in your hallucination?' grumbled his friend. All the same he asked Enquiries for the number of the Donati Clinic and then pressed the digits on his phone. From the conversation it was clear the clinic would be delighted to receive a visit from a client of such a distinguished lawyer as M. Soumier. Greg said a fervent thank you as he was shown out of the apartment, but it was drowned out by his friend's advice to give up the whole idea.

From Geneva to Interlaken was something over two hundred kilometres, mostly on fast motorways. Reaching the ski resort before noon, he took Rousseau on the obligatory lead for a walk to the Information Office, where he asked for directions to the Donati Clinic at Mürren.

The young woman at the desk recognized the name at once. '*Ach aber*, the clinic is not at Mürren exactly, *mein Herr*. It would not be convenient for sick people, you know, because it is a car-free zone. But yet the clinic is not so far from Mürren.'

He was longing to cry, 'Well, where the devil is it then?' but restrained himself. Experience with temperamental musicians had taught him that a calm manner always worked best. He looked enquiringly at his informant.

'If you take the Lauterbrunnen road,' she said, drawing him a sketch map, 'you will see a track on the left about three kilometres after you pass Zweliutschinen. There will still be a little snow, but it is a good track. You drive up that track, and you will find a little place, Feldegrün, after about a kilometre and a half, and just beyond is the clinic, with big wrought-iron gates.'

German-Swiss efficiency – she knew the way to within half a kilometre. He said thank you, put Rousseau back in the car with a promise of proper exercise later, then went in search of lunch. Soon after one o'clock he was drawing up at the clinic's wrought-iron gates. They were closed, but when he announced himself to a microphone in the gatepost, they opened majestically to allow him to drive up to the clinic's entrance. Rousseau could tell, from the mere looks of it, that it wasn't the kind of place he'd be allowed to enter.

Inside there was a pleasant foyer with parlour palms and a blond oak desk. Behind the desk was a teenage girl in a dark dress with the name tag 'Alys'. She knew which language to use in welcome, because this client from Geneva had announced himself in French at the gates.

'Monsieur Couronne? Please take a seat. I'll call *Monsieur le directeur.*'

After a murmured telephone conversation she said, 'Monsieur Deboisie will be here in a moment.' True enough, within seconds he came down a passage leading off the hall.

'Monsieur Couronne? Delighted to meet you. Monsieur Soumier said you would be here by afternoon, but have you come all the way from Geneva?'

'Yes, I'm anxious to arrange something for my sister. She's going through a bad time.'

'I see, I see. Please, come to my office . . .'

'I principally want to see the clinic, *Monsieur le directeur.* My sister is a very sensitive person . . .'

'Of course, of course, but first a few medical details. Please, this way.'

They went into a very handsome room with a splendid view of Mount Sulegg. Deboisie ushered his guest to a maroon leather chair by his desk, while he himself took the executive desk chair. He picked up a pen. 'Now, monsieur, your sister is how old?'

'Twenty-seven, and very sensitive.'

'Yes, you mentioned the fact. She is married?'

'Divorced, and that has made her very vulnerable.'

'And her name is . . .'

'Marianne Grussen, although she thinks of returning to her maiden name, because the marriage was a disaster and has made her very insecure.'

'Exactly. And what problem does she present with which I could help you?'

'Well, you know, when she found out that Emil was having an affair, she felt in need of comfort, so you can understand

147

that she looked about for something that would ease her pain, and one thing led to another, so she—'

'Has she been taking drugs? Or does she have problems with alcohol?'

'Well, you know, it's quite understandable . . .' The prince had decided on a drink problem, because drugs might lead to difficulties he couldn't handle. He knew several musicians who turned to drugs in times of crisis, but other than that he was an ignoramus. He said in a low voice, 'I'm afraid Marianne drinks too much.'

'I see, I see. Has she had medical treatment for her addiction?'

'Addiction?' Greg said, sounding affronted. 'She only has a small problem.'

'And her doctor has recommended our clinic.'

'Oh no. Your clinic was recommended by a member of the Paroskolos family.'

Dr Deboisie stiffened. 'The Paroskolos family?' he said in a strained voice.

'Yes, Costa Paroskolos. Perhaps you don't remember him. He was a patient here for a while.'

'Ah, Costa,' echoed the doctor, with relief but without enthusiasm. 'Yes, indeed, we had the pleasure of helping him not too long ago. So you know Costa?'

'Only socially. We met at a yachting event. He told me quite frankly that you had changed his life and, you know, he was so understanding about Marianne, and said he'd already recommended you to his brother Niki—'

'His brother Niki,' interrupted the doctor in a fluster. 'He has never been a patient here.'

'No? Have I got it wrong? Yes, perhaps you're right, I think it was Niki's wife who came here.'

The doctor gave a stiff shake of the head. 'I cannot discuss our patients, Mr Couronne.'

Greg noted that, though it was quite all right to agree that Costa had been at the clinic, it wasn't all right to discuss Elissa. 'Costa has great faith in you,' he said. 'But before I let Marianne come to you, I feel I must see for myself what the place is like.'

It was clear Dr Deboisie had been somehow shaken. He was glad not to have to continue a conversation that dealt with the Paroskolos family. He put down his pen. 'Perhaps we should do that now,' he suggested. 'Our guests will mostly be out for their afternoon stroll, so their rooms would be available for you to see. Shall we go?'

'By all means, but you understand I'm looking for something that will suit Marianne, because she's very—'

'Sensitive,' said the doctor, sighing. 'I understand.'

They went further down the corridor in which Deboisie's office was situated, then along a glass-roofed colonnade joining the office block to another. This was a rectangular single-storey building with a central hall where there was a nurses' station. A man and a woman in white uniform were chatting there. 'Nurse Geidel and Nurse Adlerfeld,' said the doctor as they passed. The two looked up, gave a nod, and went back to their conversation.

The doctor led on to a corridor where doors stood ajar. He pushed them further open for Greg's inspection. 'All the rooms are basically alike,' he said. 'We encourage our guests to bring their own belongings, but I must tell you at once that such items as personal computers and cellphones are not allowed. We wish our guests to concentrate on their cure, without distraction.'

'Oh, now, Marianne would miss her phone . . .'

'There's plenty to do here, I assure you, so that your sister would be happily occupied.' He showed the way to another passageway and to other rooms. All were cheerfully decorated in pastel shades, with plenty of lamps and attractive views of the mountainside. The beds looked comfortable, each with a pile of pillows and a bright duvet.

'How many patients are there?'

'At the moment, we have fourteen guests here,' said Deboisie, with a slight emphasis on the word 'guests'.

'And in that building,' asked Greg, nodding out of the window of the room in which they were standing.

Joined to this block by another colonnade was a similar building.

His guide shrugged and moved towards the door. 'That is for residents whom we might more easily speak of as patients,'

149

he said. 'I dare say you know that our director-in-chief is Dr Tony Donati, a renowned neurologist. The patients in that wing are suffering from various disorders of the brain that require medical intervention, whereas our guests here are undergoing therapy in which they must take part themselves.'

'A neurologist, you say? I believe Costa said something about that. Something about his sister-in-law and Dr Donati?'

Deboisie merely bowed in acknowledgement.

'I'd like to meet Dr Donati,' said Greg. 'Not that Marianne needs anything like that, but it would be nice to meet him.'

'Dr Donati is not here at present.'

'Oh? When will he be back?'

'Not for some time, I'm afraid.'

'Oh, well, I could stay over in Lauterbrunnen for a few days—'

'Dr Donati's absence is likely to be longer than that.'

Greg stopped so as to direct a gaze of irritation and anxiety at his guide. 'You mean that if I were to allow Marianne to come here, she wouldn't receive treatment from the head of the clinic?'

'Oh, your sister would receive the very best attention, I assure you,' the doctor hastened to explain. 'My speciality is the treatment of dependency, and I think if you read our brochure you will see that we have had great success—'

'But Marianne is such a sensitive girl . . . She'd feel diminished if Dr Donati were not to be her consultant. When will he be back?'

Dr Deboisie dithered. 'Well, that's uncertain. However, from what he tells me, it may not be long. A week or two . . . perhaps a month.'

It was all the prince could do to retain his bland inanity at this news. A week or two, perhaps a month. The problem of Elissa Paroskolos and her immense inheritance was to be dealt with in short order, it seemed. The girl now living in Elissa's shoes was to have her confidence built up after that unforeseen setback at the birthday party, the signing of the trust transfer would take place without troublesome witnesses, and the money would come into the hands of the heiress – within a month.

Then, of course, the real Elissa Paroskolos would die and the husband would inherit; but in order for Elissa to be certified dead, there had to be a body. So, logically, the real Elissa had to be hidden away somewhere so as to depart this life in a legal, normal fashion and at about the right time.

Where better than in the Donati Clinic at Mürren?

'May we inspect the medical block?' asked Mr Crowne, flapping a hand towards it. 'I shouldn't like Marianne to be upset by any very sad cases there.'

'I'm afraid that's out of the question,' said Dr Deboisie. 'It would be impossible to have open house there. Only friends and relatives of the patients are allowed to visit; but, as you can see, the quarters for patients who need psychiatric counselling are very pleasant indeed and the facilities for sport and recreation are excellent. We encourage skiing on the lesser slopes in winter, and in summer, of course, there are extensive walks—'

'Yes, yes, I understand all that; but I'm perturbed at the idea that there are sick people here. I hadn't understood that. It needs some thought.' He allowed himself to be led back to the main building while the doctor gave him endless information about regimes, menus, and hobbies that were encouraged, such as bird-watching.

When he got back into the Mercedes, he said to Rousseau, 'That got us nowhere, old chap; but if Elissa is anywhere in this world, it's likely to be in that block where the medical cases are treated.' Because that, of course, was where Elissa must have gone for treatment of her meningitis attack.

He drove out of the clinic, the gates opening silently to let him pass. About a kilometre down the road he drew up to think things over.

It was very, very worrying. Dr Donati would apparently not be needed at Kerouli much longer – might be back at his clinic within the month. His role at Kerouli was clearly to keep Nancy Lanan under control. Shortly, Nancy Lanan would be paid off and sent home. Elissa Paroskolos would be produced in time for a dignified demise. Niki Paroskolos, the grieving widower, would inherit her estate.

Elissa might be in the medical block that he hadn't been

allowed to inspect. In what state? Kept sedated so that she couldn't protest? But was it possible to keep someone under drugs to that extent and for so long? Over a year . . . Mr Crowne knew almost nothing about medicine. All he could do was speculate, and give himself an attack of the horrors.

In the meantime, though, it was now mid-afternoon with the swift Alpine evening ready to descend. If he intended to stay overnight, he must find a hotel. He drove back down to Lauterbrunnen, where he had no trouble in getting a room at Der Goldene Kreis.

He then drove around until he found an area of hillside where dogs were allowed to roam free and without a lead, which Rousseau greeted with a bark of joy. He walked for an hour while the setter raced about after every scent and flicker of movement. He fed the dog from a bag of dry food and gave him a drink, then drove back to the town in search of an evening meal for himself. Rousseau, enjoined to stay in the car and be good, draped himself obediently along the back seat with his head towards the tiny window opening that gave him air.

After dinner, the prince took the funicular up to Mürren. Once there, he had a drink in a *Stubl*, got chatting with a group of high-slope skiers, and had no difficulty learning that the imposing chalet of the Paroskolos family was about ten minutes' walk to the east of the village. He set off along a well-kept track. When the Chalet Lamerle came into view, his hopes were raised by the sight of a display of lights from several windows. That must mean, surely, that Elissa was there with a train of nurses and household staff.

Alas, no. When he threaded his way among the potted evergreens on the wooden veranda and rang the bell, the door opened to reveal an elderly woman in thick trousers, sweater, and gaily patterned socks. '*Ja*?' she said.

'I'm looking for the Paroskolos party – I was told just to drop in,' he said in German, lying with the practised fluency of the concert agent.

'Ah,' she said in quick sympathy, 'who played a trick like that on you? This chalet belongs to the Paroskolos family, I understand, but they're not here at the moment. Just a group of us grey-heads, back from a long day on the mountain paths.'

From behind her in the house came the sound of conversation. She turned her head to call, 'Willi, are the Paroskolos expected here soon?'

'Not that I'm aware of,' said Willi, appearing behind her eating a large chunk of bread spread with Camembert. '*Wie geht's?*' he said to Mr Crowne. 'Are you lost?'

'No, one of those stupid kids told him there was a party here tonight.'

Willi laughed. 'We get a lot of that. Want to come in?'

He accepted the invitation. The entrance led into a wide passage from which there was a step down to a huge living room floored in maple and with Berber rugs strewn about. Seven or eight elderly persons were sitting or lying on comfortable sofas; there was a coffee pot on a low table, bread, crackers, cheese and pâté were being consumed, and it was clear they were relaxing with a snack after hours of hard walking. The television was showing a home-made video involving, as far as Greg could make out, lichens or mosses on trees, and one of the men was pointing with his cracker and making explanations.

Mr Crowne's arrival caused only faint interest. They were too tired to want to be sociable. They gave him coffee and sympathy but were disinclined to do more. They weren't even interested in the Paroskolos family whose house they were renting. However, an elderly man came in to clear away the cups and the food debris. Greg noticed him perk up his ears when he heard the name.

Greg picked up a few cups and plates then followed him into the kitchen. There, a woman of about the same age as the manservant was putting a large gateau and plates and forks on a tray. She handed the tray to the man, who took it, but seemed in no hurry to deliver it to the living room.

'You work for Mr Paroskolos?' asked the prince, as he stacked his mugs and plates in the dishwasher. He followed this up by putting in items brought by the servant. He was showing himself to be a pal.

'No – for the agent, Herr Walen. Are you interested in renting the chalet?' asked the man. He studied the prince, who was clad in the casual bulk of Swiss mountain clothes.

Impossible to say whether this was a client capable of paying the very high rates charged for the chalet.

'Might be,' said the prince. 'You do the caretaking all the time, do you?'

'Oh, of course – done it for years, even before Herr Paroskolos came on the scene. Looked after old Mr Dimitriouso – now there was a tiger for you; he'd try anything: ungroomed moguls – you name it.' He grinned at the recollection. 'I'm Heinz Mannsig; this is my wife.' He put his tray on a worktop. He was ready for a break. '*Der Chef* isn't much of a skier,' he went on, leaning his back against the sink and taking out cigarettes. 'And as for Madame, she wouldn't even set foot on the pistes.'

'I hear from my girl friends that Madame is a real fashion leader.'

'So they say,' said Mrs Mannsig with enthusiasm. 'Here, of course, she wore only ski pants and jerseys; but I've seen pictures of her looking really lovely in evening dress.'

'She was never here,' Heinz grunted. 'Always off in Interlaken, having her hair done, her nails done, trying on fur jackets, buying embroidery.'

'Poor little thing; there wasn't much fashion about her when they flew her out of that clinic down the valley,' said his wife in a much more gentle tone.

'How was that?' He tried for a tone of mild interest. 'What clinic?'

'Oh, it was a big thing around here – caused quite a scare because of the meningitis, but there was only that one case; nobody else caught it, *Gott sei dank*. She went down with it almost overnight and so *der Chef* had her rushed by helicopter to the Donati Clinic; it's quite well known, takes in drunks and – what's the English word? – people for detox.' He grinned round his cigarette. 'The brother of *der Chef* spent some weeks there, getting himself dried out.'

'Now, Heinz,' his wife reproached him. It was clear she did this often, for the scoffing tone as he called Niki 'the Boss' announced that Heinz had no love for the Paroskolos clan.

'I think I've heard of the place,' murmured Mr Crowne. 'But it doesn't sound suitable for anything as serious as meningitis.'

154

'Oh, it has this serious side, where the big doctor treats brain fevers and such. So Madame was whipped off to it and then, when she was a bit better, they flew her out again – to Bern, for the international airport. That's what you can do when you're rolling in money.'

'Money doesn't bring happiness,' said Mrs Mannsig with a sigh. 'I was at the clinic that day; I thought she'd need some of her clothes and things, so I packed up some stuff – personal things that she might be missing: her hairbrush, her special perfume . . .'

'Yes,' said Heinz, 'she went all the way down on the funi and so on to this back-of-beyond place outside Lauterbrunnen, but *der Chef* told her he didn't need the stuff, so you wasted your Christian charity, didn't you, little angel?'

'But you saw Frau Paroskolos being taken aboard the helicopter, did you?' the prince said to Mrs Mannsig.

'Oh, yes – just happened to be there when this great thing came down with such a clatter on the clinic's big forecourt. Poor little thing! All that lovely dark hair cropped off and her poor little face half-hidden by some sort of protective mask – she didn't look like herself at all; I'd have said she was still too ill to move, but I'm no doctor, of course.'

Heinz finished his cigarette and pressed on the visitor the name and address of the agency that looked after the chalet in the absence of Mr Paroskolos. Mr Crowne said goodbye and went out by the back door, to return to the village for a *funi* back to Lauterbrunnen.

On the journey, he thought about what he'd heard: a woman with short hair had been loaded into the helicopter, according to Mrs Mannsig; and he had no doubt she was a good witness, because she was interested in Mrs Paroskolos as a fashion model. So perhaps Nancy Lanan had been the woman she had seen, because Nancy Lanan had short hair in the photograph.

The helicopter had flown to the airport at Bern. There the patient had been transferred to a private executive jet and flown to Athens. At Athens the porter had seen the patient – a woman with short hair – loaded aboard a helicopter for transfer to Kerouli. After about a year, a young woman with the bounteous dark tresses of Elissa Paroskolos was

155

being introduced to relations and friends as the heiress to the Dimitriouso fortune. A year was plenty of time to grow long hair, and a good hair stylist could easily reproduce the Hollywood look that Elissa had favoured.

Specially styled hair, brown contact lenses, low-heeled shoes to disguise the fact that she was taller than Elissa – the whole thing worked in perfect sequence. It seemed likely – it seemed almost perfect logic – that the woman who had left the Donati Clinic the previous year had been Nancy Lanan.

So where was Elissa?

The question was almost like an echo in his mind. About two and a half years ago a similar question had been asked – by the Dimitriouso family, by the press, by the members of the world of finance: *where was Yanni Dimitriouso?*

Dimitriouso had gone out alone in his smart little 505 sailing dinghy, as he often did. He'd been heard to say that it helped him think things through if he had a problem: the wide seas around him, the struggle with wind and tide, the open sky above him with its pageant of cloud. These, he used to say, reduced human questions to their proper proportions.

He failed to return by nightfall of that day. A search was begun. At first there was no sign, and the media began to wonder if, like others before him, he'd staged a disappearance because of financial problems. For a few hours hysteria had seized the markets.

Then the dinghy was found. The boom was damaged from a fracture midway along, the mainsail was flapping from ruptured cords. The centreboard and its starboard support had been stove in, the boat listing badly to that side with seawater washing in and out. It had seemed clear the *Martina* had been in collision with another vessel.

This was only too likely in those crowded waters. Big ferries, cargo boats, oil tankers, high-powered pleasure boats belonging to wealthy playboys – they all careered around the Greek coasts.

Dimitriouso wasn't aboard the *Martina*. So once again the press were asking: where was Yanni? Was it a set-up, arranged after he'd been taken off on another vessel? More hurried buying and selling on the stock exchange, more headlines demanding an investigation.

Elissa Paroskolos remained in seclusion, comforted by her husband of six months. Reporters besieged their Athens apartment. Niki came forward with a statement denying that there was any trouble with the funds of the great Dimitriouso Corporation.

Ten days later the body had been found washed up among the rocks of a little islet, badly damaged by sea creatures, by the washing to and fro among the boulders and by the effects of immersion, but easily identified. The autopsy produced a finding that most of the damage was caused by the sea after death, that Dimitriouso had probably been dead from a blow to the head received during the collision.

Dimitriouso had died from an accident. Had he?

Mr Crowne found himself asking that question now. He remembered the opinion of Niki expressed by his friend Severo Konialidis from the Athens Bourse: 'Even if he's going down the tubes, his wife's money is still there.'

Troubles among the airlines hadn't begun recently. Niki Paroskolos might easily have been hoping for help from his father-in-law two and a half years before.

Had that shrewd and cool-hearted old man said no? Although the prince had never met him, he knew his reputation – all the more impressed upon him because, despite being known as tight-fisted, Dimitriouso had treated the von Hirtensteins with great generosity. Old Yanni had had his likes and dislikes; to his friends he could be extraordinarily kind. But to those whom he chose to cold-shoulder he could be almost cruel; and it was a safe bet that he knew more about Niki's financial prospects than Niki did himself. There might even have been a suspicion – natural enough in such an experienced old warrior – that Niki had married Elissa for her money.

No, said the prince to himself, come on; you're building up a case on absolutely no evidence.

All the same, old Dr Dragorasie had found it strange 'that Yanni Dimitriouso should die in a boating accident!' And this particular accident – collision – was one that every yachtsman was on guard against. Mr Crowne himself sailed as often as he could on the Swiss lakes, always on the watch for the lake steamers, or some thoughtless power-boat owner. He considered now that Yanni Dimitriouso would have been very unlikely to let himself be run down; and if there had been a crash, who was the culprit? No one had ever been found, suspected, or charged.

What if Yanni's son-in-law had motored up and asked to board, then smashed his skull with an iron bar . . . ? Throw the body overboard, bash the dinghy enough to make it look as if there had been a catastrophe, leave the rest to time and the sea . . . Elissa inherits the money, and Niki persuades her to invest in his airlines. Problem solved.

This shocking train of thought made him feel chilled to the marrow. He was glad to escape from it as they arrived at Lauterbrunnen. Walking towards his hotel, his stubborn mind took up the problem from a different angle.

His question to himself had been, *Where is Elissa?* She wasn't on the island of Kerouli. She wasn't at the Donati Clinic, because Mrs Mannsig had seen her carried out to the helicopter. But wait – that might have been Nancy.

What if Elissa had actually died at the clinic from the meningitis attack? What if Niki, in desperate need of money, had seen the trust fund vanishing away before his eyes? It was almost certain that Yanni would have arranged for his fortune to go to some other legatee – someone of true Dimitriouso blood – in the unlikely event of Elissa's death before the age of twenty-five.

So then Niki found himself facing financial ruin. If he had indeed stage-managed the accident to his father-in-law, it had all been for nothing because, with Elissa dead too, he was disinherited. But he knew of a girl who could impersonate Elissa with a bit of cosmetic transformation and a lot of training in the family history. For a large sum of money she agreed to do it.

Yes, possible; very possible.

He was almost at the hotel when he stopped short, struck by a terrible thought. A pedestrian coming behind him bumped into him. 'Sorry,' said the prince, and walked on, shocked to the depths of his soul by what his mind had brought up.

Whoever was to sign the trust deed and claim the money – whether the real Elissa or a replica – someone had to die so that Niki could inherit. There had to be a body and a death certificate; and if Elissa had meanwhile died from the meningitis, then . . . then . . . it was Nancy who would have to die.

He needed to know more. He needed to find out if Elissa was still at the clinic, too severely disabled to be capable of signing the trust deeds. Or if she had died a natural death and the fact had been registered in their files.

His car was in the hotel's car park. He got in. Rousseau woke up and laid his head on his master's shoulder as they drove out into the valley. Somehow that was comforting – and he felt in need of comfort.

In the dark it was rather more difficult to pick out the track leading to the clinic, but he found it and parked off the road in some long, tough grass. He took a torch out of the glove compartment, and let Rousseau out, attaching his lead. If anyone challenged him, he was taking his dog for a last walk before bed.

It was still only about eleven o'clock, but the Swiss go to bed early, and the staff of a Swiss health clinic even earlier. The stately gates, of course, were electronically closed, but the wall on either side was only two metres high, decorative rather than protective. He climbed over while Rousseau quietly slipped past the palings of the gate, his lead trailing. There was only a dim glow behind the glass panels of the front door. When Mr Crowne quietly toured the perimeter of the building with Rousseau padding at his side, he saw at first only the glimmer that comes from electric night lights.

The medical block seemed totally asleep; but from the back of the office block there was the sound of a television quiz, which presumably came from the room where the night staff were on duty. Mr Crowne guessed that 'night staff' would consist of perhaps one nurse, ready to answer any bell that was rung by a patient from either the medical or the psychiatric area.

The patients undergoing detox seemed to be asleep, but there were one or two windows slightly ajar to the crisp night air.

He pressed his face against the glass, making out a figure on a bed under a duvet, and hearing a faint snore.

He took off his walking boots. 'Stay,' he whispered to Rousseau. The dog obediently sat down beside his boots. He slipped his hand inside the window, unlatched the stay-bar, pulled it open, and climbed in.

His thick socks made no sound on the carpeted floor. He closed the window to its former position lest the draught wake the sleeper. He walked past the bed, opened the door to the corridor by a few inches, and slipped out.

There he paused. Should he make his way to the medical block through the colonnade? But once there, what could he do? Open every door to see whether the occupant was Elissa Paroskolos?

Better to look at the files to see if she was here and, if so, where she was housed. He padded down the corridor until he came to the central area and from there found again the corridor down which he'd been led to Dr Deboisie's office. He tried the door. To his surprise, it opened; but then this was civilized Switzerland, where citizens didn't expect burglars.

Deboisie's desk yielded nothing of interest except correspondence in the in-tray. A quick survey of the room by torchlight showed nowhere for documents to be stored. He went out to look at the other rooms in the corridor. One was rather splendid, presumably the office of the owner and director-in-chief, Dr Donati. The second one he came to had a plaque: *Arztliche Aufzeichnungen* – Medical Records. He tried the door. It opened at once.

But the filing cabinets did not. Disconcerted, he paused. A moment's thought suggested that, if the efficient Swiss locked up their files each night, they'd want to unlock them quickly each morning. He played the light of the torch around the walls until he came to a key panel, where inspection provided him with a pair of keys for the cabinets.

He unlocked the one labelled M–Z. He soon found the file for Paroskolos, but it was about Costa, not Elissa. A tweak or two among nearby tags showed that nothing was out of place; there was no file for Elissa. He unlocked the A–L cabinet to look at Dimitriouso, in case for some strange reason she was registered under her maiden name: nothing. He looked under 'L' for Nancy Lanan. Once more, nothing. He closed the filing cabinets, locked them and put the keys back on the board.

There was a computer on the desk. Unwillingly he approached it. He switched it on. After some flashings and murmurings the screen announced itself as *'Fertig'*. He was surprised to be let in; he'd expected to be asked for a password, but perhaps general files weren't regarded as very confidential. He typed in *'Arztliche Aufzeichnungen'*. Obediently the screen changed to show the beginnings of an alphabetical list. Being no computer buff, he ran down it using the arrows until he came to the letter D for Dimitriouso. He found nothing. Next he inspected P and found Costa, with his name and address in Paris, followed by some very technical terms about diagnosis and treatment.

There was nothing about Elissa. Nor, under L, about Nancy Lanan.

One or other of these two women had been loaded on to a helicopter and flown away; but as far as the clinic's records showed, they had never been here. They had become non-persons.

Some fictitious name might have been used to list them, but he'd no idea what it might have been.

If Elissa had died from the effects of meningitis, it must be surely be in the files in some form? He floundered about for a while, but eventually under 'Discharged etc.' he found what he was looking for. There had been one death in the medical wards in the past eighteen months – a male patient whose certificate had been signed by his personal physician as well as Dr Deboisie. No other patient had died.

So neither Elissa nor Nancy was registered as a patient, nor had any death occurred to a female. That disposed of the idea that Elissa had succumbed to her illness and had had her death registered according to the law. Of course, if their names had ever been on the computer under any form, they'd been deleted; and because he fought shy of computers, he had no idea how to find deletions. He closed down the machine.

He was suddenly very eager to get out of the clinic. There was something here that lay hidden yet conveyed an intense sense of dread. He went out of the office and very quietly through the reception area to the front door. He tried it, but it was locked and bolted. He made his way back to the room through which he'd first entered, padded to the window, opened it wide enough to climb out, whispered 'Quiet, Rousseau' to his dog, and joined him on the flagstones. He pushed the window back to its original position and was vexed to hear it give a slight squeak.

He put on his walking boots. 'Heel,' he murmured to Rousseau, moving as softly as he could to the grass-covered ground beyond the flagstones. They were about fifty metres down the slope when a light shone blindingly into his eyes.

'Stand where you are!' said a voice.

Security patrol?

'*En garde*, Rousseau!' the prince commanded. The setter crouched at his side, uttering a menacing growl.

The beam of light at once moved to the dog. Discovering that he wasn't being challenged by a Doberman, the man with the torch flashed it into the prince's face again; but by that time Greg had pulled his scarf up so that it covered his chin – not exactly a robber's mask but enough to make his features less recognizable.

'Turn off that damned torch!' he protested in his deepest baritone.

'Who are you? What are you doing here?'

'I'm Heinz Mannsig and I'm walking my dog. What d'you think I'm doing?'

'This is private property—'

'There's nothing to say so! What's things coming to if a man can't go out for a stroll and a cigarette last thing at night?'

'Let's have a look at you . . .' The torch danced about as the man reached out for him.

'Keep your hands off! Who do you think you are?' The prince batted away the hand reaching for his scarf. The other hand with the torch wobbled in a wide arc. He turned sharply so that the man trying to catch hold of him was jostled. He stalked away. 'Come on, Rousseau. This guy's an absolute madman!'

He was pretty sure that without some stronger justification

162

than finding him on the grounds with his dog, the watchman – if that's what he was – would give up. He marched on, muttering protests loud enough to be heard, with Rousseau trotting obediently alongside. When he reached the perimeter wall, he shinned over.

The Mercedes opened with an old-fashioned key. With some difficulty he got it into the lock and fell into the driving seat with relief. Rousseau stood looking up at him, wagging his tail. He opened the back door for him. Rousseau leapt in and he drove away.

It was some moments before he recovered enough to see the funny side. What an embarrassment it would have been if the ex-crown prince of Hirtenstein had been arrested for breaking and entering.

'All the same, Rousseau,' he said with a long sigh, 'this is growing very un-funny indeed.'

Thirteen

He had booked an early-morning call. At the telephone's summons he dragged himself out of bed, pulled on the clothes he'd worn yesterday, and went out to drive Rousseau to the allotted hillside where he could roam free.

Other dog-walkers greeted him fraternally. He responded as little as possible. He was never at his best in the early morning, and moreover he had woken with a dreadful thought.

Yesterday he'd been supposing, as a solution to some of the mysteries, that Elissa Paroskolos had died of meningitis in the Donati Clinic.

Well, if so . . . Why had the death gone unrecorded? The reason suggested itself at once: Niki didn't want his wife to be dead until after she'd come into control of her father's fortune; but if Elissa had died of meningitis in February of last year, what had happened to the body? Had she been registered as someone else? Had she been buried, or cremated, under another name?

Nancy Lanan had come to the Bernese Oberland at some point. Quite why, Mr Crowne didn't yet understand. She'd left her home in Bloomington, Illinois, telling her friends she was going to write a book and at some point had been invited . . . conveyed . . . bamboozled . . . into the Donati Clinic. There, in some way, she'd been put into the role of the ailing Mrs Paroskolos, taken by helicopter to Bern, and flown to Athens.

Elissa Paroskolos had remained in Switzerland. Whether she was dead or alive, he couldn't be sure; but if she had died, there had to have been a body to dispose of. And Nancy Lanan was a possible name under which to register the death.

The problem now was: how did you find out if someone

called Nancy Lanan had died and been buried? The answer was: you asked the authorities.

This was Sunday however. The *Zivilstandamt* would be closed. His mind busy with the problem, he watched Rousseau cavorting on the hillside in company with a little terrier. Yes, the *Zivilstandamt* would be closed but if Nancy had 'died', surely her death would have been reported to the United States Embassy, which would never be closed to any problem concerning one of its citizens.

When he returned to the hotel he tethered the setter to a specially labelled post in the car park, promising to be back soon. He ordered coffee and croissants to be sent to his room, took a quick shower and a shave, dressed in fresh clothes, and ate quickly. The time was now almost eight o'clock – a respectable enough hour to ring Marcel Soumier, for although the Swiss go to bed early, they also rise early.

Marcel was playing with his four-year-old daughter when he picked up the phone. 'Quiet, Lucille; Papa needs to talk to someone.'

'Marcel, this is Grego. You know what I was talking to you about yesterday morning?'

'Yes?' Marcel said, alarmed.

'Do you have any lawyer friends in Bern?'

'Ssh, Lucille. In Bern?'

'Yes, anyone you can refer me to.'

'Ahem . . . For what purpose?'

'I need to go to the American Embassy and be taken seriously.' There was a silence at the other end. He waited.

After a moment Marcel said, 'Lucille, go and ask Mama to put your coat on. We'll be going out in a minute.' Joyous sounds greeted this; the little girl could be heard calling Mama, then Marcel said, 'It so happens I actually know someone in the Embassy itself. Nobody very important – a minor legal advisor, or some such thing. His name is Cyrus Guttman. Wait a moment; I'll have to go into my study to find his telephone number.'

During the pause the prince employed himself throwing his belongings into his overnight bag. By and by Marcel came back. 'Ready to write this down?' He read out an address

165

in Bern and a telephone number. 'That's his home. I've got his extension at the Embassy, but I don't think he'd be there on a Sunday. He deals with the legalities when Americans buy property in Switzerland, which I imagine is a pretty much nine-to-five job; but he could put you on to the right people to handle whatever it is you want handled.' He hesitated. 'I'm almost afraid to ask. What is it you want handled?'

'I want to find out whether the American girl I told you about – Nancy Lanan – died in the Oberland in February of last year.'

'Died?'

'Yes, I just want to find out.'

'Grego, are you sure you're not just having some sort of mental breakdown?'

'No, I'm not. That's the worst of it.'

He disconnected and immediately called the number in Bern. It rang so long he was about to give up, but at last a breathless voice said, *'Bitte, bleiben Sie am Apparat!'*

'Sure thing,' said Mr Crowne in English, for the voice had been unmistakably American. He waited as requested.

There was a clinking and clanking, then the voice said, 'Sorry about that. I'm in the garage, trying to find the picnic hamper.'

'Are you going out for a picnic?'

'We thought we would. Nice day, and all that. Who is this, anyhow?'

'My name's Gregory von Hirtenstein. Marcel Soumier gave me your number . . .'

'Oh, Marcel the Maestro, eh? Tell him I'm going to bankrupt him the next time we play.'

'Play?'

'Poker. So Marcel put you on to me – is it about a house or a business purchase?'

'Neither. Mr Guttman, I need your help to get in touch with someone at the Embassy.'

'Call me Cy. Who'd you wanna contact?'

'Someone who could tell me if an American citizen died in Switzerland some time in February last year.'

166

'Oh, gee, I'm sorry. I didn't realize it was something serious.'

'That's all right; it's not a relative or friend. I just need to know because of a problem.'

Cy became cautious. 'What kind of a problem?'

'I'd rather not discuss it on the phone, and besides, it would take too long. But Marcel Soumier would vouch for me. I'm not a troublemaker or anything like that.'

'Who'd you say you were again?'

'Gregory von Hirtenstein.'

'Say . . . Haven't I read something about you somewhere . . . ?'

'You may have. I arrange concerts, classical music.'

'Oh, and this person that's died – it's a musician? An American musician?'

'No, a journalist.' He wanted to say, 'Stop asking questions that don't really concern you, and just give me a contact at the Embassy.' But the man was being friendly and he didn't want to offend him. 'Could you just tell me who to ask for?'

'Couldn't it wait till tomorrow?' Cy asked, reasonably enough.

'It could, I suppose, but I'd like to get it sorted out today while I'm near enough to call in at the Embassy in person, if need be.'

'You're where?'

'Lauterbrunnen. I could be in Bern by mid-morning.'

'Okay. This journalist – was he resident or visiting?'

'Er . . . visiting.'

'Then listen: you need to call the Embassy and ask for the Visitors' Emergency Office. There'll be someone on duty, and just tell them what you've told me. Okay? Do you know the Embassy's number?'

'I'll get it from the phone book here. Thank you, Cy.'

'No problem. Have a nice day.'

The phone pages under Bern yielded the number of the Embassy. He was connected at once, asked for the required office, and was put through. A bright female voice said, 'US Visitors Office, Alison Brooks speaking; how may I help you?'

167

Once again the prince went through his routine. Ms Brooks at once became sympathetic. 'Oh, dear, what was your friend's name?'

'Nancy Lanan, of Bloomington, Illinois. She probably travelled to Switzerland in January or early February last year.'

'Just give me a moment; I'm calling it up on the screen. January or February last year . . . No, there was no report of an American citizen's death at that time.'

'It would be reported to you?'

'Oh, sure. Her passport and so on would probably be surrendered to us.'

'Later in the year, perhaps? March? April?'

'There were two deaths on the ski slopes in March – one a woman, but she was Alanna O'Reilly and her parents came over to claim the body. Then a couple of heart attacks – both male. There was a traffic accident in April resulting in fatalities, but they were a husband and wife and the name doesn't match.' A pause. 'A journalist might use her maiden name. She was how old?'

'Twenty-four.'

'Oh no, Mr Hirtenstein; the woman in the road accident case was over forty.'

'Could you just . . . Would you mind looking to see if the name comes up at any time in the year?' he asked despairingly.

'No problem, I'll just . . .' A pause while she looked at her screen. 'No, the name doesn't match anything, and those that appear – their passports and papers have been handed in and most of them were taken Stateside for burial back home.'

'I see. Thank you very much.'

'If you've lost track of your friend,' said Ms Brooks in a gentle tone, 'there's no need to think the worst; it might just be a missing persons case. Have you been to the police?'

'Not yet,' he said with a sigh, 'but that's next.'

This was a moment that had been moving towards him inexorably since he'd left Kerouli. His purpose had been to find out if Elissa Paroskolos was at any of the likely places in the Bernese Oberland. Although he had no positive proof she was *not* there – because it's almost impossible to prove

168

a negative – he was satisfied that the woman who had been taken from the clinic and transported to the island was, in fact, not Elissa but Nancy. That in itself was a police matter. Nancy Lanan was an American citizen. When she had been flown out of the country her passport should have been presented. If a passport had been offered, it had been that of Elissa Paroskolos. A fraud had been committed. Ergo, officialdom ought to be interested.

For such a relatively minor matter he wouldn't have dreamed of calling up special resources; but he was now convinced that something very serious had happened: that Nancy Lanan was acting out the part of Elissa because Elissa was dead.

So he took from his wallet a small card encased in clear plastic. On it was a telephone number. He entered the digits. At once a brisk male voice said: 'Office of Special Security. Is there an emergency?'

'No.'

'Please give your code name.'

'Serenade.'

A series of clicks. Another voice, heavier and older, said: 'Code name Serenade accepted. Identify yourself, please.'

'Gregory von Hirtenstein.

'Residence?'

'Bredoux, Geneva.'

'Thank you, sir. Is there an ongoing event?'

'No, but there's a problem. I need to speak to someone about it.'

'Is there urgency?'

He thought about that. 'I'm not sure. Something bad may happen within a week or so. If it's to be prevented, I need information.'

There was a grunt of amused surprise. 'You need information from us?'

'Yes, and there *is* urgency about that. I'm in Lauterbrunnen; I can be in Bern in an hour or so. Is there someone I could speak to?'

'Hold,' said the official voice. The prince sat on the hotel bed and waited.

After a short interval a different voice said, 'Your Highness,

169

if you come to the reception desk of the headquarters of the Federal Police Force, someone will be there to meet you.'

'Thank you. Shall we say soon after ten?'

'Agreed.'

He paid his hotel bill, collected his dog from his tethering post, fed and watered him, put everything in the car and drove off. He was feeling rather absurd. Each of the three members of his family had a card with the special number, but the only one to have used it had been his grandmother, the ex-Queen Nicoletta.

She'd been in a department store in Zurich when it was picketed by a group of animal rights campaigners. For some reason the local police got it into their heads that a hostage situation had developed. One customer became hysterical, a sales assistant fainted, the campaigners grew overexcited and began hitting out at bystanders with their placards. Nicoletta telephoned the special number. A small group of tough-looking young men arrived. Although they seemed to do nothing very excessive, within fifteen minutes they'd dispersed the crowd, calmed the local gendarmerie, shepherded away the hysterical and revived the sales assistant who fainted. The whole thing was over. Very efficient.

However, Grossmutti had been reprimanded for calling in the Special Security Force for such an episode; and her grandson rather suspected he was going to meet the same fate.

On the outskirts of Bern he gave Rousseau another run. He thought, as he drove into the city, that one or two uniformed city policemen gave him serious glances, which probably meant they'd been told to look out for his car, the make and registration of which were, of course, known to the authorities. 'We're under inspection,' he told his dog, 'so when I leave you in the car, behave yourself.'

At the reception desk a burly fellow in a roll-neck sweater and tweed trousers was waiting for him. As soon as he'd uttered his name the other took him by the elbow to steer him towards the lifts. On their upward journey they made small talk about driving, the state of the roads, and which route he'd taken from Lauterbrunnen. They turned left at the top of the building, went

170

along several corridors, and finally entered a room overlooking Bubenbergplatz.

At a desk absolutely clear of paperwork sat a bony, grey-haired man in a charcoal business suit. He rose, holding out his hand. 'Your Highness.'

'Oh, please . . .' murmured the prince dismissively, shaking hands.

'Ah yes, here in Bern it would be Herr Krone, *nicht*? Very well, Herr Krone, what can we do for you?' The prince glanced at the officer who had brought him in. 'That's all right, Schuls is my second-in-command. I'm Commander Melchinahr, by the way.' He led his guest to a seating area with a set of leather chairs. Schuls remained where he was, leaning by the door.

Greg had thought the matter through on his drive from Lauterbrunnen. He went through his story in logical sequence, pausing now and again for comment but receiving none. When he ended, Melchinahr raised an eyebrow at Schuls, who gave a brief nod and slipped out of the door.

'We'll find out if Nancy Lanan flew in around the time you mention – January or February last year. Fill me in about the Paroskolos clan: are they *very* rich?'

'Very. At least, Mrs Paroskolos is – she is already, and when the trust money is handed over, I believe she becomes a billionairess.'

'*Ach* . . .' He clasped his hands behind his head, leaned back, and studied Greg. 'And is there more you want to ask us? Apart from the flight information, which is a nothing.'

'Well . . . I'm inclined to think that . . . that Elissa is dead; but if she is, the death would have to be registered under the name of Nancy Lanan. At least, that's what I worked out. But, as I said, the Visitors Office at the Embassy has no record of Nancy Lanan's death.'

'And they would have it if someone thought of as Lanan had died, because she's a US citizen. Um . . .' He stared past a bony broken nose at his visitor. 'So you are asking . . . ?'

'Whether there are any unidentified bodies?' he said and, having said it, felt a terrible tremor of premonition.

Melchinahr sat up straight. He allowed a small smile to twitch at his mouth. 'You're no fool, are you?' he remarked.

He picked up a telephone from a table between the chairs, muttered into it, then nodded at Greg. 'We'll get a printout in a minute or two. There's always a few "unknowns", as you'd expect: road accidents, avalanche victims . . .'

The door opened to let in Officer Schuls. 'Nancy Lanan flew from Chicago to Munich on February second last year. According to the airline she had a one-way ticket only, which she picked up at the departure desk.'

His boss held up a finger. 'Probably means somebody bought her ticket for her. And, of course, she wasn't expecting to travel home in the near future.'

'She was expecting to write a book,' Greg put in. 'Perhaps a biography of Elissa Paroskolos.'

'Right. She flew to Munich. It seems likely she was picked up there. Brought on by car, perhaps. You know, in February, with the ski season in full swing, road traffic is heavy. She could have gone through without being noticed at a dozen points along the way.'

'If she was flown in by private jet,' enquired Greg, 'would there have been much checking of passports?'

Both men shrugged. The unspoken answer was, 'Probably not.'

A young woman came in with a couple of sheets of paper. Melchinahr took them, ran his eye over them; then, on reaching the second sheet, said, 'Describe Mrs Paroskolos again?'

'Age twenty-three at the time, height a little over a hundred and fifty centimetres, weight . . . let's say about fifty-seven kilogrammes . . . Long, thick, dark hair; brown eyes, small hands and feet.'

The commander was shaking his head. 'You were supposing that she died in the February? Nothing matches.' He went on studying the sheet of paper. 'Wait a sec.'

'What?'

He was reading as he replied. 'Let's suppose she died in February last year, yes? But suppose her body wasn't found until October?'

The others looked at him, waiting. Greg felt as if an iron bar were pressing down on him.

'We've got human remains, found partly in a stream in the

Jangerle Forest on the Schilthorn, about eleven hundred metres above Lauterbrunnen.'

'Remains?' Greg echoed. He heard his own voice, thin and unrecognizable.

'Part of a skull, ulna and radius of the right arm, both tibia, some fragments of other bones, part of a red ski jacket, one ski pole, two boots badly fractionated, some scraps of paper that might have been in the jacket pocket . . .'

Nobody made any response.

The commander read aloud: 'Remains indicate a female subject approximately one hundred and fifty centimetres tall, approximate age between eighteen and twenty-five, in good health at the time of the accident. Dental work in mandible suggests Australia or America.'

'That's appalling,' said the prince.

The other men were respectful but more accustomed to facts like these. Schuls said: 'You have to remember, sir, that she'd been there nearly seven months by the time she was found, if it's Mrs Paroskolos. Animals and birds would tear off fabric from the clothes for nests and burrows. If she was dumped partly on the ice over the stream, she'd have gone into the water at the thaw – and you can imagine what happens to a body during three or four months in water. But before that, there are wild cats and lynx up there, to say nothing of eagles and crows and owls.'

'Yes.' He'd glimpsed them himself on cross-country ski trips. He pulled himself together. 'It must be Elissa Paroskolos. The age and height seem about right, and the dental work . . . I think Elissa had a lot of cosmetic work done to her teeth while she was at college in the States. She made a big effort, you see – when she got there she was an overweight little frump, but her classmates probably made her . . .' He heard himself maundering and fell silent.

'The question is: what do we do now?' remarked the commander. 'In a straightforward case, where we got a possible identification, the canton police would take over and ask a relative to verify it.'

'No! You can't tell anybody connected with Elissa! There's a young woman on Kerouli playing out her role as the heiress.

If Niki Paroskolos gets the slightest idea he's been found out, that woman's life isn't worth a sou.'

The other two were nodding in complete understanding. They dealt with ruthless people all the time.

'We have to go to the dentist, then,' said Schuls. 'You know the family, sir. Do you know who would have done the dental work?'

'No . . . But I think I know someone who *would* know. He used to be the family doctor; his name's Basil Dragorasie and he lives on the island of Spetses.'

'Right. We'll ask the Greek police to—'

'No, don't do that.'

'What?'

'Don't contact the Greek authorities. The Paroskolos family, and Elissa's own relations, the Dimitriousos – they're a hotbed of gossip and they've got gossipy friends and relatives in all sorts of high places. If word were to get out . . .'

'We'd warn them to be discreet . . .'

He was shaking his head. 'You don't know the set-up. The family talk about each other all the time; they're intensely interested in every little detail. It needs only a whisper to reach Niki, and it's all up.'

'Well . . .' The two security men exchanged serious glances. 'We could handle it direct from here,' said the commander. 'Schuls, get the telephone number for this doctor – he is on the telephone, isn't he, sir, on his island?'

'Oh yes, but the thing is, he went to stay with relations.'

'Great,' said Schuls.

'No, wait – there's a taverna on the quay at Spetses; the owner is the kind of man who keeps an eye on everything and he was clearly a friend of the doctor's. The taverna was . . . was . . . the Lithrini, I think . . . Yes, that's a kind of fish; it was a fish restaurant. Ask International Enquiries for the Lithrini taverna on Spetses. I'm sure I can talk the owner into telling me where old Dr Drago has gone.'

'Oh,' said Schuls, 'we can probably get the Lithrini taverna number on the tourist page on the Internet, no problem.'

However, it took him longer than he'd expected. Then it wasn't exactly easy to get the café owner to divulge the

174

whereabouts of Basil Dragorasie. He had gone to stay with relations in Megara. Once again Schuls got the number, and once more the prince adopted his most persuasive manner.

'But why do you want this?' said the old doctor in amazement.

'There's a good reason. I'll tell you all about it one day soon.'

'It's confidential information about a patient. I can't give out that kind of thing.'

'Do you even remember?' challenged Greg. 'It was a long time ago that Elissa had her teeth straightened.'

He'd hit the right note. The old doctor didn't want to be thought of as senile. 'Oh, because I'm getting on in years you think I'm past it? Nothing of the sort.'

'So who did she go to? Someone in the States?'

'So you know all about it already, do you? Why do you need me?'

'Come on, Dr Drago. Just give me the name of her dentist and I'll stop badgering you.'

'All right then; the man's name was, I think, Tullot, and he had his office in Boston. Herbert Pleydon Tullot, if memory serves and you want it in full. Don't tell me there's anything wrong with my memory! And I think you're really strange to ask such a question!'

'Your memory is first-rate,' said Greg, added his thanks and respects, and hung up. He wrote down the name on the pad Schuls was holding out.

'Not bad, sir,' said the officer. 'Might offer you a job here.'

This time he quickly got the information they needed – Boston was easier to call up than Megara. He came back from his office with chapter and verse about the dental surgeon.

This time it was the commander who made the call. In excellent English he announced himself to the dentist's secretary, who was so delighted to receive a call from a police officer in Switzerland that she interrupted her employer while he was with a patient. Dr Tullot came on the line to say he was busy for the moment but would return their call in about ten minutes.

'Right,' said Melchinahr, 'time for a little refreshment, I

175

think.' He opened a cupboard, brought out a bottle and glasses, and poured whisky for all three of them. 'No ice, I'm afraid, but there's water.'

'This is fine,' said the prince, taking a reviving swallow. He glanced at his watch: twenty minutes to twelve. He'd been here more than two hours. He got up. 'I'll have to leave you for a minute or two – my dog's in the car . . .'

'Oh, if you'll give me the keys, I'll have someone give him an airing,' said Schuls. 'That's if he's okay with strangers?'

'He speaks French,' said Greg. 'Just tell him, "*Doucement*", and he'll wag his tail.'

Grinning, Schuls went out. His chief said over the rim of his whisky glass, 'This looks as if it will turn out to be a very bad business, sir.'

'I'm afraid so.' He shook his head. 'Poor Elissa. How did she *get* out there on that mountainside?'

The commander had already thought it out. 'I imagine it was meant to look like a skiing accident. There's a long descent from the Piz Gloria, some of it tricky. Even a very good skier could get off-piste and go crashing into the trees.'

'Well, that rules out Elissa getting there on her own, because she never skied at all if she could help it.' He shook his head. 'Someone must have taken her there . . .'

'Yes, probably by ski-mobile from Lauterbrunnen. Got her to dress up in her ski clothes, bashed her on the head . . . Or perhaps bashed her on the head first and put the clothes on after . . . Or, you know . . . body and clothes could have been separate in a plastic bag, because if you covered her over with snow, she probably wouldn't be found for months, so it wouldn't matter if she was dressed—'

'Please stop,' Greg said. 'This is someone I used to know.'

'Sorry, sir. I was letting my enthusiasm run away with me.'

'I never liked her. She was a selfish little monster as a child. And from what I hear she grew up pretty disagreeable, but all the same . . . she didn't deserve a fate like that.'

The commander looked at him. The angular face was pale; the grey eyes were darkened by something that might be sorrow. 'More whisky?' he asked.

176

'No, thanks.' Despite himself he'd been caught up in the speculations of the security officer. 'You said he probably hit her on the head, but she died of meningitis – that was why she was at the Donati Clinic in the first place.'

'We don't know that, do we?

'Yes, we do. She was helicoptered from the house in Mürren—'

'We don't know that either. *Somebody* was helicoptered from the home to the clinic, but it might just as well have been the look-alike.'

'Oh . . . I hadn't thought of that.'

'And we've no proof that Mrs Paroskolos ever had meningitis. There were no other cases in the area.'

'But . . .' He broke off. He'd been going to say, 'Dr Donati diagnosed meningitis.' But the doctor was complicit in the whole affair. Nothing he said could be taken on trust. Had Elissa been a victim of murder? Plain, ordinary, cruel murder?

'But even if it's true she died of natural causes,' Melchinahr went on, 'and he was keeping it secret and just getting rid of the body, he'd have to do her some physical damage. If she's found, supposedly after a skiing accident, she's got to have killed herself in the collision, don't you see?'

'Why would he pile snow on top?'

'So her ski clothes wouldn't glint among the trees. Not that anyone was likely to notice, because the forest is, of course, evergreen, and it's dark in there even on a sunny day. Not likely to be found while the snow was lying – skiers whizz past too quickly. All the same, the killer was quite lucky. By the time some walker stumbled on the bones, the animals had made off with almost everything – and the stream would wash away a lot of stuff such as her skis during last year's spring thaw.'

The phone rang. Melchinahr picked it up. 'Yes, doctor. Yes, this is Commander Melchinahr. Thank you for ringing . . . yes, a former patient of yours. Identification, yes. Well, we could . . . No, that would be rather slow . . . We could send it to you by e-mail . . . Almost at once, you should receive photographs within the hour. Yes, I'm writing it down. Yes, thank you. I'm greatly obliged.'

'You're sending photographs of the jaw-bone by e-mail?' queried the prince.

'Exactly.' He pressed digits on his phone and was connected. 'Brebant, get on to the canton police, ask them for copies of the photographs of the teeth in the case of Unknown SCH4047, have them sent by broadband, and let me know the moment you have them on screen. They're to go to an e-mail address which I'll dictate to you. Right.'

He turned to Greg. 'So far so good. We'll just wait till that's been put in train and then I think we should go out for lunch. I hope you'll give me the pleasure of your company, sir?'

Truth to tell, the prince wasn't at all hungry. The news of the morning had made him queasy. On the other hand, the whisky that he'd swallowed rather rashly was having its effect on a nearly empty stomach so that he felt he ought to eat something.

So when the pictures had been sent on by e-mail and all they could do was wait for the result, he went with the commander to a nearby restaurant, busy because Sunday is always a day for going out to lunch. He ate grilled barbel with *rösti* and drank wine from the Ticino. When they got back to police headquarters, he was feeling more himself again. But the improvement was washed away by the news.

Dr Tullot could say with certainty that the work on the teeth pictured from Bern had been done by himself; and the jaw in which they remained had belonged to Elissa Dimitriouso, who had later married Niki Paroskolos.

Fourteen

About six o'clock that evening, Mr Crowne telephoned Bredoux to say he'd be staying away at least one more night. He was relieved and pleased when the phone was picked up at the other end by his grandmother.

'Ah, *c'est toi!*' she said. 'I got home just before lunch expecting to hear all the gossip from Kerouli, and your father tells me you're in Lauterbrunnen. What a disappointment!'

'I'm in Bern. And likely to be there for at least another day.'

'Bern? Ah well, *amuse-toi bien*,' she said with irony, for she had a poor opinion of the entertaining qualities of Bern.

'Grossmutti, since you're there, could you come to Bern tomorrow so as to—'

'Bern? On a Monday? You're joking. On a Monday in Bern everything is closed.'

'Dear Grandmama, it's no joke. I brought Rousseau with me and it's not a good situation: I'm closed in with officials talk-talk-talking, and the poor beast has to stay out in the car.'

'Alas for Rousseau,' said his grandmother without much sympathy.

'But you will come? And take him home . . .'

'I have other plans for tomorrow. I'm not driving all the way to Bern and back. I just drove all the way from France this morning.'

'There's no need to drive both ways. Come by train, and then you can drive Rousseau back in the Mercedes.'

'No, my dear, I don't find that attractive.'

'Then fly. You know how you love to fly.'

'Who is paying for all this, may I ask? You, out of your puny earnings as a concert manager?' This was one-upmanship, for

179

ex-Queen Nicoletta had just pocketed a very handsome cheque for her work on the drawing room and dining room of a French computer tycoon.

'The Swiss authorities will pay.'

The old lady gave a cry of disbelief. 'The Swiss authorities? Are you quite well, dear boy? They have been very kind to us, but never in the matter of money.'

'Well, this time they'll finance your trip, I can almost guarantee it. Because you see, when you come, you'll be bringing something important with you.'

'Shall I? And what is that, may I ask?'

'A wine glass.'

'A wine glass?'

'Yes, a very important wine glass.'

She snorted. 'And which of our supply of medium-quality glass do the Swiss authorities wish me to transport?'

'It's not one of ours. I brought it from Kerouli.'

There was a little pause. Then she said, 'From Kerouli, the island paradise where the Paroskolos couple dwell in marital bliss?'

'Yes, Grossmutti. From that very paradise.'

'Aha. The soup thickens.' Any possibility of intrigue always delighted Nicoletta. 'So I shall fly to Bern, hoping for a refund from the Swiss government, and I shall bring a wine glass.'

'And then drive home with Rousseau – yes.'

'The latter part I view with less interest, but I will do it. So where is this wine glass?'

'On the dressing table in my room.'

'Very well.'

'But, Grossmutti, it's wrapped in a handkerchief. Don't unwrap it.'

'No? *Warum nicht?*'

'Because it's got fingerprints on it.'

'Fingerprints of whom?' she cried.

'That remains to be seen. I'm hopeful that when the experts examine the glass and compare the prints, we'll know whose they are.'

Nicoletta was by now fully engaged. 'So I bring with me the wine glass and I take back the dog. I agree to all of it. This isn't exactly the gossip from Kerouli I was looking forward to, but perhaps it's even better. *Mon cher*, I expect a full explanation when we meet tomorrow. Will you come to the airport?'

'Of course.'

'And give me lunch?'

'That, certainly, but an explanation, no.'

'Why not?'

'Because it's all very confidential.'

'Hush-hush?' she asked. She loved to show off what she thought of as her colloquial English.

'Very hush-hush.'

Delighted with the whole thing, she was about to ring off when she thought of something: 'By the way, Grego, are you going into engineering?'

'Into what?'

'Engineering? I ask because you never showed any interest in it before.'

'I'm showing no interest in it now. Why do you ask?'

'Because there's an e-mail in the Inbox for you about hydraulics.'

'Ah!' The thought that something had appeared dealing with his everyday life gave the prince comfort. This day that was now coming to an end, and the one before, had been dismal for him. 'You misread it; it's not hydraulics, it's *hydraulis*. A musical instrument. What does the message say?'

'Some professor says the thing can be available for you during the early part of next year if Emilios agrees.'

'Splendid.'

'Who is Emilios?'

'The man who is having the *hydraulis* made. I wonder if he'll want to be paid or if mere pride of ownership will persuade him to let me put on a performance for nothing.'

'Why should he be proud of this thing?'

'Because it's over two thousand years old.'

'But you just said it was being made.'

'Well, it's being reconstructed. It's a water organ.'

'What?'

'A pipe organ powered by water.'

'Grego, I think you should take an aspirin and lie down. You're talking nonsense.'

'Never mind,' he laughed. 'What plane shall you take?'

'Oh, nothing early – I'm not going to get caught up in the businessmen's rush hour. Let's say something about eleven o'clock.'

'I'll be there to meet it. And, Grossmutti – don't forget the wine glass.'

'Of course not. I shall bring it, wrapped, and handled with lamb gloves.'

'Kid gloves.'

'Kid? That is a small child, no?'

'Yes, but it's also a baby goat.'

'You only say that to annoy me. I shall bring the wine glass safely. And you will buy me a very good lunch.'

When he had disconnected, he rang Liz's number in London. He got an answering machine. He knew it probably meant that she'd gone out of London over the weekend. In some big provincial department store, summer fashions would be hung on the clothes rails, the windows would be dressed for a big sales drive starting on Monday, and Liz would be in her element, urging, arguing, watching her darlings being set out to tempt the customers. She wouldn't want to be distracted by personal calls on her mobile.

He left a message asking her to ring when she could and giving the number of the Bern hotel chosen for him by the Special Security Office. It was a comfortable place, and he was glad of it, for he had had a gruelling day. All afternoon he'd been in close discussion with the commander and his associates. They were trying to decide what to do, for if the case was as the prince described it, it was a minefield.

At least three governments were involved: the Swiss, because the death of Elissa Paroskolos had occurred on Swiss soil; the Greek, because if the prince was right, a major fraud was being carried out in Greece; the United States, because one of their nationals was implicated – was perhaps a ringleader – in the fraud.

The officers had tried to work out who would have jurisdiction. Switzerland would want Niki Paroskolos and Dr Donati extradited: they had colluded at least in concealing a death, and perhaps in a murder. Greece would perhaps wish to contain the case within its own borders because the chief part of the fraud, the procurement of the Dimitriouso fortune, had been planned to happen there. The United States would be concerned about their citizen, Nancy Lanan, sure to be charged with participation and, at the moment, perhaps in considerable danger.

In the end they'd decided to consult with the United States Embassy. An appointment was made for the following day. Commander Melchinahr pitched his request on the grounds that he was worried about the fate of a young American woman who seemed to have disappeared in the Bernese Oberland during the previous year.

The mere fact that it was Commander Melchinahr making the request rang alarm bells at the Embassy. They knew Melchinahr didn't concern himself with minor matters. Barron, the security officer who took the call, was afraid the missing woman was some kind of agitator. The United States was at present very concerned about agitators and terrorists. He asked: 'What exactly have you got on the girl?'

Melchinahr hesitated. He didn't want to go into a long explanation on the telephone. Mr Crowne, who was listening on an extension, covered his receiver and prompted: 'Fingerprints.'

'Fingerprints?' Melchinahr mouthed in surprise.

Mr Crowne nodded emphatically. 'For him to verify.'

'Fingerprints,' said Melchinahar into the telephone, 'for you to verify.'

'Okay,' said Barron. 'You got anything about where she comes from – address, associates?'

Mr Crowne had already supplied Nancy's address and such information as he had about her career. Melchinahr passed these on.

'Okay, bring the prints and we'll have a meeting – say, two p.m. tomorrow?' He hung up, clearly much perturbed.

Mr Crowne then explained to the commander that there was a wine glass at home in Bredoux with the fingerprints of Nancy Lanan, and guaranteed he'd get someone to bring it in time for the meeting. He hadn't thought that the someone would be his grandmother, but in a way it was a relief. Explaining the project to his unworldly father and asking him to send someone with the wine glass would have been almost impossible.

The commander wanted to provide an escort to the airport next day, especially when he understood that the courier was none other than ex-Queen Nicoletta of Hirtenstein; but he was dissuaded, so that the prince set out with only Rousseau as companion.

Rousseau greeted his master's grandmother with politeness but little enthusiasm. Madame didn't like him coming into the house, scolded him for digging up the few flowers they were able to grow in the stony soil, disapproved of his hair shed on car seats; but he was resigned to going home with her and not entirely displeased. Running on the hillside at Lauterbrunnen had been fun, but in the city of Bern he had to be on a lead. Back at Bredoux, he had freedom within the boundaries of the old farm and was allowed to trot alongside the riding students when they went out.

So when, after lunch (a reasonably expensive one), the old lady took the wheel of the old Mercedes outside the restaurant, he climbed into the back without protest.

'So,' she said to her grandson, 'when shall you be home?'

'Who knows?'

'I begin to see that this is serious.' This she had deduced during lunch, when her grandson had avoided giving her any background on this mysterious business with the wine glass. She surveyed him with snapping dark eyes under an outrageous orange knitted cap. 'Take care, my child.' She offered her cheek to be kissed, smiled at him, and drove away.

He went into the office building with the precious glass wrapped in its handkerchief and in a cardboard box supplied by Grossmutti. Schuls took it out, placed it gingerly on the commander's desk, and bent to study it.

'Beautiful,' he said. 'Thumb and three fingers.'

'But what if they've nothing to compare it to?' he murmured.

'Oh, the FBI will have been at work by now – gone to this girl's home in wherever it was . . .'

'Bloomington.'

'Yes, there, and found prints—'

'But it's months since she was there. She rented the place out for the period of her trip abroad. The tenant or tenants—'

'*Ach, Mensch*, there are always prints if you know how to look for them. And the FBI are experts. They'll have something ready to compare.'

So it proved. At the Embassy, after the preliminary introductions, the wine glass was handed over to a technician, who disappeared with it. Mr Crowne launched into his account of what he thought had happened to Elissa. He even touched briefly on his fears that her father Yanni might not have met an accidental death, for he was growing more convinced of that the more he thought of it. Bob Barron, who'd expected a tale of protesters or dissidents, listened with growing alarm. This was far worse than a group of dopey college students waving banners about globalisation.

He was still asking apprehensive questions when the technician came back.

'Perfect match,' he reported. 'She'd rented her apartment furnished, but she'd locked her computer and stuff in a closet for safety. So we got prints off the keyboard and, for verification, from a photography file – you know, some old-style transparencies she'd supplied to various magazines before she went digital. The prints on the transparencies are undoubtedly those of Nancy Lanan, and they match the prints from the wine glass.'

Greg had had no doubt of it, yet having it confirmed seemed somehow to make it more frighteningly real. His heart sank into his footwear. Nancy Lanan was part of a conspiracy to commit major fraud. Moreover, she was likely to meet an untimely end once the fraud had achieved its desired result, unless he and the men with him did something to prevent it.

'What happens now?' he asked, stifling a groan.

'That's the million dollar question,' said Barron. 'You're saying that this woman's on this Greek island, impersonating the wife of a millionaire?'

'She's impersonating the wife of an airline owner who's in considerable trouble, and who wants to inherit the fortune she'll control once she signs the trust deeds.'

185

'You say "inherit?"' queried Barron.

'Well, we're sure the real Elissa Paroskolos is dead. I think it's probable the fake Elissa will be dead before too long.'

Melchinahr was nodding agreement. 'You see, Bob, this young woman from Bloomington is a journalist, not a professional criminal. How she got sucked into all this is a mystery – but if you'd carried out a swindle as big as this, would you keep an amateur hanging around, someone who could get a fit of conscience and turn state's evidence?'

'Unless Niki intends to go on for ever living with this stand-in?' Schuls suggested. 'Did you get the impression he was in love with this girl? I mean, it could actually be a crime of passion, getting rid of his real wife because he'd fallen for this look-alike.'

That was a thought. But when he'd given it consideration, Greg shook his head. 'I think *she's* very much under his influence, relies and depends on him, like a young girl in the throes of her first romance. Niki was always very attentive and caring with her. But as to any evidence of a grand passion . . . no, I don't think that came into it.'

'You say she relies and depends on him?' Barron asked.

'Yes, because of the effects of her illness – her memory and so forth . . .' He trailed off into silence. The others looked at him, waiting. 'But of course this is Nancy Lanan. She never had meningitis. It was Elissa who got ill.'

'Yeah,' said Barron, 'Elissa got ill. According to who?'

'According to Dr Donati.'

'Who's there on Kerouli with the fake Elissa.' Barron looked grim. 'You can't believe a word that doctor said. And that opens the possibility that Ms Lanan is there under duress—'

'No, excuse me. My friend Liz Blair and I took Elissa – I mean Nancy – for a day out in Athens. She went back to the island absolutely willingly, made no attempt to get away.'

'Oh, hell,' said Barron, and was silent.

'Which means she's part of the plot,' Melchinahr said.

'Yeah.'

'We've got to inform the Greek authorities,' Melchinahr went on. 'One of their nationals has died under suspicious circumstances in Swiss territory. Her place has been taken by another woman, undoubtedly for the purposes of fraud.'

'Do you know anybody at the Greek Embassy?' Greg asked, as a general question.

The others exchanged glances. 'Well, no, not personally,' said Barron. 'It's a consulate and it's in Zurich, so we don't meet often except at government events and, of course, they have a party on their national day in March . . .'

'Same here,' said Melchinahr.

'What about CIA contacts? The Greeks have security problems like everybody else, Mr Barron. Don't you consult from time to time?'

Barron looked uncomfortable. 'Greek problems aren't my sphere.'

'But you could find someone here in the US Embassy who could make contact?'

'Ye-es.' He had the diplomat's usual reluctance to admit that anything undercover was going on in, near, or around an embassy.

After much polite fencing Barron agreed he could get someone to contact someone among the small Greek diplomatic fraternity in Switzerland. 'What we'll do,' he suggested, 'is get them to agree to let a couple of our people go to this island – what is it, Kerouli? – to assess the situation. I've already asked the guys in Athens if anything unusual's been happening there, and so far it's all quiet, but I'd like a closer look-see.'

'No,' said Mr Crowne.

'What d'you mean, no?'

'Niki isn't going to allow any strangers on his terrain – especially not now, when things must be very fraught for him. He's got this sick girl on his hands—'

'But hang on a minute: I thought you said it was Elissa who was sick . . .'

'Ye-es . . . But the fact is,' Mr Crowne said, frowning and shaking his head, 'when I called Nancy by her real name, she fainted.'

They all sat for a moment, considering that fact.

'Well, that's not strange,' Barron suggested. 'It meant they'd been found out, didn't it?'

187

'Yes, and she must have told Niki . . .'

'Hey,' said Barron, 'she told Niki you'd found them out, but you've been gone three days and apparently done nothing about it! And neither has Niki. How d'you explain that? To Niki it must seem weird. Ever since you left this dinky little island, he must have been expecting the sky to fall in on him.'

'Unless . . .'

'What?'

'Unless she never told him.'

'But surely she would have to tell him, sir,' objected Melchinahr. 'It meant the whole scheme was falling to pieces.'

'I think . . . I think she probably forgot that I called her Nancy.'

'Aw, come on, Your Highness; you couldn't forget a thing like that!' Barron cried.

'Well, so you would think, but there *is* something really wrong with Nancy's memory. It's what first made me think something odd was going on. She had – I don't know how to describe it – sort of flashes when things came into her mind. She blurted out these scraps about visiting the snake-handling place, and dancing to Cajun music . . .' He got up and moved about restlessly for a moment or two. Then he went to stand behind his chair, staring at the others. 'I'm beginning to wonder if perhaps it was *Nancy* who had meningitis. That's something we've never even thought about.'

There were muffled exclamations and a long indrawn breath from Barron. After the first shock of the suggestion, he began to experience some relief. It meant that the American citizen at present impersonating the wife of Niki Paroskolos could plead mental incapacity. But after that came the thought that, if this young woman were really sick, she was an even greater danger to Niki once the trust deeds were signed. She was unstable, unreliable. Her life expectancy seemed greatly reduced by the prince's suggestion.

'We've got to get her out of there,' he said.

'Absolutely,' said Melchinahr. 'As quickly as possible.'

'I could send in a snatch team . . .'

'There's only one jetty,' said the prince. 'They wouldn't let you land.'

188

'One jetty – you mean the coast is bad?'

'Rocky . . . nothing but cliffs.'

'High cliffs?'

'Vertiginous.'

'Vertiginous,' echoed Barron, unable to repress a smile. 'All the same, we've got guys who can scale cliffs.'

'No,' said Melchinahr, 'there's sure to be security on the island: watchmen, alarms . . .'

'Yes, and if you set them off, how long do you think Nancy Lanan would survive?' added Schuls. 'Nice high cliffs – over she goes; and she's the main evidence, isn't she? If you lose her, the only case against those two evil men is that they concealed the death of Elissa Paroskolos here in Switzerland.'

They argued, put up ideas, knocked them down, and became more and more frustrated the more they talked. At last, and unwillingly, the prince said, 'Well . . . I could go. And take a Greek detective with me.'

'No, no, we can't let you do that: that'd be against protocol – no amateurs should be included in any CIA project.'

'But it isn't just a CIA project, Bob,' Melchinahr pointed out. 'That's just the point.'

'But the prince would be in danger, chief,' Schuls said.

'Perhaps not,' said the subject of his anxiety. 'Not if Nancy has forgotten I know her real name.'

'That's a big gamble.'

'No-o . . . I don't think so.' He paused. 'I got to know her a bit. The more I think about it, the more I think she may have had some sort of breakdown, some illness. I spoke to the editorial people on a magazine she worked for. They painted a picture of a girl in complete control of her life, a girl completely different from the one I met on Kerouli.'

'That could be explained simply by the strain she's under.'

'Perhaps. But I think it's because her mind is playing tricks on her. So I think it's quite likely that she's never been able to explain to Niki why she fainted, and that's why life on Kerouli is going on as normal.'

'Could be,' muttered Barron. 'Could be.'

After more discussion it began to seem that a return visit by

His Serene Highness the ex-Crown Prince of Hirtenstein was the best way of getting someone on to the island.

'We'd better send a woman agent with you,' Barron said, 'because if this Lanan woman is really out of her skull, she'll need a female escort. We'll arrange for one of our women agents to meet you in Athens . . .'

'How am I going to explain the fact that I'm coming with a woman companion?'

'You can just say she's your girlfriend.'

'But that's the point! I was there with Liz only last week! They know Liz and I are what you call an item.'

'Okay then, you can make up some sort of story . . .'

'Certainly, I can make up a story, but Niki isn't likely to believe it. You've got to put yourself in his place, Barron. He almost got the papers signed last week, but Nancy fainted. Now he's on tenterhooks, trying to get the trustees together and stage the thing again. He's not going to be keen on having me barge in with a gang of complete strangers.'

'How big is this visiting party going to be?' Schuls put in. He glanced at Barron. 'It's clear a local CIA agent has to go, and the Athens fraud squad will send someone, and there's the prince . . .' He broke off to address himself to Greg. 'Will Niki Paroskolos accept all that?'

'The thing will be not to ask him,' Greg said, thinking about it as he spoke. 'We should just turn up at his jetty and there'll be boatmen there, because they're always handling supplies and mail. They'll recognize me because I was off and on the jetty all last week.'

'And they'll let you ashore?'

'I think so. There's a little office with a two-way radio or something; they can talk to the boats and to the housekeeper up at the house. I can be put through to the house and say . . .'

'Yeah. Say what?'

'Say I'm on my way somewhere else and just stopped by to bring a present for the invalid.'

'What present?' insisted Barron.

'For heaven's sake, how do I know? Something to do with clothes. She and Liz got quite close, and practically all they seemed to talk about was clothes.'

190

Barron looked thoughtful. 'Your friend Liz would be a great advantage. You say she got close to Lanan?'

'Yes, but—'

'If you arrived at the jetty with this girlfriend and a present, it would look a lot less scary to Niki Paroskolos.'

It was true enough – but uninviting. 'Just the two of us, you mean?'

'Very unthreatening, wouldn't you say?'

'Unthreatening. Yes. But then what happens?'

'You get Lanan down to the jetty somehow and we snatch her.'

'What?' cried Melchinahr and Schuls in unison.

'Yeah, why not? That's the whole bit, isn't it? Once we've got her, she's safe, and she's the witness that will put them in jail.'

'But the people up at the house will take off before you get back again.'

'Who says we're going anywhere? Look, we send a launch with whatever force the Greek guys think will be necessary. They stay on the launch, His Highness and his girl go up to the house and sweet-talk Nancy down to the pier. We grab her, then the Greek police march up to the house and arrest the big shots.'

The Swiss security officers looked startled. Strong-arm measures were seldom used in their jurisdiction. 'Isn't that kidnap?' wondered Melchinahr.

'The girl's a criminal. She's being arrested by the Greek authorities, but we get her under our protection because she's simple-minded and a US citizen. Of course, we'll produce her in court any time they want her.'

'It could work,' Schuls said to his boss. Melchinahr shrugged, to signify that there was nothing he could do about it anyhow, since this was all going to happen a long way away.

'What do you say, sir?' Barron asked the prince.

'I'm not going to involve Liz in anything where she could get hurt—'

'Who's going to hurt her? She arrives at Kerouli with you and carrying a carrier bag with a fashion-house name. The two of you go up to the house, have coffee or a drink or

191

something, hand over the present and bring her down to the jetty—'

'Trudi won't let her.'

'Who's Trudi?' said all three men in surprise.

'The nurse,' said Mr Crowne. 'Though, now I come to think of it, she's more like a watchdog. She won't let Nancy go down to the jetty.'

'Aw, come on; you can take care of that, can't you? Persuade her, or give her the slip, or something.'

'I suppose so.' He was trying to think his way through the plan put up by the American. 'There's one point you've overlooked, though. My friend Liz has a mind of her own. She might not agree to any of this.'

'Oh.' Barron looked dashed. 'She'll be scared?'

'That's not likely. But she has a life of her own: she may not want to go rushing off to Kerouli at a moment's notice.'

'But I thought you said she and Nancy had a connection going?'

'Well, yes. And that will count, of course. I'll explain everything to her and I expect she'll want to . . . to play a part in the plan . . . but I have to talk it through with her face to face.'

'Okay,' Barron said. 'I'll get going on travel arrangements—'

'Just a minute,' interrupted the commander in a wry tone. 'This has been a very rewarding conversation and I agree with what's been said. But I've got to point something out: a crime has been committed in the canton of Bern – whether a minor crime, such as failing to report a death, or a major crime, like murder, we don't know, but *the law has been broken.*' He tapped the table hard with his forefinger. 'An examining magistrate ought to be handling the case. That can't happen until I inform the canton police. I've known about this crime for over twenty-four hours. I *have* to put them in the picture before the day's end.'

Bob Barron gave a moan. He understood the demands of Swiss law. 'The minute it goes to the magistrate, you'll be asked for a statement,' he said to Greg. 'You're the mover and shaker as to the missing Elissa Paroskolos – in fact, the *only* reason for any action.'

192

'Well, I'm quite prepared . . .' He broke off. It dawned on him what he was being told. When Melchinahr informed the canton police, he'd be invited to come to the police station, and perhaps be kept there for hours while first the statement was taken and then preliminary investigations took place in Mürren. He might even be asked to go to Mürren to 'confront' Dr Deboisie with his claim that Elissa Paroskolos had been a patient there. But if he was detained in Switzerland by the Bern Canton police, he couldn't be in Greece trying to prevent a gigantic fraud and perhaps a murder.

He caught Bob Barron's eye and gave an imperceptible nod.

'I understand,' he said. 'Shall we say that I'll go to Athens as soon as I'm able to do so, and that in the meantime you, Mr Barron, will arrange things through your embassy there?'

'Certainly, sir,' Barron agreed. 'You're at the Fegerhof, yes?'

'That's right.'

'I may give you a ring – just to let you know how things are going.'

'I'd appreciate that.'

He shook hands all round and left. He was sure the others had things to say that were unfit for his ears – things about manipulating the system, carrying out acts that weren't strictly according to the rules.

He went to the hotel, where there was a seven-word message from Liz: 'I'm back in London and longing to hear from you.' He was packing his bag when his phone rang. He snatched it up, hoping it might be Liz, but it was Bob Barron.

'The others have gone back to their office to tell some tale to the examining magistrate,' he said. 'You ready to go?'

'Just got to pay my bill and I'll be gone.'

'Don't bother, we'll take care of the bill. You going to London to see your girlfriend?'

'Yes, but first I need to go home to get a few clothes.'

'Got you. Then London, and then Greece. So okay, one airline ticket Bern-to-Geneva, one Geneva-to-London, then two tickets to Athens. You can collect them from the Departures desk. You'll be met at Athens – I'm setting it up now. Bon voyage, pal.'

193

Greg took the next flight to Geneva. As Barron had foretold, tickets were awaiting him at the airport. He was home for dinner.

His elders were pleased to see him, but perplexed by his announcement that he was leaving for London by the late-evening flight. 'But, my boy, you've only just got home—'

'I know, Papa, but I have to go. And in the meantime I have phone calls to make, so can I use your office?'

'If you want to,' said ex-King Anton with a shrug. Presumably his son wanted to telephone to his girlfriend in London and wanted to do it in private. The problem was, of course, that Nicoletta disapproved of the girl, so that if a call came through on the house phone, she banged about making as much noise as she could and huffing in displeasure. In fact Nicoletta was frowning already at the thought that her grandson was going to speak to that unsuitable young woman.

However, the prince didn't telephone his girlfriend. He'd thought of something that might help Commander Melchinahr when it was learned that the chief witness in *l'affaire Paroskolos* had flown the coop. He called Marcel Soumier, his lawyer. 'Marcel, sorry to bother you again, but you know that tape I made at your apartment on Saturday?'

'Yes, it's safe in my desk . . .'

'Would you get a copy made and send it to Commander Melchinahr at police HQ in Bern?'

'What?'

'I haven't time to go into details, Marcel, but they've found remains—'

'Remains!'

'And there's an enquiry getting started. They'll need to know the information that's on the tape.'

'They'll want a personal statement, Grego—'

'Be quiet and listen. Send a copy of the tape with a declaration that you were present when it was made and can swear to its authenticity, and say that it's sent at my request. Get it there by special messenger if you have to – it must reach them tomorrow and the earlier the better.'

'There's something you're not telling me, Grego.'

'Quite right. But it's nothing serious, so don't get anxious.'

He ate a hasty meal with his family. His grandmother kept eyeing him as if she wanted to ask questions but had enough sense not to. His father was still murmuring that he was doing too much travelling and ought to stay at home a few days to get some rest.

He managed to catch the mid-evening flight to London. He didn't have to wait for baggage from the carousel at Heathrow. He rang Liz to tell her where he was and to say he was about to join the taxi queue.

'Greg!' she cried in delight. 'Why didn't you let me know? I could have come to pick you up.'

'Never mind. I'll be there in about an hour. I've something very important to say to you.'

She hesitated, then laughed. 'You're not going to propose, are you? You know that's not allowed.'

'It's about Elissa,' he said.

'Oh.' Any amusement was banished. 'What about her?'

'I'll tell you when I get there.'

She was waiting with the door of her flat open the minute he rang the downstairs bell. They kissed in greeting, but it wasn't the kind of kiss he might have got if this had been a pleasant surprise visit. He took off his raincoat; she took it and his travel bag and put them in the bedroom.

When she returned, he was sitting on the sofa with one hand out to pull her down beside him.

'Is it very bad, Greg?' she asked with an unwonted timidity.

'She's dead, Liz.'

'Oh, no!' But she'd known that was what he was going to say.

When he finished recounting the events of the last three days, she began to cry. He was astounded. He'd never seen her cry before. He took her in his arms, stroked her hair, murmured words of comfort. He heard himself saying idiotically, 'It's all right, it's all right.' But of course it would never be all right again for Elissa Paroskolos.

By and by she disentangled herself from him, dried her eyes, and got up. 'Well, I'm going to make some coffee. And then you're going to tell me why you came, because it wasn't just to say they'd found bones on the mountain, now was it?'

'No, *chérie,* it wasn't. I came to ask you to go back to Kerouli with me.'

She paused and turned at the door. 'No.' She made a gesture of pushing something away. 'I never want to go back to that place again.'

'It's necessary, Liz.'

'Not for me. And not for you either! You have no responsibility in this.'

'No responsibility towards Nancy Lanan?'

'It's a police matter, Greg.'

'In the end, yes. But Nancy's there, on that island, with two men who may well have murdered Elissa—'

'Niki and Dr Donati. A doctor . . . Do you really think Dr Donati would . . . It seems hard to think of that.'

'We don't know for sure. But Elissa is dead, and they've not only concealed the fact but set up someone else in her place. It's a situation I wouldn't wish on my worst enemy.'

'I can't believe Nancy is a plotter, Greg,' she protested. 'I only knew her during the last few days but she didn't strike me—'

'I understand what you're saying. It's begun to seem to me that perhaps she's ill. It seems she's said nothing to Niki about the fact that I called her by her real name, almost as if it made no impression on her. Her memory *did* seem strange, now didn't it? As if she's not quite right in the head . . .'

'Please don't say that, Greg! It would mean she's there, utterly defenceless, on that little island with two men who . . . who . . .'

He caught the point and took it a stage further. 'If we let things get to the moment where she actually signs those trust papers, she could be in very great danger.'

'No, wait, that doesn't follow, Greg. She might sign the trust deed and then make over the money to Niki, by some apparently legal transfer.'

'So she might. But she'd be a source of enormous anxiety to those two men afterwards, wouldn't she?'

196

'But . . . but perhaps she loves Niki enough to go on living with him as Elissa—'

'You feel she loves Niki? Is that what you felt while we were there? I genuinely want to know, Liz. Did you get the impression of a woman passionately in love?'

She stood with her head bent, rubbing one hand against another as she considered. In the end she shook her head.

'No, I didn't think there was that kind of relationship between them. She was grateful and affectionate and . . . and *obedient* – more like a little sister than a wife.' She tried to recollect what she'd seen and heard on Kerouli. 'I liked her a lot,' she remarked. 'I enjoyed being with her, but I thought of her as Elissa, who you always said was bossy and difficult. So it was a surprise to me that she was so . . . I don't know how to say it . . . so soft, weak – so dependent on Niki and Donati.'

'That's more or less how I saw her. And now we know it wasn't Elissa, it was Nancy Lanan, a woman they've brought in from outside, a stranger to them. I can't imagine they'd have much confidence in her as a sturdy co-conspirator.'

'You really think they might harm her?'

'I really do think that.'

She came back to him, leaned against him so as to hide her face. 'Well, then,' she said in a muffled voice, 'we've got to go to Kerouli, haven't we?'

Fifteen

The council of war was taking place in Mr Crowne's hotel room, in an Athens hotel far more lush and expensive than he would ever have chosen. It was being paid for by the generous Bob Barron, presumably. The room was, of course, a bedroom, but it was large and had a comfortable seating area by the window. Drinks had been sent up from the bar.

He and Liz had taken an early-morning flight and been met at the airport as promised. The CIA agent introduced himself as Jermyn ('Call me Jerry') Golfondi, and it was he who was chairing the meeting. Big and beefy, he was sipping bourbon.

Also present was Pano Tripidis of the Fraud Investigation Bureau of the Greek police. Tripidis kept giving Mr Crowne accusing glances, as if he held him somehow responsible for dropping this dreadful mess on his doorstep.

Of course, from his point of view, it *was* a dreadful mess – a career-demolishing mess, if this so-called prince from some unheard-of state in Europe had got things wrong. Tripidis had been up all the previous night, listening to the CIA man setting out the problem and his solution to it. He still wasn't entirely convinced, particularly by Golfondi's proposition.

Arrive in a borrowed launch? Stay in it, under cover, until this fellow and his lady-love brought yet another young woman down to the pier? Grab the young woman, stow her aboard, and then lead his team up what had been described as a steep winding path, to arrest – to *arrest* – Niki Paroskolos? Niki Paroskolos, owner of a well-known air-freight line, upright citizen of the Greek Republic, husband to one of the country's richest women?

It was a fantasy, a nightmare.

Yet, if what the royal nobody suggested were true, Elissa Paroskolos was dead – Elissa Paroskolos, pain in the neck to any police force because she expected protection wherever she was yet wouldn't accept restriction on her movements; Elissa Paroskolos, fashion plate, admired by his wife for her film-star appearance, her jet-style life. She was dead?

It couldn't be true, and yet documents had been faxed from the Swiss police that confirmed they had found parts of her cadaver: bones, in a grove of pine trees on a mountainside – this seemed to be all that remained of the admired Elissa Paroskolos.

So it had been ordained that he must take part in this enterprise, because the event about to happen (if all this proved true) was a monstrous fraud, which the Greek government would not permit. So he was here, taking part in what Golfondi called 'the fine tuning'.

'Barron suggested there would be some sort of security – alarms, perhaps men on patrol – can you extend our info on that?' Golfondi was asking the princeling. Tripidis snorted inwardly: he was a republican from his bald head to the soles of his bony feet. He thought all regal persons were bound to be victims of recessive genes.

'You mean infra-red lights, things like that? I didn't notice anything. Did you, Liz?'

That was another thing: his girlfriend was an active ingredient in this affair. His girlfriend! If you wanted any proof this was a crazy business, you had it in that fact.

The girlfriend was saying that she'd noticed no security. 'Except the inflexible Trudi,' she said, with a laugh. 'She stuck to Elissa like glue.'

'But she's a nurse, right?'

'A muscular nurse.'

Golfondi shrugged. He paid more than lip service to equality of the sexes but he didn't doubt he could take care of any woman, no matter how muscular. Besides, this girl and her royal boyfriend were going to distract the nurse while they snatched Lanan. It was imperative to get Lanan offstage – his superiors had stressed it to him. The fact that she might be about to be murdered was of less importance to them than the embarrassment she would cause as an acknowledged participant in this scam. Billions were involved. There had been enough financial scandals already in the past year or so.

Golfondi was more confident about the business in hand than Tripidis. In the first place, he believed in the conspiracy. Evildoing among financiers could almost be taken as read these days. So he didn't approach the matter with the near-disbelief that he sensed in his Greek colleague.

Moreover, although he was as devoted to republicanism as Tripidis, he was inclined to like this tall, angular guy with the quiet manner. He couldn't help having been born a prince, now could he? And he didn't pull rank. He'd registered in the hotel as plain Mr Crowne – couldn't get more republican than that.

Besides, he was their best hope of rescuing an American girl from a situation that would end badly, one way or another.

'What I think we have to take into consideration,' Mr Crowne was saying, 'is that by now Niki is probably in a very nervous state. So though Liz and I didn't notice any alarm systems or security patrols *then*, they may just have been switched off for the period of the birthday celebrations.'

'If there were any, he's activated them now, you mean.'

'Wouldn't you think so? Or taken at least some precautions.'

'If we could only get some inside information . . . Tripidis, have you any contacts among the ferry operators?'

'Ferry services don't operate to Kerouli. It has only its own private boat service.'

'Ugh . . .' muttered Golfondi.

'You were always chatting up the boatmen and the servants,' Liz suggested, nodding at Greg. 'Couldn't you go down to Piraeus and find someone at the jetty?'

'It would be a matter of luck whether any of the men I've talked to are around at the moment.' He ran them through his mental assize. Then he brightened. 'But we don't have to wander about in Piraeus, Liz! There's always Great-aunt Irene.'

Who was Great-aunt Irene? the two detectives wanted to know. After explanations, Jerry Golfondi was enthusiastic. Old ladies, he'd always found, were a great source of information if you had time to spend on them. Even Tripidis was impressed.

He knew from direct experience that gossip was part of the lifestyle of grandmothers and great-aunts.

'We must go at once and question her!' he cried.

'Nothing of the sort. Do you want to scare her to death? We'll invite her to dinner,' said Mr Crowne.

'What?'

'She'll love it,' agreed Liz. 'Ring her now, Greg.'

There was a delay while he found the telephone number again, but within ten minutes he was speaking to the old lady.

'Your Highness!' she exclaimed in delight. 'How delightful to hear from you again! Are you speaking from your home in Geneva?' This was to let him know she remembered everything from their previous conversation, including his few remarks about Bredoux.

'No, Liz and I are in Athens again.'

'So soon? You love us so much?'

'Yes, undoubtedly, love of Greece has brought us back. Also, a matter of business. You may remember I told you a little about a musical instrument . . .'

'Ah yes, being made by a group of students.'

'Yes, exactly; your memory is remarkable. Well, that's why we're here, so we thought perhaps you would like to come again to share a meal with us.'

There was a tiny pause. She was surprised and touched by the invitation. When she spoke again there was a faint quaver in her voice. 'That's extremely kind of you, sir.'

'Not at all. Is it too much to hope that you're free this evening?'

'I am, of course. What is there for an old lady like me except television or bridge with a few friends? And neither of them is so attractive as being in your company, sir. Of course I am free, yes, of course.'

'Then may I send a taxi as before? And we shall expect you by and by. We are at the Hotel Serena this time.'

'The Serena!' she breathed. One of the best hotels in Athens. Not only was she meeting royalty again, she was going to eat dinner in the Serena. She was ready to die of happiness.

The two men, who spoke Greek, had followed the conversation and were nodding approval. Liz saw their satisfaction and smiled at Mr Crowne, but he was frowning. 'I feel a bit of a cad,' he murmured to her. 'We're taking advantage of an old lady.'

'But it's in a good cause,' she said reassuringly. 'Besides, she'll have a great time.'

Great-aunt Irene appeared as before, clad in black; but this time it was a dress of rustling black taffeta. The pearls, though perhaps only fake because any real ones must have been sold long ago, were now matched by pearl-drop earrings. Liz, who'd packed for a far less expensive ambience, was outclassed in her white silk top and linen skirt.

Golfondi and Tripidis were eating in the hotel dining room but at another table. It had been agreed that to have two detectives in the party would make things difficult – how were they to be explained, and would Great-aunt Irene resent them? For, of course, she wanted her prince to herself. Liz Blair she could accept, because royalty was always allowed its paramours; but two men, two strangers, cramping her style? Never.

Once the food and wine had been ordered, the old lady plunged into conversation. She wanted to know what Mr Crowne had been doing, and with whom, and when she heard about his dog Rousseau she asked his pedigree and whether he had been shown at Cruft's. She was disappointed to learn that he'd never appeared there. Rousseau belonged to a prince: he should have honours too.

There was no difficulty in getting her to talk about Kerouli. 'Of course, everything is very quiet there now,' she remarked. 'All the catering staff have gone, and that lovely pavilion has been emptied and locked up, alas. And I hear Dr Donati might be leaving in a day or two.'

'Oh? Elissa is so much better?' He didn't know whether this was good news or bad.

'Not exactly, though I hear she's up and about after having had some sort of collapse.' She stopped and waited for Mr Crowne to tell her what kind of collapse, because he'd been there when it had happened.

'Yes, poor thing; she fainted when she was about to sign all the papers,' Liz said. 'Too much fuss and anxiety . . .'

'Certainly, one rather thinks Niki made too much of the birthday,' agreed Great-aunt Irene. 'So it was just a faint, was it? I heard it was some sort of a fit – brought on by the after-effects of the ailment, the . . . menin . . .'

'The meningitis. No, nothing as dramatic as that, dear lady. It was a simple faint. And so she's well enough for Dr Donati to think of leaving?'

'Ah, it's not that,' the old lady said, leaning forward so as to be confidential. 'There's been some little trouble at his clinic in Switzerland. No doubt something of the sort that happened before.'

'Oh? What happened before?' He felt his tone was too alert, but the old lady took it for the interest of a fellow gossip.

'Haven't you heard the story Costa Paroskolos tells? Ah, perhaps you didn't meet him . . .'

'Yes, he was there overnight on the first day we were there. But he was singing the praises of the Donati Clinic.'

'No doubt, for the treatment was effective for him – paid for, of course, by his kind-hearted brother. But while he was there, it seems there was a three-way romance going on between two male patients and one female – a sort of *ménage à trois* – quite blatant, and strictly against the rules. It resulted in the lady suffering a very bad setback in her recovery.' Her eyes twinkled with enjoyment. 'Love will find a way, not so? Even if it leads to exhaustion and prostration. But Dr Donati would have been severely censured if it had become known. So if he has had bad news of that sort, it's no wonder he thinks of hurrying home.'

Interesting though the story was, Mr Crowne had almost no doubt that the 'little trouble' was his own nocturnal prowl at the clinic. During his search in the records office he might have left something out of place and so attracted attention; and certainly the security patrol would have reported a stranger on the grounds.

'So in the near future there will be only Niki and Elissa and the household staff? That will be dull for them after all the recent excitement.'

'And perhaps better for Elissa. It's difficult for me to imagine her so easily overthrown by a few festivities – I never knew her well, even as a child, but she always seemed to me to be so much in control of everything. But there . . . this strange ailment . . .' She sighed.

'If Dr Donati leaves, I suppose that means Elissa's state of health is acceptable. I mean, so far as signing legal documents and . . .'

'Well, the rumour is that one of the trustees is being a little difficult on that score.'

'Really?'

'So one hears. Ignatius – did you meet Ignatius? He's Cousin Katerina's son – he has a friend in the law office of Martin Crissoulis, and there they're saying that Mr – now I forget his name, an American one who plays golf – that *he* is very unwilling to fly back to Greece unless he's given an assurance that Elissa is absolutely fit.'

The American one who played golf was Leskowski. His view of the matter might well be shared by other trustees. They were all busy rich men, unused to ordering their lives to suit someone else; but they were executors of the trust, so in the end they would have to gather to witness the signature.

However, it seemed the 'rescue team' had at least a little leeway.

During the flow of conversation it emerged that the staff on Kerouli now consisted of the house servants under the *chef de maison* and two gardeners recently hired. 'Just imagine,' snorted Great-aunt Irene, 'Niki fired Vathis and Philippos! They'd been there for almost twenty years. Who else knows what to feed those great plants in their great pots? But it seems he wanted younger men, and it's understandable because Vathis must be . . . what? Seventy-three or four. But I don't understand about the boats.'

'What about the boats?'

'He's got rid the fleet that were in use during the birth-day celebrations. That's understandable: most of them were additional to the household boats; they were only hired for that week. But ever since Yanni took over the island and made it

204

into a home, there have been three boats on the payroll, plying regularly back and forth And now only one!'

'That's a big change,' said Liz. 'How do they manage about mail and so on?'

'Well, the *Ikaris* takes out the mail in the morning and any supplies that have been ordered. Then it returns almost immediately with outgoing mail so as to catch the midday collection at the harbour.' She was shaking her head. 'Life is so different nowadays. Letters . . . Letters used to be so important, but now I imagine you young things telephone and fax and use computers.'

'I'm afraid we do,' Liz agreed with a smile. 'I shan't have any billets doux to keep tied in a ribbon when I'm old.'

'Ah, child, you'll have memories . . . nothing can take those away.' She sipped her wine, mournful for a moment, then returned to her enjoyable criticism of the changes at Kerouli. 'I hear Spiro thinks it's very bad, not having the boat moored at the island overnight – Spiro runs the boat, you know. It makes them so isolated, don't you think?' Then, with a laugh: 'But, of course, Niki would summon a helicopter in an emergency.'

'On the big day, the actual birthday when the trust was to be finalized,' said Liz, knowing the old lady would love to hear about it, 'helicopters brought the birthday cake, and the legal people. Greg and I got a lift back to the airport on one after the party came to pieces.'

'Is it thrilling to travel in a helicopter? No doubt that's how they'll transport the visitors if the sale goes through.'

'The sale?'

'Haven't I mentioned it?' She was delighted to realize there was still something else to convey. 'Some of the staff who were dismissed are saying that Niki is going to persuade Elissa to sell the island. I forget whether he had been approached, or whether he made overtures first; but the major-domo let it slip that he'd been asked for facts and figures to do with accommodation on the island, by which he gathered it was being looked at as a resort hotel.'

'Oh no!' Liz lamented. 'That would completely spoil it.'

'Dear Yanni would turn in his grave,' agreed Irene. 'And

Elissa adored her father, you know. I can't believe she'd ever agree to it.'

Since she's dead, thought Mr Crowne grimly, *she won't have any say in the matter*. But it was a sign of Niki's desperation over money. Anything to bridge the gap until he could get his hands on his wife's fortune after some conveniently arranged death for Nancy Lanan.

When Great-aunt Irene left, Mr Crowne ensured there was no opportunity for curtseys and hand-kissing. He knew that the watching detectives would think it ridiculous. She left in a state of high delight, however, because, while buying the required present in the clothes shop for Elissa, Liz had slipped into the boutique next door to buy a beautiful little lace mantilla for elderly churchgoing. Great-aunt Irene was clutching it to her heart when she entered the taxi.

'Well, what did she say?' Golfondi demanded when they gathered in the bar for a conference over bourbon and ouzo.

'Do you want the long version or the short?' Liz countered with a grin.

Mr Crowne frowned at her. 'She says the island staff has been reduced to household servants and two recently hired gardeners. For gardeners, read local toughs, I should think. Only one boat has been retained, and it goes out and back each morning with the mail.'

'He's getting scared,' was Golfondi's opinion. 'Things didn't go as expected and he's retreating behind the bulwark.'

'The trustees are being a bit difficult,' Mr Crowne continued. 'It seems they're not going to turn up imminently.'

'And Dr Donati may be leaving because "there's trooble at t'mill",' supplied Liz.

The two detectives stared at her as if she'd lost her mind.

'Pay no attention,' said her beloved; 'it's some weird Englishism – she gets like that sometimes.'

'I hope Donati doesn't leave. We want to sweep him up with the others.'

'If he leaves, you'll have to arrest him at the airport,' grunted Golfondi.

'I'd rather not,' said Tripidis. 'I'd like it all to take place as quietly as possible and out of sight of the general public.'

'Then we'd better do it tomorrow,' said Golfondi.

Sixteen

T he telephone rang with its early-morning summons. Prince
Gregory von Hirtenstein woke, stretched out a hand, said
'Thank you' into the receiver, and heaved himself upright.

Liz was gone. He'd more or less expected that. She was no
doubt in the Serena's luxurious leisure centre doing something
vigorous. He rose, stretched, and set about the business of
getting ready for the day.

He was having second thoughts about the plan of action.
Some time between falling asleep last night and waking up this
morning, his unconscious had presented him with the thought
that it might turn out a lot more dangerous than they'd at first
imagined.

Originally, the plan had been that he and Liz would present
themselves at the jetty and he would allay any fears on the part
of the Kerouli staff; but now, if Great-aunt Irene was right,
the servants he knew were gone. In their place might be two,
perhaps more, hired bruisers. Would he be able to talk his way
past them? And if he could, would the escape party be able to
get past them on their way to board the rescue boat?

It had been decided that, so as to keep things as normal as
possible, he and Liz should get themselves aboard the morning
mail boat run by Spiro. The fact that Spiro knew them and
had brought them out should persuade any watchmen to let
them go up to the house. The motor cruiser carrying the
police would follow Spiro at a distance and remain offshore
until he had set out on his return trip. Then the rescue boat
would come alongside the Kerouli pier to take Nancy and her
rescuers away.

'We'll get alongside and I'll do my dumb-American act
and wave a map at the guys on duty. While they're trying

208

to give me directions to Spetses, Tripidis and his merry men will emerge and take them in charge. So when you come down the path with Lanan, we'll be waiting to take the three of you aboard and Tripidis will go on up to the house and carry out the arrests.'

Sounded good; but in the light of day Mr Crowne could see drawbacks. What if the men on duty put up a fight when the police came ashore? What if he and Liz had trouble persuading Nancy Lanan to come down? What if Niki or Donati cut up rough?

He didn't want Liz hurt. So when she came back into the room, almost lost in the big white bathrobe supplied by the hotel, hair dripping wet, he began at once.

'I don't think you should go on this expedition, Liz.'

'Don't be silly. How are you going to get into the house without me?'

'I can say you came with me, but you're staying on the boat.'

'Oh yes? And you're going to go up to the house with a carrier bag containing bikini cover-up that I bought for her last night and get a private word with Nancy while she tries it on?'

'Well, the business about trying it on isn't necessary—'

'Greg my love, if you really think any woman is going to get a present of a Chanel wrap and *not* want to try it on, you're crazy.'

'But I could say—'

'And *you* certainly can't go into the bedroom with her, now can you?'

'I'll think of some other idea . . .'

'No you won't, because I'm going to be there and it will all be quite simple.'

'But on the island things aren't quite the way we thought they'd be.'

'Greg, if I don't go with you and help to get Nancy out, why did I come all this way in the first place?'

He couldn't think of an answer – except that when they'd first discussed it in London, it hadn't seemed very dangerous.

'Anyhow,' she said in a tone that held finality, 'Golfondi

209

wouldn't like it if you messed up his plan of campaign at this late stage.'

That was true. Golfondi was eager to get this over and done with. Late last night and under conditions of complete confidentiality, Tripidis had been given warrants for the arrest of Niki Paroskolos and two foreign residents, Dr Antonio Donati and Gertrud Weber. How long the complete confidentiality might last was doubtful. Nothing must endanger the carrying out of the operation this day, this morning, the sooner the better.

Neither of them ate much of the breakfast brought to their room. They were downstairs waiting for Golfondi in good time. 'Okay, the word is that Spiro is loading a few things aboard and waiting for the satchel of mail. We'll drop you off at the entry to the quay. Got your mobile?'

Liz held it up.

'Okay. Tap in the connection as soon as you're on the landing stage at Kerouli. We'll have the line open at our end. We'll be a couple of hundred yards offshore until Spiro leaves and then we'll be on the island, so we'll know what goes on.'

'Fine.' Liz summoned a laugh. 'But don't listen while Nancy and I are in her bedroom, chum. That wouldn't be polite.'

He patted her on the shoulder, and helped her into the car, Greg following. It sped away from the hotel. He said to the prince, 'You seem quiet.'

'Um,' said His Highness, and remained otherwise silent.

Losing his nerve, thought the CIA man. Really, it would have been better to summon an assault force and make a night attack; but Tripidis had nearly had a heart attack at the suggestion. He was still bothered as hell about whether or not the so-far respectable Niki Paroskolos had done anything wrong.

Well, they'd know soon, thought Golfondi, watching the morning traffic of Athens race alongside.

In Piraeus there was the usual busy scene. The car took them to the harbourside that had become familiar during the preceding week. Greg and Liz got out, and with a word of farewell walked to the jetty used by the private boat owners.

Spiro was sitting on a bollard drinking something from a

210

plastic beaker. He stood up when he saw them approaching. '*Yassos!*' he said in surprise. 'You're still here?'

'Yes, still here,' agreed Mr Crowne, thinking it easier that way. 'Sightseeing, you know, and that kind of thing. How goes it, eh?'

Spiro shrugged. 'Big changes, *keirie*. A lot of us have been given the push and I'm not even sure how long I'll be on the payroll. We hear Mr Paroskolos wants to sell up and leave. Sad thing, if it happens . . .'

Mr Crowne expressed sympathy and translated for Liz, who smiled at Spiro with a sad shake of the head. Then she brightened, holding up her shopping bag. Mr Crowne picked up the cue.

'Any chance of a lift to the island?' he asked. 'We bought *keiria* Elissa a present.'

The boatman looked dubious. 'Well . . . I suppose it would be all right. They're a bit funny there, at the moment; but you and your lady – you're friends of the *keiria*.' He took a long draught from his beaker then threw it in a trash bin, nodding towards the harbourside. 'Just waiting for the postman. We'll be off in a few minutes.'

The mail van was drawing up alongside. The driver came to the jetty with a canvas satchel. It seemed to have very little in it. He and Spiro exchanged a few joking remarks, the passengers stepped aboard, and they were off.

It was fine weather, warm and bright. Easter was over, May would soon be here with a holiday on its first day and then the influx of tourists would begin. Spiro remarked that even if the Paroskolos family sold the island, there would be work for the likes of him so long as tourists kept coming. Mr Crowne agreed, waiting for the little motor launch to work its way out into open waters.

Liz could take no part in the conversation. She sat quietly, watching for the first glimpse of Kerouli. To tell the truth, her heart was thumping a little despite her resolute words earlier. The first time she'd made this trip, everything had seemed sunny, friendly, kind. Now, as the tip of the island at last emerged from the sea, she saw its silhouette as harsh and dark. Even when she could see the white rock, the gleaming mansion on its tip, it no longer held any welcome.

When at last the *Ikaris* sidled in at Kerouli, only one sentinel was on duty. A tall, thick-bodied young man was lounging on a beach chair. He rose to help tie up, but drew back in consternation at sight of the passengers. 'Heh!' he said, 'no strangers!'

'But, *feelos*, these aren't strangers. This is Prince Gregorios and his lady, and they're old friends of the *keiria*.'

'No, no – my orders are: no strangers.'

'Come on now, *andras*, don't be silly. Keiria Paroskolos would be very upset if she didn't get a chance to chat with her friends, and you know the boss likes to keep the *keiria* happy.'

'Contact the house,' put in Mr Crowne. 'You've got a two-way radio, haven't you?'

'Well, of course I have, but I don't know that I should . . .'

Liz favoured him with a dazzling smile. She hadn't understood everything, but she'd picked up the word '*radiofono*' and knew this was the moment of crisis.

The sentinel gave in. He went into the little shelter that housed the radio and the first-aid kit and so on. For a long time no one replied, which meant that the servants were busy elsewhere, and in the end it was the *keiria* herself who picked up.

'Spiro has brought some people on his boat,' he complained. 'My orders were to—'

'Who has come?' she interrupted.

'Someone that Spiro, silly fool, says is a prince, and a young lady.'

'They are friends of mine. They can land.'

'But *keirios* Niki said—'

'That's enough. *Keirios* Niki didn't mean that to apply to my friends.'

'Yes, *keiria*.'

He nodded permission at the two passengers, who stepped ashore. Spiro, meanwhile, had been unloading a few cartons and packages to transfer them to the electric buggy. The guard was interested to note that the so-called prince lent a hand. The

212

young lady went to the little car and took her seat in it. On her lap lay a plastic bag with the name of a famous fashion house on it.

Under cover of the carrier bag, Liz keyed in the numbers for Golfondi's cellphone. She heard the connection, and the very faint sound of Golfondi murmuring, 'You're on.'

The goods for the household were stowed in the back beside Liz. Greg got in beside Spiro, who set the little cart in motion. They trundled up the bends of the path. When they were high enough, Greg was able to glance out and espy the motor cruiser, large and white as a floating wedding cake. Over his shoulder he said in English, 'Our friends are there.'

'And we're in touch.'

'Splendid.' He felt far from splendid at the moment, though.

The cart came in sight of the main house but, instead of going to the front, it rolled on around the flat terrace to the back. Here it whined to a halt.

Niki Paroskolos came out, in shirtsleeves and trying to look pleased to see them. 'This is a surprise,' he said, holding out his hand. 'I thought you were in Geneva, Greg.'

'Been there, done that,' the prince said cheerfully. 'But I had to come back – I don't know if Elissa mentioned to you? The day she went with us to Athens, we went to see some work, to make a reproduction of an ancient musical instrument?'

'Oh . . . yes . . . I do seem to recall . . .'

Liz waved her carrier bag in the air. 'Never mind all that,' she cried, and walked past Niki into the house. 'How is she?' she enquired over her shoulder.

'Oh, quite well, quite well. That silly upset at the party – I blame myself.' He was unusually clipped in his manner. Greg gave him a smile of sympathy and followed Liz.

Nancy Lanan was in the wide area of the open-plan ground floor, watching them come in. Trudi was at her side, one hand holding a needlework bag and the other holding Nancy's arm.

As they approached, Nancy cried, 'Oh, Liz, how lovely to see you! Wasn't it lucky I was passing the study? Otherwise no one would have answered the radio because Niki darling was in Tonio's room, trying to persuade him to stay.'

213

At the mention of the doctor's departure, Trudi seemed to flinch. Nancy wrenched herself free from her grasp, ran to Liz, and threw her arms about her.

A little surprised at this fervent greeting, Liz responded by embracing her.

Nancy Lanan said into her ear, 'When you leave, take me with you. I've got to get out of here!'

Luckily Liz was struck speechless. Meanwhile Trudi was saying in soothing tones, 'Now, now, *ruhig, ruhig . . .*' and Niki was telling his wife that she mustn't get excited.

'But it's so nice to see them,' cried Nancy. 'I didn't get a chance to say goodbye, remember, Niki darling?'

'No, and that was because all the excitement made you ill again, and you know Tonio says—'

'Oh, Dr Donati is satisfied I'm doing fine, dear, you know he is; otherwise he wouldn't be leaving, would he?'

'Dr Donati is leaving?' Greg put in, pretending surprise.

'He says it's important, but I think he should stay – my wife still needs him even though she's really pretty good these days.'

'I, too, wish he would not go,' said Trudi mournfully.

The scene appeared perfectly normal. The big living room was bright with sunshine; flowers glowed on tables. Niki was in sweater and slacks. Nancy, in a button-through dress of peach-pink linen, wore less make-up and had her hair pulled back in a simple clasp. People were smiling and nodding at each other – on the surface, very relaxed and normal.

Yet the nurse seemed preoccupied. Niki seemed somewhat strained, and in Nancy Greg sensed some unidentifiable change. She seemed less hesitant, more focused.

She was smiling now as she took from Liz the fashion boutique's bag and peeked inside. 'Oh, that looks nice!' she cried.

'It's a cover-up. For the beach. I saw it last night in the hotel boutique and I couldn't resist it,' said Liz. 'It's your colours, you see – coral and rose and magenta.'

'Come on, let's see how it looks!' exclaimed Nancy, and headed for the stairs with the carrier held in her hands like a prize.

214

Trudi immediately followed her. Liz took a quick step towards Greg, who swung away from Niki to meet her. She came up on tiptoe to give him a quick kiss. 'She *wants* to come with us,' she whispered.

'What?'

'When we go, sweetheart,' she said aloud. 'Don't forget!'

He had recovered himself enough to say, 'Right, of course,' as she hurried after Nancy and Trudi. To Niki he explained, inventing wildly, 'She wants us to pause, when we get a little way out on the boat. For a picture of the island.'

'Oh, no need. We have those,' Niki said. 'Elissa's father had them taken by a professional, somebody famous. I'll send you some.'

'Thank you, that's a better idea. Liz with a camera . . .' He shrugged to show his opinion of her skills, knowing she'd forgive this little lie; but what on earth had she meant by her whispered message? And as his host picked up a phone to order refreshments for his unexpected guests, he wondered what was going on upstairs.

The scene there was quite ordinary. Nancy was in front of her mirror unbuttoning the front of her dress, Trudi was delving in her needlework bag for her crochet. Liz was watching Nancy.

'Oh, Trudi, darling, don't hang around here,' Nancy cried. 'I know you're not interested in clothes. Why don't you trot along to Dr Donati and help him with his packing?'

Trudi zipped her needlework bag closed and got up with alacrity. 'If you don't mind, then,' she said, and hurried out of the room.

Nancy stepped to the door, closed it, and turned to Liz. 'You'll think I'm crazy,' she said, 'but I've got to get off this island! Please say you'll take me with you when you go!'

Liz took the mobile out of her shoulder bag. 'Are you getting this?' she enquired.

'Sure am,' growled Golfondi from aboard the motor cruiser. 'Ask her what gives.'

'I don't *know*,' cried Nancy, catching the query. 'I'm in a complete fog! Since last Friday – or more like, Saturday morning – I've been trying to work out what the hell is going on!'

'Ask her who she is,' prompted Golfondi.

'Who I am? I'm Nancy Lanan, from Bloomington, Illinois, and what I'm doing here being addressed as Elissa Paroskolos, God only knows.' She snatched the mobile out of Liz's hand. 'Who are you? What's this all about?'

Golfondi said something Liz couldn't catch. Nancy frowned and handed back the mobile. 'He says he needs to talk to you.'

'Yes?' Liz said.

'Get her down to the jetty. We don't want long explanations at the moment. We'll come in for you straight away.'

'Right, we'll be on our way as soon as I can manage.' She said to Nancy, 'There's a boat standing by to pick us up—'

'But the guy on the pier won't let anybody come in.'

'Don't worry about it. Just act normal.'

'I should be so lucky!' exclaimed Nancy. 'I don't know what normal is any more!'

'Come on, let's get downstairs. I've got to explain to Greg.'

'How the devil does he come into it?' Nancy was asking as they went out.

'Never mind for the moment. Just play along and make a chance for us to go. Ah, there you are, sweetie!' she carolled as they reached a point on the staircase where they could see Greg and his host, drinking coffee. 'The wrap is a great success; Elissa likes it, don't you, dear?'

'It's lovely, and thank you for thinking of me.'

'Of course we think of you,' said Liz. 'We couldn't pass up this chance to see how you were, now could we?' She went to Greg and gave him a playful cuff on the shoulder. 'Greg and his funny old pipe organ – you remember how bored we were when he went on about it that day in Athens?'

'Oh, that day – what fun it was! We ran away and went shopping, didn't we?'

'You can laugh,' Greg said, seeking for a path through this mystery, 'but that instrument is tremendously valuable now it's been completed. That's why we're personally taking it to Cousoulis – he lives on Spetses, you know.'

'Of course she doesn't know, Greg – she doesn't have

216

friends in obscure parts of the music world; but I'm sure you'd like to see the finished product, Elissa. Come down to the boat when we leave and take a look at it.'

'I'd love to,' agreed Nancy. She poured coffee for herself and Liz. 'Dr Donati will be leaving too. He's just finishing his packing now.'

'Ah,' said Greg, 'how is that going to work out? Spiro was going to take us to Spetses after he left here . . .'

'Dr Donati can wait for your return journey,' Nancy interrupted. 'It's not particularly important which flight he takes.'

Niki gave her an odd glance, in which there was puzzlement mixed with approval. Greg was puzzled too. Nancy wasn't any longer the trembling little violet of last week; there was some assurance in her manner. A few days ago the idea of being deprived of Dr Donati's care would have crushed her.

'We don't want him to go, do we, darling?' she went on, giving Niki a little pout of regret. 'But he seems set on it, and of course he'll have to come back to get his research papers.'

'Research? The doctor has been doing research?'

'Only as a very detailed case history,' Niki said quickly. 'His subject is mental incapacity, you know, and my poor Elissa lost her memory almost completely after she was ill. So he's kept what you'd call a sort of diary, of Elissa's case.'

'So I'll be famous one day, perhaps,' teased Nancy. 'Won't I, Niki? In the *American Journal of Medicine* or something.'

'Now, darling, you know he said his notes aren't for publication.'

'But it's good to know I've been of use in the furtherance of medical knowledge, dear.'

Niki seemed to suppress an angry retort. He rose from his seat to move towards the open corridor that gave him a view of the back door. The whine of the electric motor could be heard. 'Spiro will be ready to go soon,' he remarked. 'There's not much to take today.'

'Dearest, that sounds quite unwelcoming,' Nancy reproved. 'You're not anxious to get rid of our guests, are you?'

'No, no, of course not! What's got into you today, my angel? You seem rather cranky.'

'Cranky? Me?' She laughed, then waved her hand in a gesture of acceptance. 'But you'd expect me to be cranky sometimes, dear – just part of the after-effects of my illness, no?'

'Oh, Elissa, I'm sorry,' said Niki, coming to her and putting an arm about her shoulders. 'What a dolt I am! I should think before I speak; I didn't mean to sound patronizing. And, of course, I know you're upset about Tonio leaving.'

'Yes, and speaking of that, shouldn't you go up and ask him if he'd like to see Greg and Liz before they leave? He'd be sorry to miss them, I'm sure.'

Niki came back far enough along the corridor to be at the foot of the stairs. 'I don't really think—'

'And perhaps Greg and Liz would like to see Tonio.'

'Yes, of course,' agreed Liz at once.

'Oh very well.' With a reluctance he couldn't quite hide, Niki began to ascend.

Nancy Lanan watched him go. She was holding up one finger for silence. As soon as his figure disappeared along the first-floor passage, she whispered, '*Now!*' and ran for the back door.

Liz went after her, snatching at Greg's sleeve as she went. Taken aback, His Highness followed with long strides.

Spiro saw them erupt out of the back door with surprise. He was in his place in the buggy, testing the controls. 'Get in,' ordered Nancy, and to Spiro in Greek, 'We're going.' She got into the passenger seat in front; Liz and Greg fell into the back.

Obedient to the commands of the mistress, Spiro set the cart in motion.

'Hurry, Spiro,' urged Nancy.

'This thing can't hurry,' he grunted.

'Oh, quick, quick!' She grabbed his arm in her distress. Astonished, Spiro turned to stare at her.

'Watch where you're going!' cried Mr Crowne. The buggy rocked as it took the bend that brought it on to the path down to the landing stage, but stayed upright.

'Is something wrong, *keiria*?' Spiro asked.

'Never mind, just put your foot down.'

218

'That wouldn't make any difference, this cart—'

'Calm down, Nancy,' said Mr Crowne. 'This sort of thing can't go above a set speed.'

She turned to look at him over her shoulder. She went almost white. 'Yes,' she gasped, 'it was you . . .'

She'd gone so pale that he was afraid she was going to faint again. He put out a hand to steady her, but Liz gave a cry. 'Where's the cabin cruiser?'

A turn in the path had brought the landing stage into view. Spiro's boat swayed at its moorings, but there was no lofty white cruiser alongside.

And behind them Trudi Weber was on the path shouting, '*Nein! Nein! Sie mussen nicht entgehen!*'

Liz clutched Greg. 'He said they were on their way!' she wailed. But the rescue boat could be glimpsed, ghostly white in the rising heat haze, about two hundred metres out on the water.

Seventeen

Trudi was pelting down the track. She had to grab at the handrail from time to time so as not to fall. She couldn't hope to catch up with the cart while it was moving, so the gap was still considerable; but they would stop on the turn-around by the jetty. Her headlong descent would bring her there while they were still getting out. And the guard was coming out of the little office, staring at the approaching cart, moving to stand in its way.

The rescue boat was still out on the water, and the *Ikaris* was tied up, its engine at stop.

'Drive right up to the boat,' commanded Mr Crowne.

'What?'

'Don't stop on the apron.'

'But I always—'

'Do as you're told,' snapped Nancy in her mistress-of-the-house voice.

Folding his lips together in disapproval, Spiro fixed his sights on the jetty alongside his precious boat. The guard from the office gave a shout of surprise as the little truck came unswervingly towards him at about 5 kph. He got out of its way but thumped hard on its windscreen as it went past. Spiro flinched, and the cart made a lurch.

Trudi was now coming round the final bend. She was running, gasping and clutching her side, but her feet were on the straight track that led to the turn-around.

A long way up the cliff side, another figure could be seen running. Niki was in hot pursuit.

The golf cart trundled over the boards of the jetty, the hired man running alongside. 'Get on board, start the engine,' ordered Mr Crowne.

220

'But—'

'*Do* it!' As he said it, the prince threw himself out of the car and tackled the guard, who was jogging alongside. In the next few minutes Mr Crowne had no idea what else was happening. He was locked in a tussle with the other man, and he was losing. The guard was tough, strong, and a street fighter.

Then it seemed to dawn on his opponent that his job was to stop the entire party. His attention was distracted for a moment as the engine of the *Ikaris* mumbled into life. He half-turned.

The prince pulled him so as to make him turn even further, kicked his legs from under him, and sent him sailing into the water.

The fight had been going on while Liz tried feverishly to take the mooring lines off the posts. At the splash she whirled about, saw Greg still there, and didn't even bother to look at the man flailing in the oily water behind the *Ikaris*.

Nancy, looking as pale and fragile as a lily petal, was arguing with Spiro. The boatman was in a dilemma. The boss lady was telling him to leave, her nurse was staggering across the concrete turn-around calling 'Stop! Stop!' The boss man himself was coming down the path with one of the new henchmen, signalling something with his arms.

All in all it looked as if the majority had voted that he should stay; but then the prince-person stepped in the way of the nurse. He straight-armed her so that the palm of his hand collided with her left shoulder as she arrived. She staggered backwards and careened into the guardrail at the landward side of the pier. Her left arm was between her body and the rail. She gave a howl of pain: broken arm.

'*Entschuldigen*,' said the prince politely as he turned to wait for Niki.

'*Theos!*' muttered Spiro. Everything was turning nasty. Better to go.

'Greg!' shrieked Liz as the boat began to move.

He shouted, 'Go, go! Get out there to Golfondi!'

'Come *on*, Greg; they can't go anywhere, *we've* got the boat.'

'"*Niki would summon up a helicopter.*" Get Golfondi here with some men, quick!'

221

The quotation from Great-aunt Irene struck home. Of course – if they didn't do something, Niki and the others would get themselves flown out. A million thoughts whirled. She wanted to stay with Greg, but someone had to make Spiro drive his boat out to the *Vanda*. Nancy Lanan couldn't do that; she didn't even know anything about the cabin cruiser. Nancy was, moreover, on the verge of collapse.

So Liz would have to go. She jumped aboard the *Ikaris* just as the gap became almost too wide. 'That-a-way,' she commanded with grim humour, pointing towards the haze in the south-east where something could be glimpsed, tall and glimmering white.

Niki was yelling, 'Stop! Come back!' as he pounded on to the boards. The second of the hired men was at his heels, some sort of club in his hands. Trudi was lumbering to her feet, holding her left elbow in her right hand.

From behind him, Prince Gregory von Hirtenstein could hear the man in the water calling for help as the wash of the *Ikaris* swept him away from the quay.

Noblesse oblige.

The prince took a lifebelt off a hook and cast it into the sea as near to the helpless man as possible – very strange, how often it happened that people who lived by or on the sea never learned to swim.

Niki came up. He was out of breath and utterly perplexed. Gregory von Hirtenstein was standing with his back to him, watching the man in the sea make grabbing motions towards the lifebelt. 'He's going to drown,' he commented to Niki. The other hired hand arrived, breathless. 'Can you swim?'

'Wh-what?'

'Swim?'

'Yes . . . hah . . . of course . . .'

'He a friend of yours?'

'Yes.'

'Then you'd better help him or he's not going to make it.'

The other stood irresolute and panting. Niki gasped, 'Go on, we don't want a death on our hands.'

The man kicked off his shoes, pulled off his jacket, and dived in.

222

Greg took Niki's arm in a firm grasp. 'You're in big trouble, my friend. Can you see that big white shape out there?'

Dazed and still not recovered from his impetuous dash down the path, Niki shaded his eyes and looked. He nodded.

'That's the police, and within about fifteen minutes or so they'll be here.' Why aren't they here *now*? he was asking himself. But that was a question he couldn't deal with at the moment. His present task was to keep Niki from doing anything silly.

'The police?' Niki repeated. He put a hand up to his brow and, feeling the sweat on it, inanely produced a silk handkerchief to mop it. 'What are the police doing there?'

'They're waiting to arrest you and Dr Donati. And, no doubt, the faithful Trudi.'

'You must be mad. There's no reason for the police to be interested.'

'Here comes the doctor,' remarked Mr Crowne, pointing. The doctor was indeed coming down the path, much more sedately than the others. Trudi lumbered to meet him. Some yards away they stood together as Trudi, with nods and shakes of her head, explained what had happened.

'She's telling him it's all over,' suggested Greg.

'I've no idea what you're talking about!'

'I'm talking about a little heap of bones on the side of the Schilthorn. I'm talking about a missing wife and a stranger in her place. I'm talking about a huge inheritance, Niki.'

Niki's black eyes widened. A string of emotions raced across his handsome face – incredulity, fear, desperation. He made a sudden movement as if to run, but stopped even before Greg could touch him. Where was he to go? He had trapped himself on this little island.

The man rescued from the sea and his rescuer came up, looking like drowned rats but trying to act tough. 'You want us to thump him, boss?' asked one. At the uncouth Greek words Niki closed his eyes in misery, shaking his head. He knew when he was beaten.

Donati had finished his descent with one arm around Trudi to help her. They paused a few paces away. 'Miss Weber

223

tells me you attacked her,' he asserted. 'Has Your Highness gone mad?'

Greg smiled. 'My Highness is quite sane. But I'm sorry I had to manhandle you, Miss Weber.'

'*Schlechter Tölpel!*'

'Harsh words, *Fräulein*, but you're not without blame yourself.'

'I've done nothing that earns blame.'

'You looked out of the window of Dr Donati's room, saw us driving down, and raised the alarm?'

'You had no right to take Dr Donati's patient anywhere without his permission.'

'Nancy Lanan isn't his patient.'

The doctor, who had been content to let his nurse carry on the attack until now, gave an audible gasp. Trudi, quicker of wit, said at once, 'Who is Nancy Lanan, may I ask?'

'The girl who just sailed away in the *Ikaris*.'

'That was Mrs Paroskolos.'   .

'A very sick young woman,' said Donati, rallying. 'And you will be in court, sir, if you don't stop interfering.'

'Oh, give it up, Donati! I told Niki a moment ago, the police will be here any moment.'

'That kind of threat will get you nowhere, you fool—'

'No, Tonio, he means it,' Niki interrupted. 'Listen!'

They paused. From the south-east came the sound of a boat's engine – but not the loud, proud rumble of the *Vanda*: this was the small businesslike drone of the *Ikaris*. Mr Crowne's heart sank. Did this mean that Tripidis and his doubts had triumphed, that the police had withdrawn from the campaign?

They all stood, silent and motionless, until the little motor boat came close enough to let them see its passengers. The first to be noticed by the crown prince was Liz, standing by the wheel and waving. But the man running the boat wasn't Spiro, it was a uniformed policeman. And behind this stranger stood Tripidis, looking through binoculars at the group on the pier.

Niki gave a groan. Dr Donati and the nurse turned to begin a hurried ascent of the cliff path. The two half-drowned thugs moved themselves a little apart from their employer, totally at a loss about what was going on but sensing trouble in a big way. The *Ikaris* glided in. A plain-clothes man jumped ashore to handle the mooring lines.

Liz took a running leap off the boat and threw herself into Greg's arms. 'Darling!' She grabbed the lapels of his jacket, drawing him as close as possible. 'Are you all right?'

'Perfectly. How about you?

'Worried sick, you bonehead! Don't ever do that to me again!'

'I can't imagine there will be any need.'

'Don't be so ruddy calm! I thought they might be shooting you or something.'

'No, no, Niki isn't a physical type—'

'But he hires them!' Her eye rested on the two wet men. 'Did you push the other one in too?'

'No, I sent him in to rescue his pal. How is Nancy?'

'Ah . . . Pretty much done in, I'm afraid. She just had enough strength to keep giving orders to Spiro until we reached the big boat, and then she sort of fell to pieces.'

'And why isn't that great useless vessel tied up here now?'

Liz let go sufficiently far to give him a rueful grin. 'Some piece of plastic wound itself round one of the propellers. There's a chap in diving gear down there now, trying to free it.'

'But why couldn't they come in on one propeller? Oh, I see, they might have gone round in circles.' He began to laugh. 'My word, this has been a tragi-comic rescue.'

Now that their chief concerns had been laid to rest, they gave their attention to what was going on. Two plain-clothes men had caught up with Trudi and the doctor and were escorting them upwards to the house. Superintendent Tripidis was putting Niki aboard the *Ikaris* under guard. The uniformed officer was taking the names of the two water rats.

Out at sea, there was activity. Gaps in the milky heat haze showed first one and then another fast little cutter. One was heading towards the white bulk of the *Vanda*. The other was coming towards Kerouli.

'Jerry Golfondi has called in some help,' Liz observed.

'Yes.' Mr Crowne was having some thoughts. 'His first

objective seems to be to get Nancy Lanan out of here and prevent embarrassment to the United States.'

Liz nodded agreement.

'So what do you bet that the little boat that's disappeared into the mist near the big one is about to take Nancy off and away to some discreet hiding place?'

'Um-m. Would that be a bad thing?'

'I've no idea. But it's not a good thing as far as Tripidis is concerned.'

'Ah,' she said. 'That's why he looked so unhappy when he had to leave on the *Ikaris* . . . was it? He suspected Golfondi would do something?'

'I imagine he's not having a total success. Nancy's the chief witness in the fraud case. If Golfondi gets her off somewhere and coaches her in what she's to say, who knows what effect it will have?'

'You don't think Jerry would really do a thing like that?' she said, having taken quite a liking to the burly detective.

'He'd do what his superiors told him. Jerry's role isn't to help the Bureau of Fraud Investigation make its case; it's to damp down any little bush fires that might trouble his bosses.'

'But what about Nancy?' she cried. 'After all she's been through . . .'

'We don't know what she's been through,' he responded. 'All we know is that, when we got here, she was extremely eager to leave; but that might just be because she'd realized her future was likely to be quite curtailed.'

'But she's really ill, Greg. You saw that for yourself. She was white as chalk when I helped her aboard the boat.'

'Was she? I was otherwise engaged. But maybe she was just suffering from a severe case of fright.'

She drew in a deep breath but said nothing. She was unwilling to think the worst of Nancy Lanan.

Tripidis approached. 'I'm taking Paroskolos to the mainland. Do you want to come?'

'Yes please,' Liz exclaimed.

Mr Crowne followed more slowly. He said to the superintendent, 'I'd make sure your men confiscate all Dr Donati's papers.'

'Oh, certainly, but it's unlikely he'd put anything down on paper about the financial chicanery.'

'I wasn't thinking about the financial side. Donati's been treating Nancy Lanan as a patient for over a year – at least that's the story. It would be interesting to know what sort of treatment he's been giving, if any, and if he's kept any notes.'

Tripidis nodded, turning to one of his men to give the instruction. A group of four got into the electric buggy amid much suppressed amusement, and headed upwards to the house to carry out the necessary searches.

The *Ikaris* landed at the quiet inlet used by the private boat owners. Nobody noticed that the jet-setting Niki Paroskolos was being brought ashore under arrest. An unmarked police car bore him away. Dr Donati and his faithful nurse would probably follow later. Left to themselves, Liz and Greg decided to take the Metro back to the city.

They found a quiet *kafeneion* for coffee and a plate of sesame-scattered ring-shaped rolls. They were hungry, for they'd eaten almost nothing at their early breakfast and it was now almost noon. They sat in the shade of an old arbutus tree at the back of the café, speaking very little.

After a while Liz ventured, 'I'm worried about Nancy.'

He nodded, but he busied himself breaking off another piece of *koulourya*.

'I can't believe she's a criminal, Greg.'

'Perhaps not.'

'Be a little more enthusiastic.'

'It's not good sense to be enthusiastic when you don't know all the facts.'

'Oh, stop being so rational! I like Nancy, I don't want her to be in trouble.'

'Sweetheart, you have a very kind heart,' he said, smiling.

'We have to *do* something!'

'What, exactly?'

'Well, *I* don't know! You're the one with all the brains. What do you suggest?'

He pushed away his plate, leaned back, and stretched. 'I suggest we go back to the Serena, have a swim in its luxurious pool, have a late and leisurely lunch, and then spend some time enjoying ourselves.'

She gave him a reflective glance. 'By enjoying ourselves, what do you mean exactly?'

'Oh, I'm sure we'll think of something,' he said.

Eighteen

L ate that evening there was a telephone call from Jerry Golfondi.

'Sorry about the cabin cruiser,' he said. 'They got it back in action after a couple of hours.'

'Is everything going well?' Mr Crowne enquired.

'Not bad. We're still debriefing.'

'Debriefing! What does that mean, in plain English?'

'Well, Tripidis and I are kind of working out who's going to do what. I can't go into it over the phone, man. But we've got a lot of stuff to look at – that tip you gave Tripidis about the doctor's papers was good: he kept a detailed account. Tripidis let me have a look.' Golfondi gave a snort. 'Overconfident. Never seems to have occurred to him that somebody else would read it one day.'

Without covering the mouthpiece, Greg said to Liz, 'He's been reading the doctor's papers.'

'What about Nancy?' Liz demanded, ignoring the information.

'Liz is worried about Nancy,' he said into the receiver.

'She's okay, she's good. We've put her in a nice spot – get her reconnected with reality, kind of, you know.'

Mr Crowne's antennae went alert. 'A nice spot? What does that mean?'

'Sort of a rest centre – we use it for our own people when they need some time out.'

'Listen, Jerry,' exclaimed Mr Crowne, 'that girl, for whatever reason, has spent more than a year shut off from the world. What are you doing to her now ?'

'Calm down, calm down; it's all good stuff. You'd approve if I could tell you the whole enchilada.'

'Why can't you tell me?'

'Not on the phone, bro. And not now. Perhaps in a day or two.'

Liz was standing at his elbow, listening hard. She took the phone out of his hand and said, 'Tell us at least – is she being charged?'

Golfondi waited a moment before saying, 'Not as of now. That's all I know, pals; I can't say any more for the moment.'

'When?' insisted Liz.

'In a day or two. I promise.'

He put the phone down, and Liz slammed down hers. 'Something's going on,' she groaned. 'And we're being kept out of it.'

'*Carissima*, that's to be expected. It's a terrible situation. Switzerland probably wants her, Tripidis needs her information, the US Embassy is probably having a heart attack over her.'

'Politics! That girl isn't just a puppet! I came all the way here to help get her out, and between us we did that, and we deserve to be told what's happening!'

'I agree, I agree. But give it time, Liz.'

This was hard advice, but she had to give in to it. That day was Wednesday. Nothing appeared in the papers nor on television about the arrest of Niki Paroskolos. By Friday she was out of patience. 'Greg, I've got to get back to London. I have work to do, you know.'

'Of course.'

'But I'm not going without finding out what's happening about Nancy.'

'Ah.'

'Have you got a telephone number for Jerry Golfondi?'

'Well, I . . .'

'Because I want to ring him and give him an ultimatum.'

'Good heavens.'

'And if you don't have a number to contact him, I'm going to march down the road to the Embassy and cause a fuss.'

He began to laugh. 'Sorry, sorry,' he sputtered when he saw it was making her furious. 'I've got a number you can ring.' He fetched his jacket, found his pocket diary, and handed it

230

to her open at the page with the number. As she picked up the phone, he said quickly, 'Don't forget that phone calls are probably recorded.'

'What?'

'Well, they may be. Just don't say anything rash: you might get arrested.'

Liz gave him a glare. She tapped in the number and was put through without much delay. Jerry Golfondi said, 'Yes, Liz?'

'Jerry, I want to know what the story is about Nancy.'

'I told you, kid, there's a lot of debriefing going on—'

'Debriefing, nonsense! I want to know if she's in trouble, and what you're doing, and let me tell you this, Jerry Golfondi: if I don't get some reassurance that she's being treated well, I'm going to start chatting to some journalists in Chicago who'll be very interested because they know Nancy.'

'Liz!'

'I mean it, Jerry. Tell me where and how she is.'

'Ahem . . . Now isn't the time, dear.'

'You said that before. When are we going to get some straight talk?'

'You need some TLC, girlie; I can hear it in your voice. Let me take you out for a drink and some soothe.'

'Where and when?'

'How about this afternoon? You know the open-air café near the Folk Art Museum?'

'The Folk Art Museum?' Liz repeated to Mr Crowne. He nodded yes. 'Greg knows it. We'll be there.'

'Three o'clock, then.'

Liz went out to spend the interval in her favourite pastime: shopping. Mr Crowne rang Golfondi again as soon as she left. 'Jerry, this is serious. Don't put her off with rubbish. She talked to colleagues of Nancy's on a Chicago magazine a couple of weeks ago; she'll go back to them if you try to put her off.'

Golfondi groaned. 'Women's lib,' he sighed. 'What has it done to us? But okay, okay, I hear you.'

The café was a simple place, with awnings for shade and wrought-iron tables. Golfondi was already there when they arrived, sipping something pale and shiny in a tall glass. It turned out to be apricot juice with soda: 'Got to keep my head clear for this interrogation,' he said with a grin.

They joined him, ordered drinks, and looked expectant.

'First thing,' he said, 'that girl is one sick puppy. She's been through some very hard times.'

'So where is she? What are you doing to her?'

'She's in a spa, out in the mountains to the west of Athens,' said Golfondi.

'A spa?'

'Oh, yeah, there are a lot of them in Greece. Used to be sacred springs, you know – that sort of thing. Now they're pretty lush places, treatment for arthritis, asthma – you name it.'

'You mean you've got her cooped up in some sort of medical prison!'

'No, no, Liz, honest; it's a sweet place – our own people go there for R and R. And to set your mind at rest, no kind of prison is going to be involved. Our little lady is absolutely innocent of any wrongdoing.'

'Innocent?'

'Yes, sir, Your Highness, she's Snow White.'

' *"Pura e disposta a salire alle stelle"*?' quoted His Highness with some scepticism.

'I don't know about mounting up to the stars, but she's pure, yeah – she's as pure as the poet would have wanted.'

Liz said, with a weary shake of her head, 'Listen, Jerry, I don't want Nancy to be hurt, but Greg and I were there; we saw her acting out the part of Elissa Paroskolos.'

'She wasn't acting,' said Golfondi. 'She really believed she was Elissa.'

Liz and Greg exchanged glances. 'I beg your pardon,' said Greg.

'She was Elissa. She'd been taught to believe that.' He surveyed their bewilderment with some enjoyment. 'She was brainwashed.'

This time the gaze of his listeners remained fixed on him. Then the prince said, 'Oh. I see.'

Everything fell into place in his mind: Nancy's hesitation

232

and uncertainty, the supposed lost memory, the flashes of recollection that couldn't be accounted for . . .

'Of course. That's Donati's specialty – disorders of the brain.'

'Right.'

'And Nancy's been able to tell you about it?'

'Not too much. We got on the track after we put her through a complete physical, because when I first got her to the Spa Hermes, she was in a state of collapse. The docs found traces of all sorts of chemicals in her bloodstream. They did specialized tests on her liver and so on. That clued them to the fact that she'd been subjected to some modern form of paraldehyde at first, and nitrazepam, and a bunch of other things I can't remember.'

'Oh!' cried Liz, and threw her hands up to her face to prevent the tears that were springing up.

'What else did the doctors discover?'

'They're still working on it. Unfortunately, we only got a little go at the records Tripidis gathered up. He says he'll let us have copies, but when, there's no knowing. Donati was keeping a diary of his patient's progress—'

'His patient!' Liz exclaimed. 'His victim, you mean!'

'Yeah, now you're with me, see? This kid did nothing wrong. What she remembers is that she was to go to Mürren to begin writing a book about Elissa. Elissa had been taken with the idea when Nancy had interviewed her just after her father's death. It seems they thought they had some ancestral tie, or something. Nancy went via Munich, where Niki met her and took her on by private jet to Bern. She remembers being surprised at Niki showing any enthusiasm about the project, because she had got the impression from Elissa that things weren't too hot between them. Money problems, she thought.'

'Probably she thought right. Niki was beginning to be in deep trouble over his airline. I'm pretty sure he asked his father-in-law for help, and when Yanni was fished out of the sea, he was hoping Elissa would supply the money.'

'Yeah, Nancy says she got the impression during that interview – the one she did just after the father's funeral

233

– that Elissa was going to be as tight-fisted as her dad over giving any handouts.'

'She doesn't sound a very nice person,' muttered Liz, who was trying very hard to feel sorrow over Elissa's death. She gave Greg a frown. 'And don't you say I told you so.'

'It never crossed my mind. But it does look as if Elissa signed her own death warrant by refusing to give Niki any financial support.'

'Yeah, it was a bad scene, all right. Well, Nancy got to Mürren – no sign of Elissa. She remembers feeling unwell but put it down to jet lag. Then everything goes blank. She thinks she recalls a hospital room, and a sound that went on and on—'

'A sound?'

'It's called "white noise".' Golfondi sighed. 'Poor kid. She says her head was bandaged so that her eyes were covered, and she couldn't seem to move her hands or feet. She doesn't remember being given anything to eat so we think she was fed through tubes. She *does* remember the bandages being taken off, because she was so relieved to find she wasn't blind.'

'Don't,' begged Liz. 'Don't tell us any more. It's awful.'

Mr Crowne said, 'And when she could see, Dr Donati was there being kind and good to her.'

'Yeah,' said Golfondi, surprised. 'You know something about this?'

'Not a thing. But it stands to reason she was confused and scared, and someone would have to reassure her. Donati's the man with the knowledge of how to do it. He runs the clinic in Mürren – which is where she was when she woke up, I suppose.'

'You got it. The medical boys tell me she was probably there about four or five days for the session of complete sensual deprivation Now Donati tells her this yarn about meningitis—'

'Can we just sort that out? Did anybody actually have meningitis?'

'Not a soul. The real Elissa had been disposed of – your Swiss pals are working on that and they think she was probably hit on the head before she was put out on the mountain. Small pieces of a black plastic bag lead them to think she was carried in that.'

'Oh, don't!' Liz said.

'Sorry, there was no need to tell you that,' Golfondi apologized. 'We're talking about what happened to Nancy, not about Mrs Paroskolos. Well, Donati now has Nancy believing she's had meningitis. Donati tells her it's affected her brain, she's been having some delusions and her memory is damaged. Of *course* she believes him. He's a nice kind doctor.'

'If I ever get near him again, I'll strangle him,' said Liz in a stifled voice.

'S-sh,' said Greg. 'Go on, Jerry.'

'She doesn't know when she was taken to Kerouli. We can sort all that out from witnesses and airport records if we want to. Anyhow, there she is on this island in the Saronic Gulf, and life is pretty good: lots of lovely food, fresh air, long sessions with the dear doctor to get her memory back using old home movies and photographs, dressmakers coming to measure her for new clothes, her hair all done up in waves and curls – it's not bad, when you summarize it like that, eh?'

'A teaching process. She was being taught how to be Elissa.'

'Exactly. And it worked, to a great extent. If she had moments when she saw pictures in her mind of things that didn't fit, Donati would be there to soothe her and explain it was all due to the after-effects of her illness.'

'Diabolical—'

'Liz, shut up. Go on, Jerry.'

'Our psychological experts say that the treatment could only have a temporary effect. Sooner or later her true personality would be bound to reassert itself. They go on about the ego and the superego, stuff like that.'

'Niki only needed a temporary effect,' Greg supplied. 'It only had to last until she'd signed the trust deeds.'

'Yeah.' Golfondi snapped finger and thumb. 'And then – kepow! A few weeks later, poor Mrs Paroskolos, so young and beautiful, will have an accident or die of some after-effect of the meningitis.'

'Not that, Jerry,' said Mr Crowne, momentarily confused. 'There would have to be a death certificate.'

'And who would sign the certificate? The faithful Dr Donati.'

'I *will* say it, Greg: he's a monster!'

'No, no, Gertrud Weber says he's a genius.'

'Oh, her! She's probably in love with him.'

'She says Niki blackmailed him into it. She won't say what he used as a threat.'

'Oh, there was some hocus-pocus at his clinic a couple of years ago – naughty sexual games . . .'

'Do you know everything about the get-go of this business?' marvelled Golfondi.

'We got it from Great-aunt Irene. It would have wrecked his reputation if it had come out.'

'Well, Weber is saying that her darling doctor agreed to do some work on Nancy but he had no idea Elissa had been murdered; and he didn't know Nancy was being groomed to carry out a fraudulent signature.'

'But he was going to get a large sum of money from Niki once she'd signed.'

'Well, that's what I think, Greg, but Weber says he did it for the furtherance of medical knowledge.'

'Nonsense! He could never publish any of that! And what does Fräulein Weber say to justify her own conduct?'

'She was carrying out the doctor's orders.'

'*That* has a familiar ring. But she must have known the treatment was being administered against Nancy's will.'

'Not at all. She says Nancy agreed to it.'

Both Greg and Liz gave a groan of incredulity. 'She can't think anyone's going to believe that,' Liz cried.

'Well, Nancy isn't in a position to deny it. She doesn't know what she did when they first got hold of her – of course she doesn't believe she agreed to anything criminal, but under cross-examination by a clever attorney, what could she say? She really doesn't remember. There's a chance we may get something from Donati's medical papers. They're in the evidence files of the Greek police at the moment.'

'Can they be used against Niki?'

'Who knows?' sighed Golfondi. 'As far as I can gather, Niki is saying as little as possible. He says he knows nothing about the bones on the mountainside. He says Elissa went out skiing and never came back—'

'No she didn't; Elissa hated skiing.'

'Yeah, you're probably right, sir, but that's his story. He's also saying that when Nancy Lanan heard that he, Niki, was going to be deprived of Elissa's fortune—'

'He was?'

'Sure was. According to the trust deed, if Elissa died before the age of twenty-five, about half the money was to be divided up among twenty or so members of the Dimitriouso family and the rest went to a list of charities.'

'Do you mean,' asked Liz, brightening a little at the news, 'that those poor old things that we met on the island might actually get some money? – Great-aunt Irene?'

'Looks like it. Can't tell you names, but the lawyers gave us that much. So to go back to Niki: he's saying that when Nancy heard that the trust had to be signed but Elissa had disappeared, she volunteered to take Elissa's place and help him get the money. His story, of course, is that he thought Elissa had flounced off in a pique about something and that he expected her to come back. So Nancy suggested she act as stand-in.'

'Absolutely not!' shrieked Liz.

'Well, I agree with you. And in view of the medical reports our guys have handed in, and the evidence we hope is in Donati's files, his lawyers are telling him to ditch all that. There's absolutely no doubt that Nancy was drugged and manipulated and there's very *little* doubt she would have been finished off in the near future. So Niki's lawyers are building up a case so he can cop a plea of diminished responsibility.'

'You can't mean he's going to get away with it!'

'Liz, dearie, I don't know what's gonna happen. All I know is that I did what I was told to do: I got Nancy out – with your help, of course.'

'Huh! How do I know you're telling us the whole story?' she riposted. 'For all I know Nancy might have been shipped home on the first available plane and she's sick and penniless in Bloomingdale—'

'Bloomington,' corrected Mr Crowne. 'Is she really at a health spa, Jerry?'

'She is, honest. Look, I've told you a lot more than I was supposed to. You can see that this is a very touchy affair, now can't you! Three governments are involved, and even the Germans are muttering that she was kidnapped from one of their airports, so they want their ten cents' worth.'

'So you're treating her as if she's part of an international incident? That must be fun for her. Nearly fifteen months in the hands of criminals and now she's being – what was the word? – debriefed?'

'Look, she's okay, she's having medical care—'

'She was having "medical care" on Kerouli. I bet she's scared every time someone in a white coat comes into her room!'

'She isn't scared; she knows we're her friends, Liz—'

'Friends! A bunch of strangers! I think Greg and I should do some hospital visiting—'

'No, no, that's impossible.'

'What do you mean, impossible? Is she a prisoner?'

'Calm down, calm down. I mean it's better for her to have complete quiet.'

'What do you think we're going to do – take a brass band with us?' In her anger, Liz knocked over her glass. She and Greg mopped at the liquid with inadequate paper napkins. During the tidying up, Golfondi could be heard muttering in Brooklyn-Italian a couple of sentences that included the word *imbecille*.

'*Anche tu!*' the prince said sharply. 'Listen, my Machiavellian friend: it's no good trying to keep this so covered up that well-wishers can't be part of it. That poor soul has been through a form of torture, and you're denying her the comfort of seeing a couple of friends.'

'That's right!' agreed Liz. 'We're the only friendly faces she's seen since she left Bloomingford—'

'Bloomington,' corrected Golfondi. He huffed a little, but looked apologetic. 'This thing's so sensitive, you see.'

'Sensitive or not, I insist on seeing her,' she said.

'Whereabouts is this spa?' asked Greg.

'Well . . . It's about an hour's drive from the city.'

'So we could go there and back this evening.'

'This evening?'

'Well, we're leaving tomorrow,' she explained. 'There's a department store in Glasgow expecting me. And I'm sure there's a temperamental soprano somewhere who needs Greg to hold her hand.'

The information seemed to cheer Golfondi. He was probably thinking that he could take them there and back without asking permission, and if anybody wanted to see it as a problem afterwards – well, they'd be gone.

'Let me think . . . Okay . . . Okay, then, it's a deal.' He looked at his watch. 'It's nearly four. I've got a few things to do at the office, so give me a coupla hours. I'll pick you up at the hotel at six.'

Mollified, Liz gave him a smile. He hurried off. Mr Crowne said to his beloved, 'That was a side of you I've never seen before: the warrior queen.'

'Take note of it, then. If you get out of line, you'll get some of the same.' But she kissed him on the nose as they got up to leave.

Back at the hotel they had coffee and the Greek version of a sandwich. Then Liz decided they must take a present to Nancy. 'You can't visit an invalid empty-handed,' she said.

They went into the flower shop of the hotel. There she rejected most of the offerings as being too ordinary, although they were, in fact, beautiful. Her gaze fell at last on a container of copper from which arose three stems of a yellow orchid. 'I'll take that,' she said.

Mr Crowne was about to check her, because the price tag on it was horrendous and his own credit card – and probably hers – had seen a lot of use; but she shook her head at him. When it came to paying she gave their room number. She was putting it on the tab for the US government. He smothered a grin, took the plant in its cellophane wrappings and followed her out.

'That'll larn 'em,' she growled in a mock-menacing voice. 'Trying to keep the poor lass in solitary! Should we buy her some chocolates?'

'Why not? Even if they're not allowed because of medication or something, it'll show we're thinking of her.'

So they bought an expensive box from Switzerland. Support home industries, thought Mr Crowne.

Golfondi drove them out of Athens as the evening rush hour was beginning to die down. They headed west then north on good roads, past signs that said first 'Elefsina' and then 'Stefani'. They were soon in the mountains, and next came a road sign depicting a big earthenware water jug. After that there was an arch across the carriageway with lettering in Greek and English: 'Spa Hermes'. A stream was rushing by, its waters tinged with gold by the setting sun.

The buildings were of stone blocks that somehow looked old, but the place was very modern, with a lot of glass and bright awnings. There were gardens of flowering shrubs and trees, their perfume sweet on the air. 'Golly,' Liz whispered as they got out of the car, 'I think I had the wrong idea about this place.'

It was certainly no prison. Golfondi led the way through a marble-paved reception area where a man at a desk nodded in salute. They went past a pool and then a gym. At the end there were a few steps and then a line of doors. Golfondi tapped on the second. It was opened by a nurse in a pale-blue uniform. They went in and she went out, closing the door gently behind her.

Nancy Lanan was reclining on a cushioned lounger. She swung herself to sit upright as they came in. She was wearing a long pink flannel nightdress, a dark-blue bathrobe, and slippers in the form of bunny rabbits.

'Hello,' she said. 'Jerry let me know you were coming.'

'Hello,' said Liz. It wasn't at all what she'd expected. 'How are you?'

'Not bad.' She offered her cheek to Liz, and her hand to Greg.

'Love the slippers,' he said.

She gave a little laugh. 'They had to lend me things. All my own stuff seems to have vanished.'

'Huh!' said Liz. 'We should have bought you a snazzy nightie instead of these.'

240

Greg offered the orchid. Nancy made as if to take it but decided instead to let him place it on a nearby table. 'I might drop it,' she explained. 'I'm kind of trembly.'

'No wonder. But you're feeling better?'

'Better than the day you got me out. I was hanging on by the skin of my teeth that day.'

'Say, sit down, folks,' said Golfondi. 'I'll go and rustle up some coffee or something.' He went out with a faint smile at the prince, as if to say, 'See, I'm leaving you alone with her.'

The evening sun was streaming in from open French windows. Nancy shaded her eyes with her palm. 'Could you pull down the blind a little? Direct light seems to be a bother to me, but the doctors say that'll pass.'

Her eyes were a clear, deep blue. Her hair had been cut so that it fitted close to her head in a cap of short curls. In her homely night things she was no longer Elissa Paroskolos by any stretch of the imagination.

'Jerry told me it was you who worked out what was going on,' she said, waving them to chairs. 'I can't imagine how you did it, because *I* didn't even know who I was.'

'It was the Musical Maestro here who got suspicious,' Liz replied. 'He didn't like the way you spoke English.'

'I beg your pardon?'

'He thought you didn't speak it with a New England accent.'

'That's for sure,' Nancy said with a faint laugh. 'I grew up in Illinois.'

'And went for a course on photography to a university in Louisiana,' put in Mr Crowne.

'To put me ahead as a photographer. Right . . .'

'That accounted for the Cajun dances. You suddenly began talking about going to places where they played Cajun music, which was impossible if you were Elissa Paroskolos,' Liz continued. 'And there was the snake thing . . .'

'Ooh, that,' Nancy said with a shudder. 'It only earned me peanuts, but it was the bravest thing I ever did!'

'And a thing Elissa would never have done, according to Greg. But the big thing was the contact lenses. We took them to an oculist and he said they were purely cosmetic. Then Greg realized you wore flat heels because you were taller than Elissa, and we began to get really worried.'

'You weren't half as worried as I was,' sighed Nancy. 'All the time I was there on the island I'd have these little glimpses of things that seemed to come from another life. But Dr Donati kept soothing me, and believe me, he knew how to wind me round his little finger. He'd tell me it was delusional, that it often happened after an illness like mine—' She broke off. 'But I was never ill in the first place!' she cried. 'That's what I can't seem to get my head round! They made a fool of me, they got me playing their games – they made me believe I was that poor woman.' She looked at Greg. 'Is she really dead?'

'I'm afraid so.'

'And I would have been too, wouldn't I?' He hesitated, and she nodded. 'Oh yes, I realize now what those rats had in mind. It was after the big day, when you called me by my name, remember?'

'Shall I ever forget?'

'Well, they carted me up to my room – Elissa's room, I mean; and when I recovered from the faint, or the collapse, or whatever, I was lying there, trying to think what had happened. It wasn't too much later – about twenty minutes, I think. I knew I was Nancy Lanan in a sort of way, but I couldn't understand why I was Elissa Paroskolos too, and my darling husband Niki was talking to Dr Donati and blaming him for not getting his measurements right.'

'His measurements?'

'Of the drugs I was given. I lay there with my eyes shut trying to make sense of it. Dr Donati was saying he could get me ready again in a week or ten days, and Niki said he'd round up the trustees again, and after that they wouldn't need me any more and I could be disposed of. Thank heaven, he said, because I wasn't as easy to handle as the doc had promised.'

Neither Liz nor Greg could think of anything to say. Nancy went on, 'I was really too stupefied to be scared at first. I said nothing, asked nothing, just played absolutely dumb for a day or two. And I grew certain that I really was Nancy Lanan, because I remembered being in my apartment in Bloomington,

242

and going shopping in Chicago, and a lot of stuff about my real self.'

'Oh, poor soul,' said Liz, and took her hand. 'You must have been scared out of your wits!'

'*Terrified.* I was terrified. I hadn't a clue what it was all about. I thought I was going crazy. Yet I had enough sense to understand that if I took the pills that Trudi kept dishing up at regular intervals, I got sort of confused and over-relaxed. So I began keeping them under my tongue then spitting them out when she'd gone. And I kept on being Nancy Lanan when I was off the stuff, but I never let on about that.'

'Golfondi says you were fed quite a cocktail of specially designed drugs,' Greg suggested.

'I think that may only have been at first. After the first few weeks, once Donati had me under his thumb, I think he reduced the dose to something fairly simple, though I was often woozy – out of focus, at a loss. And that *weasel* would tell me I must expect after-effects and I *believed* him.' She clenched her fists and thumped her chair arms. 'It really galls me! I was played for a complete sucker all the way along.'

'But you got the better of them in the end,' Mr Crowne reminded her.

'You bet! Because after that birthday party scene, I stopped swallowing the stuff and began to understand I was in a helluva trap. If I let any of them see that I knew I wasn't Elissa, I'd be drugged up to the eyeballs again. I looked around for a way of getting off the island – I thought I'd slip aboard one of the boats—'

'But they reduced the service to one boat a day,' Liz said.

'And when the boat came I was never alone, because Trudi was always there ready to grab me. I was desperate. Then you turned up.'

'Bearing gifts.'

'Yeah, that beach wrap – I left it when we ran, darn it!' She laughed, pleased with her brave joke.

'Never mind, it's still there somewhere. Tell Golfondi you want it.'

'I might, at that. He's not a bad guy, but it's clear he and the medical staff are concentrating on what I know,

243

what I can remember – and that's still a bit of a muddle.'

'How long do they think of keeping you here?' Greg asked.

'Not too long, but in a way it's up to me. They say I should be able to leave the spa if I want to in about a month, but it's pretty decent here so I'm not in a hurry. Because, you know, I couldn't afford a hotel or anything. I think I'm broke. My credit cards and stuff have all gone. Do you think there's any way I can claim compensation?'

'There's no need to think about that yet,' Mr Crowne said, rather taken aback.

'But I want to get back to the real world as soon as I can.'

'Of course you do. And then,' Liz said soothingly, 'you must put it all behind you and try to forget.'

'Forget?' cried Nancy, with unexpected animation. 'Are you *nuts*? This is the best story I ever landed and nobody is going to write it up except me!'

'Nancy!' protested Liz.

'I was promised a book, wasn't I? I was tempted into going to Mürren to write a book about Elissa. Well, it's *my* story now, not Elissa's. I'm sorry she got killed and all that, but I've got to think of myself. So when my head is on straight again, I'm going to do the deal of the century with a publisher!'

'Good for you,' murmured Mr Crowne.

They stayed about an hour; then it seemed a meal would be coming for Nancy, and she was growing visibly tired. Golfondi drove them back along quiet roads and under a canopy of stars. This is a beautiful country, thought Liz. I bet I'd love it under different circumstances.

At the hotel she rang her Glasgow contacts to say she would be with them next day, although it meant taking the shuttle straight on from Heathrow. The prince rang his one-room office in Geneva to hear a few tales of woe from his 'assistant', Amabel, a mother of two who gave him what hours she could when her children were in school. They left the Hotel Serena for a daybreak flight next day. They would go as far as Paris together; then she'd head for London and he'd head for Geneva.

On the plane, they settled in. He said to Liz, 'You're a bit subdued?'

She sighed. 'I've been thinking about Nancy. I thought it was a bit mercenary, the way she talked about writing her book.'

'It's probably a good idea. She'll get it out of her system – exorcise whatever demons are left when the doctors at the spa have done their best.'

'But just at the end there, she didn't come over the way I'd pictured her. You know?'

He gave her a comforting pat on the hand. 'You've been thinking of her as someone who had to be helped, to be rescued – something like a deer in the power of tigers – but she's not, really. She's a career woman.'

'I think I liked her better as Elissa. She seemed nicer.'

'A better class of person?'

'Well, sort of.' She thought for a minute. 'I suppose she will really make a lot of money with the book?'

'Ah . . .' He was silent while the attendant came trundling up with breakfast. When she'd gone he said, 'I doubt the book will ever be published.'

'What makes you say that?' she asked, amazed.

'Well, in the first place, it may be years before the cases come to court. All the governments involved will study the evidence back to front and upside down, because they won't want to create an "incident" or make themselves look foolish.'

'And we'll be called to give evidence, shall we?'

'Probably. And we'll figure in the book, I suppose.'

'Well, fancy that. That hadn't occurred to me.'

'It had occurred to me, sweetness, and it's the last thing I want; but I comfort myself Nancy will get tired of waiting and give up the idea.'

She applied herself to buttering a roll. 'But does she have to wait until the courts have done their stuff?'

'I'm not sure. In Switzerland they wouldn't let her publish anything for fear of harming the defendant's rights. Apart from that, I'd take a bet the US government will do all they can to prevent anything in print. All that about brainwashing? They're probably working out how to get hold of Donati's documents so as use the treatment themselves on recalcitrant prisoners.'

'That's cynical, darling.'

'But perhaps true. And then there's the lawyers – if she says, for instance, that Niki murdered his wife, he'll sue her, because he swears he knows nothing about Elissa's death and there's no proof he does. So that would have to be left out. And both Niki and Dr Donati are claiming she took part in the impersonation of her own free will, so anything about being a victim will have to go. The only thing left is the intended fraud, and she doesn't really know anything about that out of personal knowledge, because you can bet they never discussed it with her.'

'Doesn't leave much, does it?'

'Not a lot.'

Liz ate some buttered roll and was silent, following her own train of thought. 'You know, she never even said thank you to us!'

'No, that's true.'

'And we saved her life, after all!'

'I think that's true, too.'

She gave a little nod of satisfaction. 'I'm glad it wasn't us that paid for her orchids,' she said.

That made him laugh. 'You mean you'd begrudge spending your own money because you've taken against her?'

'Is that what I mean?' She shook her head at herself. 'That's small-minded of me, isn't it. But it's true: I've gone off her quite a bit.' She finished her orange juice and put down the glass. 'So she's not going to get a big contract for the film rights?'

'Doesn't seem likely.'

'That's a pity. I rather fancied seeing my part in the film being played by Meg Ryan.'

He gave her an amused glance. 'You'd better choose an actress who's eighteen years old at present, because it'll be ten years before they make the film, if ever.'

'In ten years' time I'll have my own chain of fashion shops, one in every major capital. I'll be too busy to care about who plays me in the film.'

'That's the ambition, is it?'

'Yes, it is. What's yours, Greg?'

246

'To stage a recital with the *hydraulis*, one in every major capital.'

It made her giggle. 'You and that old contraption! Anybody hearing you would think you were an old fuddy-duddy.' She leaned against him, a close body contact, and when he turned to look at her. she mimed a kiss. 'But you're not a fuddy-duddy, even though you are a crown prince.'

'Kind of you to say so,' he replied. 'You know how much I value your opinion.'

He was thinking that they would be meeting again fairly soon. Lawyers and officials would want to speak to them about *l'affaire Paroskolos*; and tedious though that might be, they'd find time outside the lawyers' offices to be together.

So it wasn't a bad outcome.